PENGUIN BOOKS

The Lost PRINCESS

Connie Glynn has always loved writing and wrote her first story when she was six, with her mum at a typewriter acting as her scribe. She had a love for performing stories from a young age and attended Guildhall drama classes as a teenager. This passion for stories has never left her, and Connie recently finished a degree in film theory.

It was at university that Connie started her hugely successful YouTube channel *Noodlerella* (named after her favourite food and favourite Disney princess). After five years of publicly documenting her life and hobbies to an audience of 900,000 subscribers on YouTube, Connie closed the book on the Noodlerella project in a bid for more privacy and to pursue her original passions in the performing arts. Connie now writes music and fiction full-time.

Follow Connie on YouTube, Twitter, Instagram and Tumblr
@ConnieGlynn
#RosewoodChronicles

The Rosewood Chronicles
UNDERCOVER PRINCESS
PRINCESS IN PRACTICE
THE LOST PRINCESS
PRINCESS AT HEART

THE ROSEWOOD CHRONICLES

The Lost PRINCESS

CONNIE GLYNN

PENGUIN BOOKS

This book is dedicated to the rat who lives
in the bushes outside my building
(I've named it Zooms)

PENGUIN BOOKS

UK | USA | Canada | Ireland | Australia
India | New Zealand | South Africa

Penguin Books is part of the Penguin Random House group of companies
whose addresses can be found at global.penguinrandomhouse.com.

www.penguin.co.uk
www.puffin.co.uk
www.ladybird.co.uk

First published 2019
This edition published 2021

001

Copyright © Connie Glynn, 2019, 2021

The moral right of the author has been asserted

Printed and bound in Great Britain by Clays Ltd, Elcograf S.p.A.

The authorized representative in the EEA is Penguin Random House Ireland,
Morrison Chambers, 32 Nassau Street, Dublin D02 YH68

A CIP catalogue record for this book is available from the British Library

ISBN: 978–0–141–37997–5

All correspondence to:
Penguin Books
Penguin Random House Children's
One Embassy Gardens, 8 Viaduct Gardens, London SW11 7BW

Prologue

There was something in Emelia's eye, a speck of dust that caused tears to stream down her cheek. Sniffing, she rubbed her face, not caring that it left a black panda smudge. Honestly, she didn't really care about anything any more.

'Emelia, *bella*! Are you OK?' her mother called over. Emelia's parents sat side by side on the Italian designer sofa, but her father didn't even glance up from his book.

It was almost a year ago to the day that Emelia's whole life had been turned upside down.

'I'm fine, Mother,' she replied sweetly, the ring of mascara making her left eye look like an empty socket in her skull. 'Just something in my eye.'

Last year Emelia had been kidnapped along with a deaf boy named Percival Butter. He was the son of Richard Butter, owner of the Butter Company and a direct competitor to her father's confectionary company Hubbub. Although they could not remember a single thing from the time they were held captive, they'd been found safe, unharmed and with no obvious impact on their health or well-being. Which meant the only remaining question was . . .

'Emelia, I think it's time for you to go to bed. You have track practice in the morning.' Her father turned another page, still not looking at her.

Emelia glanced at the window. 'But it's not even got dark yet,' she protested.

'I said go to bed.' His tone was dark and oppressive, extinguishing any chance of further conversation.

She resisted the temptation to scowl at him, knowing she'd be picking a fight she could never win. She grabbed her track team schedule off the gilded coffee table and marched up the marble stairs to her bedroom, fighting the urge to slam the door behind her and scream.

As she'd been thinking – before she'd been so rudely interrupted – the only remaining question was: *If I've been returned safe and unharmed, why is my father so clearly disappointed?*

Ever since her return, her dad had turned distant. At first he had watched her like a hawk, as if expecting something of her. Whatever it was, she never found out. Instead she watched his hope turn to disappointment and now to this – a cold withdrawing.

She'd been upset, of course. She'd taken up every improving hobby imaginable to try to satisfy him. She excelled in school, tried to assist him with work. But nothing pleased him.

Emelia carefully unpinned her white hijab, folding it neatly to put away in the pristine gold armoire where she kept all her headscarves. They looked up at her, in a variety of colours, but the white one had always been her favourite.

It made her feel neat, straightforward, covering up her annoying hair and turning her into someone to be taken seriously, and now she was going to make sure she felt like that underneath it too. She took one deep, furious breath, letting go of all the rage and hurt as the reality of the situation settled in her belly.

She went through everything she knew. A few months ago, Percival Butter had been admitted to hospital after a mysterious group called Leviathan had made a kidnapping attempt on the princess of Maradova. Fact.

She knelt down and reached far under her four-poster bed to pull out an unassuming wooden box. She eased back the lid. Inside were piles of curling newspaper snippets, everything she'd been able to find on Leviathan, Percy and the princess of Maradova.

Percival Butter had been brainwashed and couldn't remember a thing. His father had known and allowed this to happen. Fact.

Emelia had been kidnapped by Leviathan a year ago along with Percival. Fact.

Emelia's father, for reasons she still didn't understand, was disappointed that the brainwashing had not worked on her, making her useless for whatever plan they had. This was speculation, but there were two things Emelia was absolutely sure of, deep in her gut.

One. Leviathan had ruined her life.

Two. She was going to make them pay.

At the very bottom of the box was what she needed, the things that would let her feel like herself again. Free and true.

Emelia had spent her whole life being the perfect daughter, the perfect young woman, always doing what was expected of her, but it had never been enough.

She strode over to her lavish dressing table and sat down, grabbing a fistful of thick, curly ebony hair. With decisive cuts, she allowed the silky locks to fall like water through her fingertips, leaving a little halo of black around the top of her head. Then, without hesitation, she turned on the electric razor she'd retrieved from the box. Vibrations coursed through her fingertips, a low buzz of power in her hand as she raised the rotary blades to her scalp. She brought it closer . . . closer still . . . keeping her eyes trained on the mirror until she felt the halo fall around her feet. When she allowed her glance to fall she saw the curls glimmering on the white-marble floor like writhing black snakes.

There. It was done.

She ran a hand over the shape of her skull, newly exposed. Silky spikes of freshly shorn hair covered her scalp like a glistening helmet. Her eyes somehow looked bigger, more soulful – dark orbs staring out from an unrecognizable face. She smiled at her new friend, a real smile, welcoming the familiar stranger in the mirror.

A buzzing from the bed caught her attention. The caller ID simply read '4', but she knew immediately who it was.

'Hello, Riri.' She grinned down the phone, still admiring her reflection in the mirror. 'How's our little project going?'

The girl on the other end of the phone pondered, a melodic hum that sounded out over the noise of engines revving.

'We're still trying to decipher the puzzle.' Her tone was thoughtful, distracted, and Emelia could imagine the exact expressions on her face. 'How are you holding up?'

'Pretty good.' Emelia sat down on the bed, absent-mindedly reaching to curl a lock of hair round her finger. It was no longer there. She turned to stare at her new image again, her head feeling lighter, her body free. She smiled again. 'You're not going to believe what I've just done.'

PART ONE

お邪魔します

Ojama-shimasu

Japanese greeting:
'Excuse me for disturbing (you)'

1

All she had to do was get through the gate.

'There she is!' a lone voice cried out from the crowd of people closing in around the car.

The school rose up behind the gilded gates of Rosewood Hall, its windows winking in the sunlight, the stone pillars carved with roses. Their safe haven. Yet here, outside it, this sea of strangers spread like an awful stain.

Journalists.

The gates usually did a good job of keeping them at bay, but the pavement outside the school walls was a no-man's-land in this fight for privacy. Anything went – and Lottie was the best story these journalists could get. Until she passed through those gates it was open season.

But first she had to get Ellie away from these sharks.

'Nikolay,' she whispered, 'please sneak Ellie into the school. I'll distract them.'

'But, Lottie –' Her princess tried to protest, sniffing loudly.

'It's fine, Ellie. Don't worry.' She threw her a reassuring glance. 'This is what I've been trained for, remember?'

They'd dealt with the press after the incident at the Tompkins Manor, and Lottie had answered their questions well, but then she'd had the king's advisor, Simien Smirnov, to coach her. He'd warned that the dam would eventually break, that they'd get hungry for more. And, from the looks on these journalists' faces, that moment had come.

'I'll see you inside,' Lottie assured her princess, putting on her best smile as she watched Ellie disappear, rubbing her nose.

In the two years Lottie had known her, not once had Ellie ever had a cold. It was strange to see the red of fever on her pale olive skin, the deep shadows beneath her eyes and the dry, chapped lips, all weighing heavy on a body usually so full of life.

Seeing Ellie ill filled Lottie with a furious determination. She was her Portman, meant to take on the burdens of being a princess so Ellie could play the part of a normal girl. Getting sick was what happened to stressed and worried people. Not a princess.

Lottie was meant to do the worrying.

When Lottie stepped out of the car it was cloudy but warm, the staple of a British summer. The air crackled with the threat of a storm.

Well, come on then. Let it break.

Lottie walked confidently into the fray.

'Has there been any more information on the mysterious Leviathan?'

'Why haven't you been out in public since the incident? Are you afraid?'

'Can we see a smile?'

Kind, brave, unstoppable! Kind, brave, unstoppable! Lottie repeated the words over and over in her head, tapping the wolf pendant at her chest, then moving her hand up to adjust her tiara nestled in her hair.

The crescent-moon opal at the top of the tiara rose to greet the sun when she lifted her chin boldly, the strength of the intricate silver headpiece coursing through her, reminding her that she was never alone, that she always had a piece of her family with her.

In a great display of poise, she walked calmly down the line of reporters. At her side, where the princess's Partizan should have been, was a hired bodyguard. Samuel was a nice-enough man, and Lottie had to keep reminding herself that it wasn't his fault Jamie wasn't with them. Because Jamie had been very clear that he didn't want to come with them to collect their exam results.

Instinctively Lottie clasped the wolf at her heart. It was a pendant she shared with her princess, a gift that had welcomed her into the royal family, the weight of it a reminder that they were all connected. Only now Jamie had broken their link, and she felt it like a wound in her chest.

A microphone was suddenly shoved into her face, grasped by a hand that stank of cigarettes.

She stared at the reporter holding it as he aggressively repeated his question.

'Has any more progress been made on finding out why Leviathan are after you, Princess?'

Lottie took a deep breath to steady her voice. 'It's still the same information. As far as we're aware, Leviathan . . .' Her throat went dry at the name, memories of Ingrid and Julius swarming around her. They were the deadly duo that had nearly kidnapped her. 'As far as we're aware, they're targeting the children of important and influential families, but their objective is still unknown.'

Samuel put an arm round her and smoothly guided her away from the reporters. Lottie couldn't help cringing at her answer.

Her words had been true. Almost.

But the whole truth was much less easy to digest – because the truth was they had no idea what Leviathan were really planning. All they had was a terrible theory, that they might want to control those influential children, and that Lottie and her friends may very well have given them the tools to do so when they had found the Hamelin Formula, a dangerous mix of chemicals that could be used to brainwash people.

'This must have all been awfully difficult for you!' a man's voice called after her, rich with fake sympathy. The temptation to roll her eyes was almost unbearable. 'How have you coped with adjusting back to normality?'

Barely.

Lottie had to shush the voice in her head, turning to smile pleasantly at the crowd.

These were the questions they asked the most. Personal questions. A chance for them to get to know this mysterious Maravish princess who'd somehow landed herself in the centre of an evil conspiracy.

Lottie couldn't help imagining the looks on all the reporters' faces if they found out she wasn't even the real princess. A professional fake, only a cover for Ellie, who was already safely inside the school gates, thank goodness.

'They just want a good story,' Simien had warned her. 'And a good princess.'

Heeding his words, Lottie swept a stray lock of hair from her face. She'd scooped her curls up in a meticulously arranged chignon, a request from Simien when he'd declared her 'frowsy tresses' to be too long and unruly for public appearances. She just couldn't bring herself to cut it.

'I have a wonderful support network,' she said now, 'and with everyone's kindness and patience I have found my studies both comforting and a welcome distraction.' Lottie put on her absolute best smile to let them all know just how much she loved studying.

Look at me, look at what a great student the Maravish princess is.

A camera flashed, sending dots dancing in front of her eyes. She brushed a hand over her face, staggering.

'No photos or videos,' Samuel ordered, shielding Lottie.

The next question was painful to hear, yet she should have been used to it now. After all, they asked it every single time.

'We love your dress, Princess! Who are you wearing?'

Lottie imagined how Ellie might answer something so ridiculous. '*I'm wearing the skin of the princess formally known as Her Royal Highness Princess Eleanor Prudence Wolfson!*'

Laughter caught in her throat and she swallowed it down.

She smiled again, going pink in what she hoped they'd think was humility and not irritation. 'I'm wearing a modern take on the traditional sarafan dress in Maravish style. From the A-line shape, the sun embroidery and distinctive design, I'm sure you can recognize the work of Léon Marie.'

She could practically hear Ellie gagging in the distance, and she wouldn't have blamed her. There was a giant conspiracy

13

afoot, yet all these fools wanted to know about was her dress. Part of her wished they'd take it more seriously.

A wish she'd quickly regret.

Samuel eased her further along, nodding to let her know she was doing a good job. The gate was just moments away now, the rose gardens coming into view. Only a few more steps and she'd be free.

'We were told the princess was attending a fencing tournament?' A calm and steady voice sliced through all the other questions, a Pacific Northwest accent that dripped with the confidence of a big city. 'So why exactly were you in the manor and not watching the match?'

Lottie's blood ran cold. This was the first time she'd been asked such a suspicious question, and her eyes snapped on to the mystery inquisitor. A smartly dressed young woman with thin rectangular glasses and a sharp-cut black bob stared back at her. She seemed to inhabit a space all of her own in the crowd of journalists, standing out like a beacon. A name tag on her blue blouse read AIMEE WU, CLEAR LINE MEDIA.

Lottie reminded herself that she needed to keep moving, yet the look on Aimee's face froze her to the spot.

'We were looking for the Hamelin Formula,' Lottie responded smoothly, gathering herself. She could almost touch the golden gates behind her. The familiar, sweet scent of roses and lavender drifted around her, urging her to step inside to safety.

'That's the dangerous formula that Leviathan were attempting to recreate?'

'Yes.'

'Why didn't you tell a teacher about it? And what exactly happened to this Hamelin Formula?'

Heat rose in Lottie's chest. She didn't know which question to answer first.

The other reporters fell silent, everyone's attention now locked on Aimee and Lottie.

'Unfortunately Leviathan took the formula and it is unclear what they plan to do with it or if it works. As for your other question, we wrongly believed that we –' Lottie's throat went tight again, remembering the magnitude of how wrong they'd been, and the terrible consequences of their mistake. It had all been a trick; they'd led Leviathan to the formula like obedient dogs. Aimee instantly took the opportunity to launch another question as though she was throwing a hand grenade.

'Who is "we"?' Before Lottie could answer, another question was hurled across the space. 'Also, I must ask, we were told at the Tompkins press dinner that the Hamelin Formula had been locked away with no way of finding it. So how exactly did these Leviathans end up with it?'

'*We* is my friends . . .' Samuel was right beside her, urging her to step through the gate, but when she tried to answer the phantom scent of icing sugar from the factory caught in her nostrils, nearly choking her.

Leviathan was not the only memory to torment Lottie. She also remembered the taste of a kiss, sweet from the sugar in the factory. A moment of joy before everything had gone up in flames. She was so sure it had meaning, that she and Ellie had shared something special, and yet afterwards her princess had claimed it was nothing at all.

15

So why, Lottie wondered, *if it really meant nothing, does Ellie refuse to talk about it?*

'Princess?' Aimee urged, dragging Lottie from her thoughts.

'My friends from Rosewood and myself,' she said a little too quickly, 'and Leviathan found the formula because we discovered the key to where it was hidden.'

The key, it turned out, had been a piece of music. When it was played on the Tompkins twins' grandfather's piano, the melody had opened a secret hatch in the side of the instrument where the formula was hidden. At the time it had seemed magical. But, really, it was wicked.

Lottie realized she'd lost all composure. She was gabbling her responses like a child. The way Aimee relentlessly threw questions at her made it impossible to gather her thoughts in time.

Why was no one else asking questions?

'How did Leviathan find the key?'

'They stole it from us.'

'Did you find the key?'

Lottie felt her heart thundering in her chest. She was answering these questions all wrong and she knew it. The journalists didn't need to know any of this – shouldn't know. She'd given too much away.

'I'm afraid I must leave now; I need to get my exam results.' There was a sudden breeze, and as she turned she saw rose petals float through the air, a trail of them drifting down to welcome her. Glancing back over her shoulder, she added, 'I'm expecting excellent grades.'

Lottie's gaze was fixed on one person only. Aimee Wu. Light glinted off Aimee's glasses, her eyes cast down to where she was writing in a notepad. With each flick of the pen, a thick ball of dread settled uncomfortably in Lottie's stomach.

Samuel's arm draped protectively over her shoulders, his large body shielding her from any further questions. Samuel had eased the golden gate open. 'Come on,' he said, quietly encouraging her. She began to follow him, but she couldn't tear her gaze from Aimee, who now stared hypnotically back. And just as Lottie stepped through the gate she tripped.

The ground came hurtling up towards her, and she threw her hands out to break her fall. Cameras clicked. Samuel's voice called out.

A strong hand effortlessly pulled her up. The sting on her knees told her she'd scraped them, and her arm ached where she'd landed on it. Soon there would be bruises, but that would be the least of her troubles.

Limping up the pathway, confused and hot with embarrassment, Lottie could still feel Aimee Wu's eyes burning through the back of her head, people sniggering and most likely comparing photos of a princess grovelling on the ground.

I've really messed this up.

2

'We shouldn't be here – Ah . . . Ah . . . Ah!'

'Here!' Lottie held out a tissue for Ellie just as she let out a huge sneeze.

'*Atchoo!*' Ellie hid her face in the handkerchief and noisily blew her nose, before lifting her head, eyes streaming as they took in Rosewood.

At the end of the rose-lined path stood the home to the righteous, resolute and resourceful. It towered over them, sunlight glowing round its edges like rays from the face of an ancient god and demanding just as much respect. Every step up the path felt like a step closer to safety.

Only something was off. It wasn't just her fall and the ravenous glances that followed her, but for a second the scents that usually felt like home had turned sour. She was glad Ellie couldn't smell it.

Handing her another tissue, Lottie noticed her friend's eyes. Darker, deeper, a midnight ocean that might pull her down. The two of them were almost the same height now, the distance closing in as Lottie grew taller. She could look straight into her now, falling fast into those dark pools whenever their gazes met.

'Thanks,' Ellie grumbled, blowing her nose again, the moment swiftly over. 'We should have got our results sent to us at the palace. Then we'd be safe.' Hesitating, just long enough for Lottie to notice, her princess added, 'Safe from those reporters. Look what they did to you.' Her face darkened. 'I should teach them a lesson.'

Dressed in an oversized black band sweater and ripped fishnets, Ellie was neither dressed for the warm British summer nor for a common cold. Lottie had to assume she was delirious if she thought she'd be able to take on anyone in her current state.

She was right about one thing, though. Coming back to Rosewood was starting to feel like a bad idea.

Rosewood Hall was Lottie's home in more ways than one, or so she'd recently found out. She'd uncovered a secret to rival even her highly confidential Portman agreement. In an entirely unlikely turn of events it had become apparent that the founder of the school was the runaway Princess Liliana Mayfutt, and that same princess just happened to be Lottie's ancestor. She had passed down her tiara like a shining puzzle waiting to be solved by none other than Lottie.

All her life Lottie had dreamed of being a princess. She'd thought they were the childish fantasies of an ordinary girl obsessed with fairy tales. When the opportunity had arisen to play the part of a princess on a professional level, in order to protect Ellie's identity and give her the freedom denied to most of royal blood, none of them had imaged Lottie might actually have a real royal connection. This school was in her blood.

So why had she floundered just now, as she'd stepped through the gates? This was meant to be her safe harbour, not the scene of her humiliation.

'I'm completely fine, and I doubt anyone noticed,' Lottie lied. 'Besides, it's good to get out and about, and it'll be nice to stay at Binah's for a few days.'

In reality, there was more to this trip than collecting their exam results. If it had been up to Lottie, they would have stayed at Rosewood after their last exams like most of the other students. Ellie needed to get out of the palace. It was making her ill, literally.

As if on cue, Ellie broke out in a new fit of coughing before she recovered and smiled weakly.

'Let's go and find the others. Get as far away as possible from those reporters,' Lottie suggested.

'*Atchoo!*'

'Bless you, Ellie. Hello, Lottie.'

Both girls looked towards the giant stone arch of the reception doorway. Beneath it stood a girl with dark curly hair and a yellow cloak, the rosy tint of a holiday illuminating her radiant brown skin.

'You have a cold, Ellie!' Binah's glasses glinted in the sunlight. 'I'll have to make you my honey and ginger tonic when we get back to mine. It can cure anything.'

'Yeah, maybe. I'm fine, just . . .' Ellie caught the look in Lottie's eye and immediately looked away. 'I'm fine. Let's just get our results.'

Indicating for Nikolay Olav and Samuel to wait for them outside, Ellie stepped into the reception, trying to be inconspicuous, which was not easy when she was dressed like an eighties punk rock star and Lottie like a princess on display.

The hall greeted them with a creak of floorboards, sapphire beams pouring through the stained-glass window, sending a criss-cross of light over Ellie.

It was hot inside, and the air was thick with the scent of deodorant and perfume. As the three friends made their way to the front desk, Lottie could feel the other students' gazes following them. Was there anywhere they could go without being stared at?

A red-headed prefect from Conch House stepped out in front of them, a badge on her chest reading JESS PARKER-SCOTT. She flashed a smile at them, nearly blinding Lottie with her perfectly bleached teeth. *Oh no. Not more questions.*

But this wasn't the type of question she'd been expecting. 'Excuse me, have you girls considered joining Rosewood's international partner to partake in one of our award-winning summer schools?' Her eyelashes fluttered. 'You can learn valuable skills and even earn extra marks towards your exam results, all in the peaceful setting of Japan.'

The girl shoved a glossy pamphlet into each of their hands, her perfect crimson manicure glinting like talons. 'They're still accepting late entries for Rosewood students, but you only have three days left to apply.' Her smile widened, her teeth radiating an inhuman glow.

'Thank you.' Lottie tried not to cringe away from her dazzling smile. Over the girl's shoulder she spotted a teacher handing out envelopes. Exam result time. The whole reason they were here. 'If you'll excuse us . . .'

The three girls slipped by as the prefect turned to another group of students. Lottie, Ellie and Binah approached the desk. This was the moment they'd been waiting for. When they found out if all their hard work had been worth it.

'No pressure then,' Lottie mumbled. 'Good luck, everyone.'

Liliana's secret study was cold in comparison to the warm sunshine outside. Instead of blossoming flowers, there were fleece blankets and dusty furniture, a topaz glow from the torches and fairy lights illuminating their hideout in the bowels of the school where they'd come to open their results.

Binah immediately began setting out the beanbags and cushions in a circle, while Ellie fumbled in her bag.

To the left of the study an ancient relic stood out among their decorations. Liliana's desk. Inside one of its drawers hid a centuries-old diary. Lili's diary.

With their exams finished, Lottie intended to take the diary home and learn everything she could about her mysterious ancestor.

'Oh, Lottie,' Ellie wheezed between sneezes. 'My parents asked me to give you this.' Ellie handed her an envelope, which was wax sealed with the wolf crest of the Maravish royal family.

Lottie eased it open to find a letter inside. It was only a few lines long, yet the words made her inexplicably nervous.

Congratulations on another successful year of playing the princess.

The Maravish royal family thanks you for your continued and indefinite service.

The letter was signed by King Alexander himself and embellished with his personal stamp, a crimson triangle with three surrounding circles, a symbol Lottie had only seen once before. It was a sign that he'd written this letter personally.

'What does it say?' Ellie asked, leaning over to see.

'It's just a thank-you. Nothing to worry about.' Her fingers tightened round the parchment, crumpling it into a ball.

Loud footsteps echoed down the stairwell, and Lottie quickly shoved the letter inside one of the antique drawers in the desk.

'This is stupid. *C'est ridicule.*' Anastacia's distinctive French accent carried into the room ahead of her, Micky and Lola Tompkins and Raphael following nervously behind while Percy casually brought up the rear. The five of them wandered into the study.

'How dare they?' Anastacia's voice was low, and Lottie noted she was wearing her sunglasses again, chestnut hair tied up in a messy bun, a particularly bad sign for the girl who treated her hair like a rare vintage car.

'What's going on?' Ellie asked, but they all ignored her.

'Anastacia, it's going to be OK,' Lola chirped, recoiling immediately when Anastacia furiously turned on her.

'It's not going to be OK, Lola. This is the worst news I could ever have received.'

Wordlessly Percy placed a comforting hand on Anastacia's shoulder. For anyone to shout at Lola like that, whatever news Anastacia had just received, it must have been terrible.

Lottie watched from across the room. She felt the emotional scars from the Tompkins Manor tear open like a fresh wound.

It was no surprise they were arguing; there was so much they hadn't processed yet.

'Ani,' Binah began, taking a cautious step towards her. 'Just take a deep breath and tell us what's going on.'

Panting like a trapped animal, Anastacia slowly began to relax, holding Binah's gaze to anchor herself, each heavy breath slowly becoming steady.

'It's Saskia.' Still angry, Anastacia shuddered. 'The Partizan council agrees that Saskia was brainwashed by Leviathan, but Rosewood's bursars are saying she won't be allowed back having missed a year. Something about their strict policy on failing grades.'

Lottie felt Anastacia's gaze on her through the sunglasses, as though Saskia being locked up in the Maravish dungeon after being persuaded to kidnap the princess was somehow Lottie's fault.

'Can't she retake?' Ellie offered with more concern than Lottie was expecting.

'It's not just that.' Anastacia planted herself on the love seat in the middle of the room, a crown of gold LEDs floating above her like stars. 'The council said they could pull some strings if she'd give them information about Leviathan, but . . .'

The atmosphere in the room froze over. They could all guess where this was going. Getting Saskia to talk about the mysterious Master of Leviathan was like trying to force-feed a lion, and just as messy. A spell had been cast on the Partizan. At the mention of the name, her gaze would turn distant. It was a vacant look – scared. Nikolay had told them what she'd said when they'd first interviewed her:

24

'I don't want him to be disappointed in me.'

Their countless interviews with Saskia had given them only one solid fact. That whoever the Master of Leviathan was, he had a stronger hold on his minions than they could ever have imagined.

'It's OK, Anastacia,' Lottie said. 'We'll figure something out. If it's still causing Saskia stress, she doesn't need to push herself.'

A wave of relief washed over Anastacia, her shoulders relaxing.

'I hate to change the subject,' Raphael chimed in. Out of all of them he looked the least stressed, his skin fresh and dewy, no sign of a restless night anywhere on his face. 'Is Jamie coming?'

Poor Raphael! He tried so hard to be a good friend to Jamie, and Lottie knew better than anyone how difficult that could be in the face of Jamie's stubbornness. Lottie had decided it was best to leave Jamie to figure things out on his own, but recently she'd started to wonder if that was such a good idea.

'He's not,' Ellie said bluntly, the edge in her voice making it clear she didn't want to continue the discussion.

Ellie and Jamie had hardly spoken, the two of them drifting apart. It felt like an impossible task to bring Jamie back into the fold, waiting for him to find his own way. And the longer it went on, the colder the space between them became.

'That's a shame,' Raphael replied at last, the disappointment on his face matching the gloom that hung over the rest of them.

Lottie fingered the envelope with her results in, wanting to get back to something normal, something solid and productive.

Micky signed in the corner of the room for Percy, and they all exchanged a knowing look.

'Is it just me?' Lola began, her voice tiny in the large, echoing room. 'Or does everything feel a bit, well, bad?'

The rest of them nodded in mute agreement. Yes, they were back at their beloved Rosewood, but it didn't feel the same. It hadn't felt the same since the incident at the Tompkins Manor.

Enough! Lottie slipped a fingernail beneath the envelope flap and prised it open, pulling out the yellow card.

'It's like something's missing,' Micky said, picking up Lola's solemn tone. 'It's as though we're not ready to be back yet.'

Lottie stared down at the numbers in her palm, the hazy glow of the fairy lights blurring her vision.

Congratulations on another successful year . . .

The king's note taunted her while she stood completely still, unable to tear her gaze away from the dreadful reality staring back at her.

It was not possible. She'd worked too hard. She was a good student; they all knew that.

'Guys . . .' She spoke with unexpected calm, still not believing it, as though detached from it all, floating above her own head. Finally she looked up at her friends, holding out the card. 'I've failed the year.'

3

The one thing Lottie had been sure of was her grades. In all her worst nightmares – that Leviathan might hurt Ellie, that Jamie would be lost forever – never had it occurred to her that something so simple would be her downfall. That she would fail the year.

It was only by a few marks, but those tiny errors would be enough to have her let go from Rosewood. If that happened, her job as Portman would be in serious danger.

'It has to be fake.' Ellie snatched the card from Lottie, and stared at her results. 'This doesn't make any sense; that English grade alone is far too low. What if Leviathan –'

'But why would they do that?' Lottie tried to rationalize it. 'And even if they did tamper with the results system, what could we possibly do about it?'

'Ellie's right,' Anastacia stated, plucking the card from Ellie with just as much conviction. 'You worked too hard; these grades can't be right.'

Part of Lottie wanted to believe that someone had messed with the grade, because she would never have allowed this to happen. Too much was at stake.

Or had she?

Before her mind had time to dwell on the doubts, she looked up to see Percy and Binah signing intently, and from her little knowledge of BSL it looked like they also believed something fishy was going on.

It was the strangest feeling to look around the half-lit study and see nothing but unwavering faith on her friends' faces. Not one of them showed an inch of doubt that she would pass the year, turning instantly to other possibilities.

'There was a break-in,' Binah announced, turning back to everyone, some sort of conclusion having been reached between her and Percy who nodded solemnly for her to continue, 'at the exam board headquarters – no witnesses and no suspects. It was only petty theft, money stolen from people's bags, but all the CCTV footage was tampered with. Percy believes, from his experience, that Leviathan easily have the tools to achieve such a thing as grade tampering, and without being caught, either by hacking or by brain-washing a member of the exam board.'

'Well, that's it then,' Raphael declared. 'Leviathan tampered with your grade. You can contest it with the exam board and this will all be fixed.'

Somehow this didn't make Lottie feel any better, because there was a much more important question than how they'd done it.

Why would they tamper with the grade? What did they want?

'Don't you see? They probably *want* me to contest the grade.' Shaking her head, Lottie turned to Ellie, who was grinding her teeth. 'It doesn't matter if Leviathan fixed it; we can't prove anything, and if we bring attention to it, people might think I really did fail the year and I'm looking for an excuse.'

Silence, brooding and sombre, spread through the room, each of them dwelling on the harsh truth. And at the centre of them all was Ellie, a look on her face like she'd been poisoned, which had nothing to do with her cold.

In the quiet, a little voice in Lottie's head wished she could get away; to take Ellie, the twins and Anastacia, all of whom had been through so much over the past year, far away from their troubles.

The thought settled in her mind, a nonsense fantasy slowly forming into an idea. All the events of the day were bringing her right up to this moment.

'So what do we do?' Lola and Micky asked.

'If we're going to fix this,' Lottie declared, 'we're going to have to think outside the box. In fact,' she added, heart thudding, 'we're going to have to fly as far away from the box as possible.'

Lottie and Ellie flew back to the palace immediately, seven hours of silence like death following them across the world. At the end of their journey waited Ellie's parents, the king and queen of Maradova, who held the power to rip Ellie and Lottie apart at the snap of their fingers.

All thoughts of the journalists, her fall at the gate and Aimee Wu had vanished.

'OK,' she told her princess, staring down the snarling wolf on the great doors of the palace. 'This will be fine. I'll sort this, and then we'll talk to your parents.'

The door creaked open to reveal an endless vista of history, stretching along the corridor ahead. Previous rulers of the kingdom glared at the girls, following them with every echoing step on the marble floor.

Ellie shuddered when they passed the black-framed painting with green irises that dripped judgement like poison. Claude, the lone wolf of the Wolfsons, smirked down at them, a shadow in the hallway that acted as a bitter reminder of what became of those who couldn't handle the expectations of the Maravish throne. Exile, complete and final.

Lottie would not let them fall to the same fate.

'Edwina –' Lottie nodded to the head of the house staff who was holding a shimmering silver tea tray – 'please make sure Ellie gets a hot drink and heads to bed; she's very ill.'

She gave one final glance back at her princess. Her lips were purple like a bruise, and Lottie felt the weight of her trust pulling at her along with the wolf on the chain round her neck.

Jet-lagged and uncertain, Lottie had decided to do the one thing she dreaded more than anything else. She was going to talk to Jamie.

You can do this, she told herself. *You can speak to him.*

Making her way through the palace, every gold-framed painting, every chandelier and rare antique seemed to judge her for the terrible mistake she'd made.

'*It wasn't me*,' she wanted to tell them. '*Someone tampered with the grade. I'm going to fix this.*'

But first she needed to get Jamie on her side.

She caught her reflection in a gilded mirror at the end of the narrow corridor by Jamie's rooms. Tired. She looked tired, but she felt good in the sportswear she'd worn on the plane journey, as good as she could in this situation, and she allowed that sliver of hope to fill her with determination. Everyone had found a way to occupy themselves after Leviathan tricked them. For Lottie that had been through training – and she was now fitter than she'd ever been. Even if Jamie refused to train with her, she wasn't going to let anything stop her.

I will be kind. I will be brave. I will be unstoppable.

If her ancestor Liliana Mayfutt could successfully run away from home, take on the identity of a man so people would take her seriously and set up Rosewood Hall, one of the most prestigious schools in the world, then Lottie could grow strong on her own, and she wouldn't let this little blip get in her way.

Pulling her hair up tight into a ponytail, she wondered if perhaps Simien had been right, that her hair *was* too long. It had sneaked up on her, just as the height difference between her and Ellie was slowly closing, her hair had grown unexpectedly. Mounds of memories and experiences were tangled up in the straw-coloured curls.

Her fist hesitated in front of Jamie's door, then she rapped her knuckles against it, hard, in the same way she'd seen Nikolay do a few times, hoping to trick Jamie into thinking it wasn't her.

After only a few seconds, he opened the door, his gaze falling much higher than Lottie's eyes, clearly expecting Nikolay, and as he took in his visitor he made no attempt to hide his irritation at being tricked.

He was shirtless, and *still* not wearing his wolf pendant. She blinked rapidly, tearing her eyes away before she could

31

fully take him in, her cheeks going red with the sudden thought that this was a very stupid idea.

Whatever had remained of the regular boy in Jamie was officially gone. In its place stood a dark, brooding tower of firm muscles and eyes sparking with anger. Somehow he was taller, his dark hair longer but tied back. He truly looked like the deadly assassin he was trained to be, and it hadn't crept up on them like Lottie's hair or height – this had happened within weeks of the attempted kidnapping at the Tompkins Manor. It was as if the event had triggered something inside him, something he might never be able to undo. He'd shed the skin of a boy and grown into a man.

'What are you doing here?' he asked, leaning an arm on the door frame. 'Why aren't you at Binah's?'

Beyond the compact muscles of his shoulder, she glimpsed a corner of his room – immaculate. Cinnamon and spice swirled through the air, mixing with the scent of roses that lingered from Lottie's deodorant.

It smelled weird.

Everything in the room was crimson. The bedding, carpets and lighting, all an ominous red. And glinting like a precious jewel on his bedside table in a box, was the wolf pendant, its gemstone glaring at her like an eye, a creature Jamie had sworn not to wear again until he felt worthy.

Lottie had tried to persuade him that what had happened at the Tompkins Manor was not his fault, that none of them could have known it was a trick, but no matter what she said he had been determined to punish himself. As a Partizan, her constant protector, he felt he should have shielded her from danger, refusing to believe that there was nothing that could have been done to change things.

Noticing her line of sight, Jamie leaned in further, blocking her view until there was nowhere else to look except at him.

'What are you doing here?' he repeated.

'Ellie's not well. I . . . we . . . need your help. It's –'

'Unless this is a life-or-death situation, I don't want to know. I have work to do, and I won't get distracted by another one of your and Ellie's silly little adventures.'

Lottie stayed firm.

Jamie always did whatever he could to keep everyone at a distance. A comment like that would have upset her a year ago, but now she knew her 'silly adventures' had led to her finding her place in the world, and that was more than Jamie could say for himself.

With Jamie preparing to close the door, Lottie shoved her foot into the doorway, holding her ground, not even wavering when he looked down at her, eyebrows raised in surprise.

'I want you to race me,' she told him.

The look of shock on Jamie's face would have been hilarious if this wasn't so important.

'Why would I ever do something so ridiculous?' He crossed his arms, biceps bulging, as if to remind her how much stronger and faster he was than most people.

'Because,' Lottie replied, 'if you win, I promise I will never ask you for a single favour again. You can just focus on your Partizan duties, and –' her next words caused her physical pain, knowing that none of this was her fault – 'I won't distract you.'

His face was impenetrable, making it impossible to tell if he liked the idea or if he was reeling from shock.

'But,' Lottie warned, 'if I win, you have to hear me out.' On second thought, she quickly added, 'And you can't get mad.'

'This is a big waste of time,' he said eventually. Lottie's heart sank, until he continued, 'But if this is what it takes to persuade you to stop kidding around, then so be it.'

He turned back into the room to get his things, leaving Lottie to catch her breath. She could hardly believe he'd really agreed.

'I'll meet you by the gate of the West Garden in fifteen minutes,' Lottie called after him, her fingers curling into fists.

And I'm definitely going to win, she added in her head. Because if she didn't get Jamie on their side before they spoke to the king and queen, then they might as well give up now.

The sky was unusually clear above the Maravish palace. Even though it was freezing outside, streaks of sunlight through the evergreen trees filled the air with glitter. Lottie batted it away, remembering the story of the Snow Queen, and not wanting her heart to turn to ice.

'First one to lap the pond and make it back across this –' Lottie unfurled a red ribbon over the gravel path – 'is the winner.'

'Pond' was a particularly unceremonious word for the great body of water in the west side of the palace gardens. With the top frozen over, and the sheer size of it, the *pond* was big enough to be an ice rink. Ellie had promised Lottie that she'd teach her to skate on it one day, but Lottie had always chickened out. It looked too deep, too cold, too deathly.

In the centre stood a mossy statue of the goddess Artemis, a bow and arrow poised and ready, pointed directly at them.

'We start when this goes off.' Lottie placed her phone on the stone steps opposite the pond and set the timer for one minute. 'Are you ready?'

Jamie shrugged, indifferent in his black vest and matching hoodie, a stark contrast to Lottie's peach sportswear. He was taller and stronger than her; it seemed obvious that he would win.

'Let's just get this over with.' He took position next to Lottie, legs braced.

Breath like smoke mingled in the air.

I'm going to win this. Lottie willed the thought to life. *I'll show you what I'm capable of.*

The timer beeped, and they were off! They tore across the frozen grass, and Lottie blanked her mind. She didn't think about the race, she didn't think about the journalists, the failing grade, or why Leviathan had caused it. Nothing could catch up with her if she ran fast enough. This is what she'd learned after the attack at the Tompkins Manor, that there was power in getting strong on your own. Not once would she have dreamed that young Lottie, puffing, aching and humiliated from a single training session, would grow to love the freedom of running. She hadn't needed Jamie to teach her. She'd only needed to be unstoppable. Her time with Ellie had taught her that.

The frozen grass crunched beneath their feet, where they left ghostly footprints with every furious step. A taste like metal flooded her mouth, her chest aching from the cold, taking in great gasps of air to propel herself forward. It wasn't until she was halfway round the pond that she realized she was falling behind Jamie, only a little, but that gap slowly spread wider, like stretching an elastic band. The pressure built up, her legs screaming every time her foot pounded the earth, and still the gap grew. They were so close to the finishing line now; he was going to win! If she didn't snap back, he was going to win.

Lottie let out a screech, feeling the elastic band pop, springing forward as they approached the ribbon.

But it was too much for her. Her knees, still sore from her fall at the gates, gave way and the world tumbled around her, the cold hard ground slamming into her body, just as Jamie's feet came down purposefully over the ribbon.

She lay sprawled on the ground, panting. Humiliated again. Jamie reached out to help her up, but she shoved him away, clambering stiffly to her feet without his assistance. She trembled as she rested her hands on her thighs, bending over to draw in ragged lungfuls of cold air. She watched a single bead of sweat drop to the ground and spread, melting the ice.

Her plan had failed, and it wasn't even until she looked up again that she realized she hadn't even made it over the finishing line.

4

'I'm not racing you again. No way.'

'But I would have won, I'm sure of it. If I hadn't fallen over, I would have won.'

Jamie barely even gave her a second glance, pulling his bomber jacket on with a dismissive flick of his hand.

It felt colder, if that was possible. The air tasted frosty, like bitter, terrible failure.

'Jamie, please.' Before she could stop herself, desperate fingers reached out for him, grabbing his jacket.

He turned back to her. Golden-flecked eyes bore into her own, and for a split second, so fast she nearly missed it, a flash of concern passed over his face.

'I failed the year.' She spoke quickly, before his concern disappeared. 'We think my grades were tampered with, but we can't bring attention to it, not with the media, and I won't be allowed back at Rosewood unless I resit. But . . .' Lottie slipped a hand into her pocket and pulled out the hand-bound pamphlet, on its cover a tranquil lily pond surrounded by wood-panelled buildings and pagodas. And, above the image, curly gold script announced the name of the school, Takeshin Gakuin.

'They offer physical and creative courses over the summer. If you get a good enough grade, it adds to your exam marks for the whole year. This could fix the problem without needing to bring attention to it.' She felt the nervous sweat from her hands dampen the pages where she held it out. She swallowed. 'Ellie wants to do the kendo class, and I think it will help build up her confidence again, but we need you on board. We need you with us when we tell her parents.'

She'd read the information about the school what felt like a hundred times, the words growing in her mind like roots, pulling her across the sea.

On the outskirts of Tokyo, set within the dense bamboo forest the Kiri Shinrin, named for its languid and thick fogs that appear mysteriously all year round, Takeshin Gakuin prides itself on both a beautiful setting and academic excellence. Said to be a school filled with secrets, Takeshin was founded by Kou Fujiwara in 1650 during the Sakoku period in Japan, when travelling in and out of Japan was strictly limited by the Japanese shogunate. Ahead of its time, with an interest in other cultures and traditions, the school quickly became known for producing graduates who showed outstanding strength of mind, body and spirit. It wasn't until the 1800s, when Japan opened up its borders to allow trade with Great Britain and America, that Takeshin formed its lasting and mutually beneficial relationship with the esteemed Rosewood Hall, and the renowned summer school had its foundations. Now students from all over the world can choose one of Takeshin's exceptional physical or creative courses and partake in eight weeks of intense learning. We hope that those who set foot in our grounds will leave with not only desirable grades but a stronger sense of self to carry them through life with confidence and passion.

'Japan?' Jamie took the pamphlet from her, his expression as cold as the air around them. 'You want to go to Rosewood's sister school in *Japan?*'

'It's not that far away from Maradova; I remember reading that the countries do a lot of business together, and it's not just about the grade – I'm worried about Ellie too.' Lottie tried to keep her voice calm and even. 'This might be the thing we all need.'

'We?' He looked up at her sharply.

'Yes, *we*. If you hadn't noticed, we're not exactly at our best right now.' The tension stretched between them like a rope pulled tight. 'It would be Ellie and me, and you, and possibly Saskia and Anastacia and –'

'No.' He tried to shove the pamphlet back at her, but she clutched her hands behind her back.

'No?'

'You need to apply for resits. You can't run away from your problems, Lottie.'

'But if Leviathan had something to do with the grade, what if it happens again?'

The beautiful calligraphy that bore the school's name trembled in Jamie's fist as he realized Lottie was not going to budge from this decision.

'You promised that if I beat you in the race, you would never ask me for a favour again.'

Any argument turned dry in her mouth. In the freezing silence she took the pamphlet back, feeling the pain in her knees, the ache in her muscles, and the scrapes on her flesh begin to throb, proof of her failures.

'Listen, Lottie, you don't understand the implications of this. Japan is . . .' He swallowed, looking up at the grey mist. 'King Alexander and his brother, they have a history there. Japan is where Ellie's uncle ran away to when he was exiled.'

Green eyes flashed through her mind. The portrait of the man that hung above them whenever they walked out of the palace, a dark reminder of Maravish tradition and what would become of a person if they broke it. It was a life Ellie must never follow.

She opened her mouth to speak when a shrill voice called to them. Lottie looked up to see Simien Smirnov, anxiety etched in his face. Smirnov – usually so fox-like and calculating – seemed worried about something. This couldn't be good.

'Miss Pumpkin, Mr Volk,' he called again down the stone steps. His breath came in gasps, as though he'd been running. 'I'm afraid you're needed in the East Screening Parlour with the king and queen.'

Lottie couldn't help looking to Jamie in the hope he might know what was going on but he seemed as confused as she was.

Following Simien through the palace in silence, Lottie felt her wolf pendant bounce against her with each step across the marble floor.

She was grubby with her scraped knees and ratty hair. The very idea that she was about to see Ellie's parents made her want to curl into a ball. Part of her worried that Ellie might have already

40

confessed about the failed grades, but as Simien led them to the screening room, the brow above his glass eye twitching with concern, it soon became clear it was much worse than that.

White double doors creaked open, hazy blue light from a mounted screen leaking across the woven pink floor.

The first thing Lottie noticed was that every member of the Wolfson family was wearing their wolf pendants. A token of solidarity. A reminder that if you wore one too, you belonged. It should have put her mind at ease to know she had a pack behind her, but the glittering eyes of the wolves nestled at the base of each person's throat suddenly felt ravenous, ready to eat her up.

The second thing Lottie noticed was her princess. Dwarfed by an antique velvet armchair, Ellie looked small and stranded in its centre, more ill than ever. Her mother and father stood at a distance, still as statues behind the matching sofa. They looked icily handsome, even beneath the dark shadow that stretched over them from the pillars that lined the room. The queen's expensive perfume mingled uncomfortably with the faint stench of Ellie's sickness.

'Lottie.' Queen Matilde attempted an apologetic smile. 'There's been some bad news. We feel it best that you, Eleanor and Jamie see this together.'

As though on cue from some invisible signal, Simien joined Nikolay by the huge desk in the corner, where a sliver of light seeped out between the closed curtains, silhouetting him. He pushed a button under the table and the screen mounted on the wall came to life.

'It's clear to me that all these children want is attention, and it's time we kept them in check.'

41

Bile flooded Lottie's mouth.

Aimee Wu, with her deceptively pleasant smile, was on the news discussing their impromptu interview at the gates of Rosewood, but it felt to Lottie as though she were listening to her own eulogy.

'*A secret formula that controls people's minds? An evil society?*' Aimee smiled again, shaking her head in pity. '*It all sounded like nonsense to me. I was glad to finally get a chance to speak face to face with the princess. Or, as I like to call her, the ringleader of this operation.*'

The screen cut to a shaky clip of Lottie fumbling over her words, half hidden by Samuel as she tried to respond to the barrage of questions. It was edited to make her look confused and tired. Then she watched herself say the worst possible thing.

'*My friends from Rosewood and myself, and Leviathan found the formula because we discovered the key to where it was hidden . . .*'

Lottie remembered saying those words, but they had been answers to two separate questions. This made it sound like they'd all found the key together, like she and her friends *and* Leviathan were working *together*.

Everything was spinning; everything was hot. She could smell the acrid tang of her sweat, an enormous pressure bearing down on her, stealing her breath.

'I thought you stopped people filming?' Jamie asked, his voice steady.

'We couldn't guarantee it,' Nikolay responded, rubbing the stubble on his chin.

They turned their attention back to the screen as Aimee Wu reappeared.

'*She was completely out of it,*' she was saying. '*She even stumbled on her way into the school.*' Then came an image of Lottie splayed on the ground, her skirts crumpled. The humiliation was like a hot poker searing her stomach, and it was followed by something far, far worse: a zoomed-in shot through Rosewood's gilded gates of Lottie and Ellie, glancing back over their shoulders at the media parade behind them. They'd officially brought Ellie into the nightmare.

'*The princess – with a close friend, who looks like a bad influence if you ask me.*' Aimee sighed – deep, regretful, as though she had no choice about what she had to say next. '*I think people have a right to know the truth.*' A pause. Aimee did not break her gaze from the camera as she delivered the final, killer question. '*And what is the truth?*'

Looking down the camera lens, it was as though Aimee was speaking directly to Lottie now, all the way over in Maradova. '*The truth is that these spoiled children are liars. This evil Leviathan group could be closer than we think.*'

Aimee's menacing glare vanished as Queen Matilde snapped the footage off. Lottie could find no relief in the quiet that followed.

Ellie spoke first. 'Wait, I don't understand. Is she saying we're lying, or working with Leviathan?'

'She's being intentionally vague; they'll roll with whatever story people cling to.' Jamie spoke matter-of-factly, but somehow that made everything feel even more out of control.

'Why would they . . . I don't understand, I . . .' Lottie had to take a deep breath to try to calm down but it didn't help; she couldn't seem to get enough air. This was her job, to make

43

people like and trust the Maravish princess. She had failed. 'These were facts. Everyone believed us. They're facts!'

'They're changing the facts,' countered Jamie.

'You can't just change facts,' Ellie fumed, her fists balling. If Jamie was resistant to the storm, Ellie *was* the storm.

The king cleared his throat, resting a hand on his daughter's shoulder. 'When people are scared they will believe whatever suits them the most.' The softness in the king's voice was unexpected. 'Unfortunately it seems the news of an unknown formula and evil society is too unpleasant; it's more convenient to believe that it's something they can control, like a group of troubled teenagers.'

A polite knock at the door caught their attention and Simien went to answer it, revealing Midori and Edwina, and, from the looks on their faces, it was more bad news. Quiet murmuring echoed through the gilded room and, though seemingly impossible, Nikolay Olav achieved a new level of grave and serious.

'Media vans have parked at the perimeter of the palace grounds; they can't get in but I will need to organize more severe security measures.'

'So what do we do?' Jamie pulled back his shoulders. 'I think the best course of action is to move both girls as far away from all of this as possible. But in such a way that will not be read as *running away*.'

'Yes, I agree. Our little Pumpkin should stay out of the spotlight, at least until things have settled.' The queen wandered over to Lottie's side, where she stroked her pink cheek.

Far away . . .

Lottie looked over at Ellie, and was glad to see that the same thing had occurred to her at the same time. Everything was coming together. Lottie needed to attend Takeshin Gakuin in order to safeguard her place at Rosewood, and it was the best way to do so without drawing attention to her failing grade. The last thing they needed was any more media scrutiny.

'Your Majesty –' Lottie bowed low – 'we must confess another problem, but before we do please allow us to present you with our solution to both our current situation, and the one we are about to share.' Reaching into her pocket for the pamphlet, Lottie looked at Jamie. She had to do this whatever he thought. 'Your Majesty,' she continued, 'I must confess that my exam grades were not up to Rosewood's standards.' She swallowed hard; she would not shy away from this. 'We believe the results may have been tampered with. But with no proof, and for fear of drawing unwanted attention, we are given little choice but to remedy the grade as quietly as possible.' Lottie continued talking quickly, not wanting anyone to interrupt until she'd said everything she had to. 'With your permission I feel our best course of action would be to attend a Rosewood-approved summer school. Not only to make up my grades, but to get away from the media and find some respite.'

'I've been looking over the courses.' Ellie took over now, and Lottie went to her, their hands searching for each other's in solidarity. 'This school will also help me build up my confidence after everything that's happened in the past year.' Her last words disintegrated into another fit of coughing, and she pulled her hand free to cover her mouth. It was clear Ellie needed to recuperate somewhere far, far away.

A muscle twitched in the king's jaw. Lottie could only wonder what terrible thoughts of his older brother she'd just summoned.

'Takeshin,' he said quietly, glancing at the pamphlet. With a sigh, he turned to face the wall, his shadow extending longer with each step he took away from them.

Strangest of all was the queen. Usually so tranquil, her face had turned rigid like she'd been frozen in place.

'I know that school,' the king said at last, still not turning back to them. 'I attended myself one summer.'

Ellie and Lottie exchanged a surprised look. Lottie knew the two countries had business ties, and Jamie had said that the king's brother had fled to Japan, but she would never have expected there might also be a far more promising connection.

'Wonderful!' the queen trilled, her face lighting up once more, as if nothing out of the ordinary had occurred. 'An alumnus in our midst. I'm sure that will help the application process.'

'So we can go?' Ellie asked, hardly believing it.

The king slowly turned his head, and Lottie imagined it would spin the whole way round like an owl, only it stopped just as his ebony eyes locked on her own. 'We will begin preparations.'

It took Lottie a moment to realize they'd been successful, and she had to stop herself from spluttering in disbelief.

The king's words should have been a relief, but the Maravish royal family was drowning in secrets. And perhaps she'd just discovered one more.

5

Pulling her cap down lower over her face, Lottie felt like a spy. Everything had happened so quickly that it was hard to keep her feet on the ground – quite literally. From the capital of Maradova, St Krystina International Airport, to Tokyo Haneda Airport took almost four hours. Four little hours to escape the clamour back home. It seemed too good to be true.

They had been told they could expect a hospitable welcome from the headmaster, Nobuo Chiba, upon arrival – a special privilege for the princess.

'I hope he's not teaching any of the classes.' As they passed through immigration, Ellie scrutinized his photo in the back of the brochure. Professor Croak, the head teacher at Rosewood, was at least capable of the occasional smile. There was absolutely nothing *smiley* about Mr Chiba with his gunmetal grey hair and sharp frameless spectacles.

'He might look mean but he's saving us.' Lottie could handle a bit of mean if it helped them out. 'Besides, I think we all know better than to judge a book by its cover, don't we?'

'You're right.' Ellie smiled. 'Remind me to thank him when we arrive.' Most people caught colds on planes, but Ellie's had almost entirely vanished, her body getting stronger the closer they got to Takeshin. Lottie was glad to see that they'd made the right decision, for Ellie at least.

Now that it was real, now that she had reached Japan, Lottie let the excitement flutter in her belly, a feeling she knew all too well, because it was the very same feeling she had when she was on her way to Rosewood Hall. The only problem was all the other students at Takeshin had already chosen their classes. Lottie had been reassured that she could choose when she arrived, but it still felt like a daunting decision.

'Can we pay attention to where we're walking, please?' They were the first words Jamie had spoken in a while, his tone making it clear how he felt about this excursion.

Lottie remembered what he'd said about running away from her problems, as if she couldn't handle reality. But, looking out of the window at Tokyo, the flow of neon lights like electric blood, it all appeared to be very real to her. She wasn't running away from anything; she needed to do this to stay where she was, in her rightful place at Rosewood.

When they emerged on to the main concourse it was not difficult to spot Saskia and Anastacia. Their attempts to remain inconspicuous did far more to draw attention to them than not. An air of celebrity surrounded them, which was not helped by their choice of large sunglasses and chic, messy up-dos. They looked stunning.

Ellie smirked. 'Guess no one gave them the memo that we need to stay undercover.'

Lottie was about to call out to them when a high-pitched squeak cut her off and she felt herself being scooped up in a hug that smelt of icing sugar.

'I'm so glad you're here!' Lola held Lottie at arm's length, still grinning, her white-blonde hair hidden beneath a yellow cap. 'This is going to be the best holiday ever!'

Her twin brother Micky stayed back as usual, his cherry lips twitching round his lollipop in what was almost a smile. Saskia and Anastacia had been obvious candidates to invite along for the trip, with Saskia needing to get her marks up to be allowed to return to Rosewood. But including Lola and Micky had been Lottie's idea. They'd been through so much the past year, with their father getting sick and Leviathan infiltrating their family's factory. Like Ellie they needed a change of pace.

'Are you both OK? After the . . . media thing?' It was difficult to know what to call it, and Lottie still hadn't seen the backlash.

The twins' faces turned sour, Lola rolling her eyes. 'Let's not talk about any of that here please. This is meant to be an escape from all that, remember?' She grabbed Micky's hand and they began walking towards the exit.

Lottie glanced at Jamie, and the expression on his face made it clear what he was thinking. *You can't run away from your problems.*

Jamie nodded at the other Partizan, not quite respectfully and with clear warning. 'Saskia.'

Cursing Saskia's giant sunglasses, Lottie wished she could read what their old nemesis was thinking.

Ellie's face split into a grin and she dropped her backpack to the floor to throw her arms round Anastacia in a fierce hug. Lottie was sure Anastacia would snap in two, but instead she pulled away and smiled.

49

'You may have beaten me in the fencing tournament, but kendo is a whole different game,' she warned Ellie, only half joking.

Lottie felt a rush of happiness as she looked over their group. Seven Rosewood Hall students, of all houses, about to embark on a whole new adventure together. She dared to hope, if just for a moment, that everything might actually be OK.

They were met on the other side of the terminal gates with the hospitable welcome they had been promised. The airport was like a first magnificent snapshot of Japan and everything that awaited them. The airport corridors were decorated to look like downtown streets, with tiny, bustling ramen restaurants and souvenir houses with red *noren* curtains wafting above their doorways. A great staircase led up to a wooden bridge that covered the terminal walkways, with a garden of make-believe cherry blossom trees growing beneath it, and in neat rows, all around them, lanterns covered with black calligraphy lit up the paths in a warm, glowing welcome.

'This is the most amazing place in the world,' Lottie whispered.

She was greeted by a confused look from Lola and Micky and it took her a moment to realize why.

'Lottie, have you never been to Tokyo before? We thought Maradova and Japan did business together?'

'A security precaution,' Jamie quickly interjected, throwing Lottie a warning glance. 'We rarely leave the country, not even for holidays.'

Lola and Micky still don't know you're not the real princess. She chastised herself for being so obviously awestruck. She couldn't help thinking how funny it was that she came from such a different world compared to her Rosewood friends – if only they knew.

'Well,' Lola continued, 'you'll love it. So many cute cafes and shops.'

'And everyone is polite and they have the best candy,' Micky added. As if to emphasize his point, at that exact moment they walked past a bright pink shop filled with colourful sweets. Lottie was so enticed by the pretty pastel colours that she almost didn't notice the men in front of her.

There were three unblinking men in black suits, peaked caps and white gloves. One of them held a sign that read LOTTIE PUMPKIN AND GUESTS with a little blue heart in a corner, at odds with their serious faces. Beside them were three others, including Headmaster Chiba. It was a small entourage, nothing over the top.

'Welcome, Rosewood students, Princess,' the headmaster said as Lottie bowed in greeting. 'My name is Nobuo Chiba – but please call me Chiba Sensei. It's a pleasure to meet you.'

Lottie shook his hand, but couldn't help glancing to his left, where stood the most beautiful girl she had ever seen. Everything about her was magnetic, like a glowing sunset. Her hair was so dark and long it looked like a waterfall pooling down her back.

Hair as black as ebony . . . A line from an old fairy tale came to Lottie's mind.

The girl's red mouth curved in a smile of welcome as she cast her eyes towards the floor with a small bow in polite greeting. Seeing her standing opposite Ellie sent an unexplainable dizzy feeling through Lottie, like some sort of déjà vu.

'This is my granddaughter, Sayuri Chiba,' the head teacher explained. 'She lives with me, and assists in our summer-school programmes. She will be happy to help should any of you require it.'

Sayuri. Lottie repeated the name in her head.

Ellie adjusted the bag on her shoulders and bowed. 'I'm Ellie.'

Sayuri raised her head, heavy lashes fluttering to reveal eyes as dark and clear as a star-filled night. 'Nice to meet you all.' Each syllable sounded like a feather floating through the air.

Chiba Sensei nodded and gestured to his other side. 'And this is her Partizan, Haruki Hinamori. He will also be assisting over the summer.'

The tall boy on the other side of the headmaster bowed as he was introduced. His hair was a fluffy copper tuft on top of his head, with little curls sticking out in all directions that reminded her of sheep's wool. Square glasses with a thick brown frame accentuated his dark chocolate eyes, and there was a faint smattering of freckles across his cheeks. A complete contrast to stern and serious Jamie, he seemed friendly and easy-going. How on earth he could be a Partizan was a complete mystery.

'Please, call me Haru.' He extended a hand – not to Lottie but to Jamie. 'You must be Jamie – it is an honour and a pleasure to have another Partizan here.' There was unexpected affection in the way he said Jamie's name, and Lottie worried how their Partizan would respond to such attention.

Jamie took his hand, but there was an obvious hesitation and Lottie was sure she could feel static when their fingers touched. 'It's a pleasure to meet you all.'

Saskia cleared her throat loudly, placing a hand on her hip with a spark of amusement in her eyes. 'Partizans – plural, I think you'll find.'

'Oh yes, *Partizans*.' He gave a lazy smile, but it faltered as soon as she gave her name. 'Hello, Saskia.' There was the tiniest waver in his voice, and Lottie assumed he must have heard about Saskia's interesting past. She hoped it wouldn't be a problem.

Three black cars took them through the city, blending with the night. They drifted through the high-voltage twinkle of neon signs and tiny lantern-laden streets. It was like a kaleidoscope, every fizzy sensation growing and fading away while they drifted by. Just before midnight they arrived at Takeshin, and it was everything the brochure had promised: a quiet, peaceful haven – a different world from the bustling, glowing urban energy of the city.

Fog greeted them as they passed the black iron gates at the bottom of the driveway. Rosewood Hall was set apart from the rest of the world by stone walls that gave way to its namesake, the Rose Wood, but Takeshin was separated from the busy streets only by the dense bamboo that grew in tight formation all around. If you squinted, the fog turned into wispy figures phasing through the trees.

'They look like ghosts,' Ellie whispered. 'Ready to haunt us.'

'Or maybe to watch over us,' Lottie suggested.

Their luggage was carted away and they were led to their dorm rooms. They removed their shoes at the sliding doors and slipped their feet into fluffy slippers. The girls had to follow Sayuri, tiptoeing quietly on the *tatami*, not wanting to wake any of the sleeping students. Memories of sneaking around Rosewood with her friends in the dark sent a pang through Lottie's chest, an ache for her home that morphed into firm resolve. She had to succeed at summer school and improve her grades; it was the only way to stay at Rosewood.

Haru led Jamie and Micky to their room, which they'd be sharing with a summer-school student from China and a Takeshin pupil. Saskia, Anastacia and Lola were put in one room, while Lottie and Ellie went to a room they'd share with Sayuri and her room-mate, who was fast asleep with a pink eyemask covering her face and what looked like blue hair.

'I hope you will find these futons comfortable, Princess,' Sayuri whispered, as she settled down into her own futon, after they'd all got ready for bed. 'We will give you and your companions an exclusive tour of the grounds tomorrow. I look forward to seeing which programme you choose. *Oyasuminasai*.'

The feathers of her voice fluttered to the floor, and the room turned dark.

'She seems nice,' Ellie whispered sarcastically.

Lottie took one last look over what was to be their home for the next eight weeks. Beyond the screen door she could hear a night-time chorus of insects, and from a small crack a sliver of moonlight cast a glowing line over the low wooden table in the centre of the room. They curled up on their fluffy futons to have their first night's sleep in a strange new world, which somehow echoed Rosewood. Safe in her warm cocoon, Lottie wondered what sort of welcome Ellie's father had received here.

As her eyelids drifted closed, the exhaustion of travel seeping through her, she floated somewhere just between sleeping and waking. Suspended in that special place, waiting for her dreams to take over, Lottie felt sure she heard a cat give a soft meow from beyond the room, and it sounded like a welcome.

6

'It's six thirty in the morning,' Ellie groaned, sleep making her vision blurry.

'Yes?' Sayuri stared down at her from the platform opposite. She was already dressed in the honey-coloured sailor top and chocolate pleated skirt that was the uniform of Takeshin Gakuin. She looked incredible, the earthy colours complementing her midnight-black eyes. It annoyed Ellie to even look at her, Sayuri's elegant demeanour a bleak reminder of the physical discomfort she'd felt recently in her own body.

'*Yes!*' Ellie said indignantly. 'And it's too early for any normal human being.' She moved to lie back down when a pillow came flying across the room and whacked Ellie in the face.

'Hey!' Ellie shot back up, and Lottie finally sat up too. But it wasn't Sayuri who'd thrown the pillow. To her side, hands on her hips, stood their mysterious room-mate. The girl was no more than five feet in height; she might have even been smaller than Binah. Periwinkle hair framed her round face in an immaculate wavy bob cut above her ears. But, most noticeable of all, was the little blue heart she'd drawn like a beauty spot next to her left eyebrow.

The blue heart on the welcome sign.

Her bedding was also blue, blue penguins to be precise, on which sat a blue penguin stuffed toy that reminded Ellie of Mr Truffles (who was still trapped in Lottie's luggage bag).

'*Yamete kudasai!*' she growled in Japanese. 'Don't talk to Sayuri like that.'

Ellie froze, unable to move from the shock, and Lottie tried not to laugh.

'Now get up,' the girl ordered. '*Hayaku kudasai!*'

So, swallowing her irritation, Ellie did.

The two of them were left alone to change into the school uniform that had been given to them, and it only took a few minutes for Ellie to realize Lottie was staring at her.

'Ellie, are you OK?'

'Yeah, what? I'm fine.' Ellie pulled the sailor top over her head, immediately getting tangled in it.

'You wanna talk about it?'

'No,' Ellie snapped, her head popping out abruptly. 'I mean, sorry, no. I'm all good, really. Just first-day nerves.'

Lottie's lips curved in a less-than-convinced smile, but she didn't push it. 'We'll be fine.'

Ellie smiled back, though she couldn't help feeling that Lottie worrying about her was exactly what had got her best friend into this mess in the first place.

Making their way to the rest of the group, it was clear to everyone that Ellie was miserably uncomfortable in the uniform, constantly tugging on the skirt hem as though it might sting her.

'I hate this stupid uniform,' she grumbled, as they reached their meeting spot by the school's cat shrine. The other Rosewood girls were already waiting between the two stone cat statues that stood tall and inquisitive on red pedestals, Anastacia and Lola looking annoyingly great in the school uniform. Lottie looked great too, but Ellie didn't mind that so much, not that she'd say anything.

'It looks like it hates you too!' Saskia cackled, pointing at where Ellie's long torso made the top sit too high on her stomach. At the same time it swamped her shoulders, simultaneously too big and too small.

Ellie refused to laugh and Saskia's face softened. 'Don't worry,' she whispered. 'I'll ask them for some boys' uniforms for us later.'

It was hard to tell if Saskia was joking or not, and, more importantly, she wasn't even sure if they'd be allowed to do that. The boys and Haru joined them, with Sayuri and the angry blue-haired girl trailing behind. Ellie managed to look up just in time to catch Jamie's eye; there was a hint of hesitancy about him, like he wasn't sure about something. In a moment of sympathy she raised an eyebrow in silent inquisition, a small gesture, but one she hoped he might respond to, but he simply shook his head and turned away.

Lottie was worried about Ellie. It was hard to put her finger on it, but she knew her well enough to be able to know that something was off. Unfortunately there was nothing she could do right then, so instead she gave herself over to the incredible sight of the school in daylight.

Takeshin was smaller than Rosewood and more tightly packed. The centre of the school was built round a large lily-covered pond, the flowers in full bloom, with big, fat koi drifting in and out of sight beneath the emerald surface. The air was sweet and warm, like biting into a fresh pastry from her mother's old bakery. They crossed bridges with red-painted edges and bronze embellishments that connected the different buildings. All the while the bamboo surrounded them, casting shadows.

The school was silent, other than the invisible insects that sang in melodic patterns. They all followed Sayuri, Haru and the blue-haired girl, who looked very out of place in the traditional setting. It reminded Lottie of the first time she'd walked through Rosewood Hall, when she'd feared that at any moment she might wake up and find it was all a dream, only this time it wasn't herself she was worried about – it was Ellie.

'This is the dining hall used during our summer school.' Sayuri took them into another large dark-wood building where people in aprons hurried around. 'You will be able to eat breakfast here every day between seven and eight –'

'Wait, wait,' Ellie said, interrupting, and Lottie felt her whole body prickle. 'Are you telling me we're expected to get up that early, even when we don't have classes?'

The blue-haired girl made a tutting noise, mumbling something in Japanese that made Haru's eyes go wide. Lottie could only imagine the colourful language she'd used.

'As Miko-san politely said,' Sayuri replied, smiling serenely and gesturing to her room-mate, 'when staying with us you will be expected to adapt to our customs. This should be easy for a Rosewood student, no?'

Ellie looked as if she were about to say more, her eyes narrowing in a way Lottie recognized all too well, and panic rushed through her.

'Yes – of course it's no trouble,' Lottie said quickly, plastering on her most accommodating smile.

'Excellent, then let us continue the tour.'

'You need to be nicer to Sayuri,' Lottie whispered to Ellie.

'I'm trying,' she replied, rubbing her forehead.

But Lottie wasn't sure that she was. What was making Ellie behave like this? Hadn't she wanted to come to Japan? She might be better physically, but it was clear there was a more insidious illness lurking inside her. Lottie just had to hope Takeshin could help her.

The second area they visited was the *onsen*, or 'hot spring'. It was a great steaming pool of water, which was heated under the ground and split by a wooden fence to separate the male and female areas.

'So we bathe together?' Anastacia asked, evidently troubled.

'The baths are not for cleaning yourself,' explained Sayuri. 'You will do that in the showers. These are for recreation. But, yes, we bathe together.'

'So it's like a swimming pool then?' asked Micky.

'Yes,' said Haru, 'but without the swimming costumes. That is why there is a separation.'

A blush crept on to Lottie's cheeks at the idea of being so exposed around people she didn't know very well. As her eyes met Miko's, the other girl smirked, clearly able to tell what Lottie was thinking.

The next room they entered was the dojo, which was tucked away up a set of mud steps. A skylight above them illuminated a wall of powerful ebony suits like ominous black knights guarding the school. It felt as if the dark empty space behind the wire masks hid spirits watching them step through the arched entrance.

'One of our most popular programmes is kendo. As four of

you have chosen this course, you may return here after breakfast for your first class. I look forward to seeing how a Rosewood student fares at such a complex practice.' Her calm manner made it impossible to tell if Sayuri was making fun of them or not.

'What are those?' Anastacia pointed at a selection of long wooden poles with handles like a sword.

'They're called *shinai*,' replied Haru, smiling. 'They're kendo swords. I teach some of the classes.' He turned his attention to Jamie as if they were the only two people in the room. 'I think you'll enjoy it, Jamie-kun. And you too, Saskia.'

It was so friendly, so effortless, the way Haru spoke to him. Jamie didn't have friends besides Ellie and Lottie, if they could even be called that any more, and after what had happened at the Tompkins Manor even Raphael had felt the bite of Jamie's coldness. Everyone waited for the inevitable rebuff, so it came as a shock when Jamie returned Haru's broad smile and replied, 'I look forward to it.'

Lottie wanted to grab Haru and shake him until he revealed his Jamie-taming secrets. Even Lola and Micky were standing with their mouths agape, looking between the two Partizans as if the world were about to split in half.

'Excellent,' said Sayuri, walking gracefully to the centre of the room. 'I look forward to seeing your progress.'

The tour continued, then Lola and Micky were left in the kitchens for their first lesson in authentic Japanese cuisine. That left just Lottie, Sayuri and Miko to finish the tour and choose Lottie a course.

Other summer-school students began to emerge and the scents of *miso* and fresh rice wafted around them when they walked back past the breakfast hall again, towards a bridge leading to a quieter area of the school. Both Miko and Sayuri were waiting to eat until after Lottie had found a course, so she couldn't get distracted by food.

'What programmes are you taking, Miko-san?' Lottie coughed, feeling awkward for being so indecisive.

Miko looked up and Lottie could see how dark her eyes were, like the bottom of the ocean rippling under heavy lashes.

'*Kabuki*,' she replied simply. 'Japanese theatre.'

'Miko-san makes beautiful costumes,' Sayuri added pleasantly.

'Costumes?' Lottie asked.

'Yeah,' said Miko, at last seeming to relax. 'For the plays, and masks and items and the back— What's that word? Sets! But the costumes are my best. Let me show you.' From Miko's blue satchel emerged an art folder with a cute penguin mascot on the front, but when she opened it a dark and magical world bled out of the pages.

The sketches and photographs hidden within her art book were both grotesque and enchanting. Hideous doll props with horns and eyes like an abyss – and the costumes! They were ghastly and gruesome in the most wonderful way. Lottie felt as though she should be afraid of the spiked and jagged demon clothes, but instead she was enraptured. It was not like any art she'd ever seen, let alone something that could be *made*, and the idea of working on such incredible things was tantalizing in a way that lit her up from the inside out.

'You like them?' Sayuri asked curiously.

'They're fascinating,' said Lottie, feeling almost breathless.

Miko looked at Sayuri, confused, and Lottie watched her face morph into a grin when she translated, nodding up at her in approval.

They were about to continue down a smaller, darker path, when a black flash darted through Lottie's legs, nearly tripping her over, before disappearing.

'Cat!' Lottie exclaimed inanely.

Another appeared, a big fat ginger one with fur that smelled like candy and a tail as thick as a log. It plodded slowly in the same direction, pausing briefly to rub against her bare legs. She attempted to stroke him but he bristled and continued walking.

'Look, there's loads of them.' Lottie blinked in astonishment when two more cats appeared behind her, both black and white but with different-coloured eyes.

Sayuri and Miko barely reacted.

'*Neko-jinja*, the cat shrine,' said Miko, by way of an explanation, and for the first time Lottie noticed that one of her teeth protruded like a tiny fang.

Sayuri bent down and effortlessly scooped up the fat ginger boy, rubbing his chin. 'It's an old superstition. Some think they're messengers of the founder of the school; some that they're here to guard her secrets.'

'Her? The founder?' Lottie asked.

'Kou Fujiwara, a strange woman, and supposedly my ancestor. She wrote poetry and kept cats. There's a silly belief that she hid something in the school that'll make its finder rich.'

Lottie's ears pricked up.

'We have her study preserved by the headmaster's office as a museum with a statue of her outside that we're very proud of. I'd be happy to show you one day.'

Lili Mayfutt! The name burst into Lottie's mind like a balloon filled with confetti and she remembered Liliana's diary, which she and her friends had found when they'd discovered the secret study. She'd left it cold and alone in Liliana's study, a museum of its own, forgotten in the mess of awfulness that had followed. The roots inside her grew, trying to anchor to the ground beneath her.

Lili and Kou. Both school founders, both writers of poetry. Coincidence? Or could they have known each other? The idea made her chest feel like it would explode with excitement. It was also laughably fantastical.

There was something magical in the idea, though; that she might have an ancient connection to Sayuri that neither of them knew about.

'I'd love to see the museum. Do you have any of her poetry?'

'Oh yes. We have her old drafts too. Although I should warn you most of her work is about cats!' Sayuri smiled, and it was the first real smile Lottie had seen from her. 'Some think the cats are waiting for someone worthy to show them the secret treasure hidden in the grounds. It's all very silly.'

'No, it's not! You should never ignore these things,' Miko protested with a mischievous grin.

'And where are these ones heading?' Lottie asked, looking at the cats.

'To the theatre.'

In a moment that felt like fate Lottie decided what her programme would be. She would join Miko and learn to make those shocking costumes. Because, as far as she was concerned, this school held the same confusing power as Rosewood. And now it had made a choice for her. Lottie was going to study Japanese theatre.

7

Ellie's hair and uniform smelled like the colour pink. Hibiscus pink, to be precise, a sticky residue from Anastacia's shampoo and soap, which she'd had to borrow after their morning kendo class. In front of her, strolling into the dining hall, was Jamie, waving goodbye to Haru. She noticed Haru shoot him back a breezy smile that was so soft she wanted to squish it between her fingers.

Only three days into the summer school there was one thing she was sure of: she loved kendo. The confidence it gave her, having an outlet for her worries – all the things Lottie had told her she needed – and it would all be perfect but for one little thing. Jamie was still barely speaking to her.

'Don't you feel like Haru's playing favourites with Jamie? It's weird to see them so friendly,' Ellie grumbled, pulling the door open to the salty scent of *dashi*, a smell that instantly made her stomach rumble.

'Sounds like sour grapes to me.' Anastacia's hair was up, and she had no make-up on after their training, yet she still looked like a model in Takeshin's sailor uniform as she joined Ellie in the queue for food.

Ignoring her, Ellie grabbed two *onigiri* from the immaculate array of food, stuffing the second one in her mouth and chewing it hard in search of the sour plum in the centre.

'Who's got sour grapes?' Saskia asked, leaning forward to take the strawberries off her cheesecake and place them on her girlfriend's plate.

The easy affection between the two always left Ellie a little bitter, and she didn't know why, clinging to the idea that it was because she still didn't completely trust Saskia.

'Ellie thinks Haru's playing favourites with Jamie.'

'Hmm.' Saskia's hand hovered over a selection of sweet canned coffees. 'Maybe it'll be good for Jamie to make a friend.' Her words left an awkward silence.

Yes, but why can't that friend be me? Ellie thought.

Making their way to a table in the centre of the room, the moment they sat down her eyes hunted for Jamie while she absent-mindedly grabbed her wolf pendant, squeezing it until the metal dug into her palms.

Her gaze found him and she watched, curious and frustrated, where he sat at a table near the back. He was with the other two boys he and Micky were rooming with. One had his face stuck in a book and the other had headphones in, while Jamie was all permanently messy hair and brown skin like a shining copper penny. It would be his birthday very soon, not that he'd ever let them celebrate it, but it always reminded her that she'd known him her whole entire life. If she looked hard, there would be a small birthmark by his nose, flecks of gold in his eyes and a natural kink in his left eyebrow.

Yet, despite knowing every trace of his face, the boy on the other side of the dining hall was not someone she knew. He didn't move the same way or share a smirk the same way; his eyes didn't glint with dry humour any more. This boy was a dark shadow of her Partizan, riddled with burden and self-blame. Blame that should have fallen on Ellie.

How could he not see? How could Lottie not see? Everything bad that happened to Jamie and Lottie was because they worked for her family, and all Ellie could do was mess up over and over again. She didn't deserve them.

A single beam of sunlight came from the dining-hall door and caught her eye, and then in came her little pumpkin princess flanked by the twins. When Ellie had first met Lottie she seemed so small and delicate, but she was taller now, hair longer and wild, her limbs dense with muscle. Yet her face still retained some of its roundness, and always her kindness shone through, soft and vulnerable, like holding a baby bird in your hands. It made Ellie want to wrap her up and protect her from the world. But Ellie had gone and ruined everything by kissing her in the chocolate factory.

The very thought made her shudder, wondering how on earth she could have thought she was good enough to kiss Lottie. They needed to think about Leviathan, and school, and fixing Jamie, and not get caught up in stupid confusing feelings that she had no right to feel in the first place.

'What's wrong?' Saskia asked.

'Nothing, just . . . Lottie and the twins are coming.'

A knowing look passed between Anastacia and Saskia that Ellie very much wanted to punch off their faces.

Lottie took the seat next to Ellie, smiling obliviously at them, flecks of paint in her fingernails from her morning art class.

'Hey, guys, the twins and I are gonna head to the library after lunch if anyone wants to join us?'

'No can do,' Saskia replied, taking a sip of her iced coffee. 'We have a compulsory meditation session with one of the martial arts –'

Before she could finish one of the Takeshin students from the ceramics course with sticky-out hair came running into the hall, hands still covered in dried clay. '*PINKU ONI-CHAN! PINKU ONI-CHAN!*' she shrieked.

All the other students jumped up, pulling out their phones in a frenzy as if someone had just announced that monsters were crawling out of the earth.

'Pinky . . . what now?' Lola asked.

Only three other students weren't checking their phones – Jamie, although he looked equally confused, and his room-mates. It looked like she had the perfect excuse to speak to him.

The boy with the book raised an eyebrow as they approached, while the boy with the headphones smirked, as if he had expected them. 'I was wondering when you'd come to collect your lost puppy.'

'Excuse me?' Lottie asked, not realizing he was talking about Jamie. But Jamie didn't seem to care, rolling his eyes in a way that was almost humorous, like they might even be friends.

It's only you he doesn't want to be friends with. Terrible, terrible you. Ellie bit down hard on her cheek to shut up the voice in her head, turning to the boy with headphones. Up close she could see that his skin was browner than most of the other students, with dyed-red hair and piercings on the top of his left ear and both eyebrows, which were thick and black like some kind of evil caterpillar. The other boy, who still wasn't looking up, had the sharpest cheekbones she'd ever seen and skin so pale it was almost translucent, drawing attention to his bruised crescent-moon eyes. He looked as if he never slept, only read.

'Hey, Micky.' The red-headed boy beamed over at him and pulled out a chair, gesturing for him to sit, which he did happily.

'Hi, Rio! Hi, Wei!' Micky replied, ignoring the tension.

Without a word, Rio winked at Ellie and she felt like kicking him.

'Obviously we were hoping one of you guys could tell us what's got everyone so excited,' Anastacia said bluntly, taking a seat next to Wei, the boy with the book.

'I like your eye make-up.' Caterpillar Eyebrow's hand moved a lock of red hair from his eyes, looking Ellie up and down. 'Very cool.'

'Rio, stop being a nuisance,' Jamie chastised, which only made Rio laugh.

But, if Ellie didn't know any better, she sensed that Jamie also wanted to know. She took a seat opposite them, spreading her legs across the bench, hoping to give off the energy of a dangerous gangster.

Thank goodness for the boys' uniform, she thought. Something about this boy was already getting on her nerves. 'Can you tell us or not?'

'It's the Pink Demon, *Pinku Oni-chan*.' It wasn't Rio who had replied, but Wei, who thrust out his phone for them all to look at, clicking TRANSLATE FROM CHINESE.

Everyone leaned over, even Jamie, the phone in the middle of the table while Lottie read aloud.

'The Pink Demon, who has been making sporadic appearances throughout Tokyo and nearby cities for the last two months, was spotted this morning in Shinjuku without her usual gang. This has now dispelled rumours that she can only be spotted at night.' She scrolled down and pressed play on the blurry video below the article.

What Ellie saw set her whole body alight.

From the video came the sound of an engine revving, a high-voltage purring in the distance getting closer and closer, until a flash of pink, so fast it could send the whole world spinning, whooshed past the camera. The video stopped just as she appeared. The Pink Demon. Dressed in a black graffiti-covered uniform, and oversized pleated trousers, she roared in the wind, mounted atop her magenta sports motorbike, with all the grace of someone riding a valiant steed. On the side of the bike was a black-painted number four in a circle like a brand, and in the girl's hand was a baseball bat, her weapon, inscribed with colourful writing and numbers. But the most shocking part of the image was the girl's head. Magenta like the bike, with two massive horns protruding from her helmet.

The Pink Demon.

Ellie didn't know if it was the bike or the girl, but she wanted to be that powerful. She wanted to be that free.

'Whoa!' Saskia echoed Ellie's feelings precisely.

Ellie looked up, her mind still a blur of pink and black and the number four.

A familiar voice sounded, bringing the fun to a sudden stop.

'Phones away, everyone.' Sayuri repeated the words in Japanese as well, standing with her hands on her hips in the doorway of the food hall, Miko at her side.

'The queen of the school has spoken,' Rio declared, smirking while everyone rushed to put their phones out of sight.

Ellie couldn't help scowling at Sayuri as she floated across the hall to a table where she pulled out her own beautifully handmade lunch. How could anyone be that perfect?

'*Takeshin Gakuin's secret treasure has long been a mystery to historians around the world, a rumour grown from one of Fujiwara Kou's poems that hints at a priceless artefact hidden "in her heart". To this day no one has been able to solve the mystery and it is widely considered to be a myth.*'

Beside the text was an *ukiyo-e* painting of Kou, depicting her with black hair flowing down to her knees, turning to the spectator with a long deadly sword in her hand. Although there was a tranquillity to the image, there was no denying it – the painting reminded Lottie of the first time she'd seen a picture of Liliana last year in a textbook. The ferocity, the sword, the edge of authority that you could taste. Lottie was getting serious déjà vu. It was far too similar to the curiosities at Rosewood, curiosities that she'd learned not to overlook.

'Secret treasure *and* pink demons!' Lola whispered in the near silent library. 'I think I love this school.'

Micky was spread out quietly opposite them on a cushion, reading over his notes from class while pushing long chocolate-covered biscuits into his mouth.

Staring down at the image, Lottie couldn't help thinking of Ellie's dad. Had King Alexander known about the treasure? Had he looked for it? Had he met Sayuri's parents?

A buzzing came from her pocket and she peeped at her phone to see a message from Ollie, her old friend from home. Without reading it she typed back: Can't talk. Busy.

It was the fifth message he'd sent her since she'd arrived in Japan, and she didn't know how she could make it more clear to him that she had important things to worry about and couldn't be messaging him all the time to tell him about Japan. She had too much on her plate right now.

The library was small compared to Rosewood's – three wooden rooms that smelled of dusty paper, separated by decorated screens, all filled to the brim with books. Non-fiction, ancient stories, poems, their ageing spines created ladders into whole new worlds.

'Do you think it's real?' Lola asked, eyes glittering.

'Maybe,' said Lottie.

'What's real?'

Feather-soft words settled on Lottie's ears, almost making her shiver. Haru leaned over the desk, his face so close to Lottie's that she could detect a faint scent of soap, but she didn't even start at his abrupt appearance; something about him was oddly calming.

Lola grinned up at him, clearly charmed by his smile. 'We're just reading up on the mystery of Takeshin's hidden treasure.'

'Have you found anything interesting?' he asked.

His brown eyes came to rest on Lottie. She couldn't help thinking that maybe Haru would be good for Jamie.

'Not really,' she admitted. 'Do you know anything more about it?'

The Partizan smiled so wide it made him look like a grinning fox. 'I am afraid I do not know much more than you. Though I have heard some people think the treasure is Kou Fujiwara's lost sword.'

With his long index finger, Haru pointed to the sword in the painting, and once more Lottie thought of Liliana and the painting, which depicted her with a sword just as fierce. 'Others think it's a secret passed down through each generation.'

'Haru, there you are!' As if summoned by his words, Sayuri appeared behind them, between bookshelves filled with Japanese history. 'We need some help with filing in my grandfather's office.' She looked around. 'What's going on here?'

'We're looking up the school's secret treasure,' Lottie said happily, but her enthusiasm didn't seem to reach the queen of the school, and all eyes in the library turned on them like she'd just uttered a curse.

The smallest frown creased Sayuri's brow. 'I'm a little confused. Could you enlighten me?' She edged towards them, her eyes fluttering in a strangely menacing show of sweetness. 'I'm not sure how things are done at Rosewood. Are you given special treatment simply because you are a princess?'

Lottie nearly choked. 'Um, no.'

'Good. Then I'm sure you understand that you should be using your free periods to work towards your final project, not entertaining a silly myth.' Sayuri's smile was so tranquil it was

73

almost impossible to believe such words had just come from her lips. Then she added, 'We wouldn't want you to leave here without the grades you need, would we?'

With a quick flick of her hand, Sayuri shut the book with a loud thud, before turning swiftly, leaving Lottie completely speechless.

Shrugging an apology, Haru followed her. As Lottie watched them leave, she couldn't help wondering how such a sharp girl could have such a gentle Partizan. It looked like their research was over.

8

Haru was . . . weird. It was the only word Jamie could think of. He was an incredible mentor, but he'd never met a Partizan like him. Partizans were calculating, serious, deadly, all the things that Haru was not, and it was hard to believe this boy was a whole four years older than him. So when Haru asked Jamie to join him in the hot springs after training he should have said no, that it was a frivolous luxury, and chastised him for being such a lackadaisical Partizan. But he hadn't. He was here.

The two of them alone in the baths, Jamie watched Haru with fascination. The smooth way he moved in the steam, the sharp curve of his jaw that bloomed like a flower when he smiled. All so relaxed, so easy. It reminded him a little of Raphael, minus the ego. His hair had turned into a remarkably silly-looking fluffy ball, but he certainly had the physique of a Partizan.

'What do you think of the Pink Demon?' Haru asked suddenly, cutting off his train of thought and making him look away, embarrassed that he'd been staring.

'I think you should always be cautious of things you don't know, especially when there's a known threat.'

Three days had passed since the frenzy in the hall and there had been no further sightings of the mysterious motorbike rider. Personally Jamie didn't see what the big fuss was about.

Haru laughed, making fun of the serious answer. 'Whoever she and her gang are, they're causing lots of excitement with the youth of Japan.'

Jamie liked how he spoke, simple, straightforward, and his voice made all his words sound like a pillow, as if you could lie down on them.

His jaw tensed at the thought. Partizans were not supposed to be *pillowy*.

'I hear it is your birthday soon,' Haru stated, casually leaning back against the stone side of the bath, unaware of the uncomfortable territory they'd just entered.

'I don't celebrate my birthday,' Jamie said frankly, hoping to cut off the discussion, only it did not have the desired effect.

Haru's expression turned quizzical. 'Why not?'

Not wanting to get into the story of his mother's passing, Jamie felt it better he should go. 'I need to check on my master.'

There was another laugh, softer this time, and it almost sounded like pity. 'Lottie is with Miko. She's working.'

Jamie tensed even more, unable to tell him that Lottie was not the 'master' he needed to check on.

'She is a sweet girl, your princess,' continued Haru. 'You two don't talk very much.'

It was not a question, but the statement caught him off guard.

'We . . .' he began. But his head turned cloudy with the heat and steam, blurry memories materializing in the misty air.

Your fault, your fault!

He'd failed, and Leviathan had taken the Hamelin Formula, and nearly Lottie and him too – and all because he hadn't been paying attention. He'd been too caught up in Lottie and Ellie and what he'd seen them do. Too caught up in Lottie the Portman, who'd insisted that she'd chosen her role and that *he* was the one who was lost.

They'll all leave you behind and you'll be obsolete.

'Are you OK?' Haru pressed the back of his hand to Jamie's forehead, making him flinch. 'I think this bath might be too hot for you.' His chocolate-brown eyes showed genuine concern and it made Jamie's chest ache in a way he resented.

'We're fine,' he said at last. 'What about you and Sayuri? You seem very happy to let her disappear off on her own.'

Haru smiled, but it was not the warm summer smile Jamie had grown used to. It was pondering, thoughtful in a melancholy way, as he leaned back against the stone side of the bath to gaze up at the night sky.

'Sayuri, Sayuri! Sharp as a knife,' he intoned, still staring at the sky as if he expected the stars to give him an answer to a question Jamie couldn't hear. 'She is like a little sister to me, and I want her to live well.'

Jamie had always felt that way about Ellie too. And that is exactly why he had to keep his distance, so he could do his job properly, whether she liked it or not. He felt better knowing that Haru felt the same, even if they went about it in a different way.

Then Haru said the worst possible thing. 'If you weren't a Partizan, what do you think you would want to do instead?'

The words were ice shards slicing through the warmth of the bath.

'I don't,' Jamie replied at last, his tone as cold as his heart. 'I don't think about it.'

Jamie climbed out of the bath, grabbing his towel and making it clear he had no interest in continuing such a distasteful conversation, when he felt Haru's fingers curl round his wrist.

The look in his eye had warped. The comforting chocolate brown had turned to the shade of oak, sombre and wise, and his grip was so tight it felt like bruises must be flowering beneath the skin.

'You should think about it.' Haru's voice was no longer a pillow, but a deep well filled with mystery. 'I've heard you're talented. Music, poetry . . . Why did you choose my class? You could have done theatre, helped with the music or the writing. Why kendo?'

For the first time in his life Jamie felt something he'd never experienced before. He was lost for words. So instead of answering he did the next best thing.

'Get off me or I will break your arm.'

Haru let go, his easy-going demeanour returning so seamlessly it was like he'd never changed. A smile bloomed once more on his face, stretching wide. 'I am deeply sorry to have offended you.' The new tone made Jamie feel foolish for reacting so harshly. Haru gave Jamie one more glimpse of his sunshine smile and added, 'I hope we can still be friends.'

Lottie loved costume making. She loved it, loved it, loved it. It combined all her favourite things: painting, decorating, storytelling and fairy tales. And – oh! – she was learning so many new fairy tales, about Japanese ghosts and demons, *yōkai* and *kami*. There were good *yōkai* and bad *yōkai* and often the most gruesome ones of all were the nicest. It was so different to the folklore she'd grown up with. She only wished she could understand Sayuri as well as she did these fairy tales.

'*Kabocha-chan!*' Miko mumbled, her mouth filled with pins. It was a pet name she'd invented after learning that Lottie answered to 'Pumpkin'. Little did Miko know it was, in fact, her real name. 'What is that thing?'

It took a second for Lottie to realize what she was talking about, until Miko nodded in the direction of the tiara on top of the worktable. Even among all the wonderful horrors that were laid out, the twisting vines of the silver tiara glittered with its own magic, the crescent-moon opal at the centre like rainbow milk.

'Oh, it's a family heirloom. I was hoping to incorporate the design into one of the outfits.'

Scrunching up her nose, Miko took a sip of a florescent-blue drink that smelled like bubblegum. 'No way! Its energy is distracting me.'

'Excuse me?' Lottie blinked, wondering if perhaps she'd actually met someone who could also feel the strange power of Liliana's tiara.

'I said, *put it away* – we need to do a fitting today. Our maiden will be here soon.'

Nodding reluctantly, Lottie slowly placed the tiara in her bag under the table. Apologizing to it under her breath as if it were a real person, she made a mental note to try to persuade Miko later.

It didn't take long to become absorbed in her work again, turning back to the intricate stitching needed to create the cat fur of her design. It was a beautiful and terrible vampire-feline-maiden-monster. It seemed like a bizarre mix but Miko assured her it would satisfy the story, although she had yet to tell it to her. The theatre students were split into groups to enact different plays at the end of the summer. Each group had two costume/set designers, two musicians, two scriptwriters and three performers. And maybe, if Lottie had been paying more attention to everything outside of her strange regalia, she wouldn't have been so shocked to find out who would be wearing her vampire-feline-maiden-monster costume.

'Hello, Princess.'

Lottie looked up from her stitching to see a bright crop of red hair and an inordinate amount of facial piercings.

'How is my costume coming along?' asked Rio.

'Sorry, Rio,' Lottie began, 'I don't think we're making your outfit. This is for the maiden.'

A smirk cracked Rio's face and Miko rolled her eyes behind him.

'Oh, but, *Kabocha-chan* . . .' Lottie bristled at the name, not liking when anyone other than Miko used it. 'I *am* your maiden.' He gave a flamboyant twirl, moving with all the grace and fluidity of a geisha, before switching back to his regular cocky self.

'He's an *onnagata*,' Miko interjected, saving Lottie. 'A boy who plays a girl in theatre. He's good.'

Good was extremely high praise from Miko.

Rio smiled, tilting his head to the side with a decidedly feminine grace. 'All appearance is performance, Lottie.'

'Well then.' Lottie finally found her voice, stepping up to Rio, already thinking about how he would complement her costume. 'Let's get you fitted.'

Stripped down and redressed in a thin black robe, Rio began to transform again into a new skin, mannerisms and expressions turning delicate and coy as if the robe itself had altered his soul.

Lottie and Miko began pinning their fabric over him with utmost care. The trick was that the vampire-cat costume must be able to rip away, turning Rio into an elegant maiden. There was an easiness between Rio and Miko, a buttery quality that could only be achieved through familiarity.

'How do you all know each other?' Lottie asked round the pins she gripped in her mouth.

'Wei goes to our partner school in China. He came to the summer school last year and we became good friends with him, so he applied to come again,' explained Rio. 'I started at Takeshin last year when I moved to Japan from the Philippines with my father. He's Japanese but my mother's Filipino. She's a doctor in Manila. She's going to come over to join us in the New Year.'

'Rio and I decided to stay on with Sayuri for the summer school this year,' added Miko in a distracted tone, still engrossed in the costume, 'to keep her company while her parents divorce.'

Divorce! Lottie had wondered what her parents must be like, and now felt a pang of empathy for the seemingly impenetrable queen of the school.

'Do you know the tale of *Nabeshima Bakeneko*?' Rio said, changing the subject, and Lottie noticed that even his voice had become sweeter, like it had been dipped in honey.

81

'I know it's about a vampire cat who turns into a beautiful maiden, but Miko has yet to tell me the rest.'

A giggle escaped the blue pixie's mouth, and she gave a half-nod to Rio, gesturing for him to continue.

'It was supposedly the favourite story of our school's founder and it is quite a gruesome tale . . .' As he talked, Lottie was transported back to her childhood, lying in bed, wearing her then-oversized tiara, as her mother lay beside her and shared the most fantastic stories. 'In Nabeshima there lived the prince of Hizen, most beloved and beautiful was he, and in his court was a woman who matched that beauty like a lily to a rose.'

Lottie was struck by the coincidental choice of flowers, the thought of them resonating deep within her.

Rio continued. 'Her name was Aoi Tōyō, and she was the prince's favourite. But one night, when she was alone in her quarters, the shadow on her wall began to move, creeping towards her until it was no longer a shadow but a monstrous black cat, who pounced upon her and choked her to death as though she was no more than a measly mouse. Upon tasting Aoi Tōyō's blood, that monster cat morphed into her skin.

'Over the following weeks, the most beloved prince weakened until he could no longer walk or speak, bedridden, clinging to life as if it were being drained from him.'

It took Lottie a moment to realize Rio had stopped talking. She blinked. 'What? Surely that's not the end?'

'Oh no, it's not. The prince was saved by one of his soldiers who stabbed himself in the leg every night to stop the vampire cat's spell from sending him to sleep. They killed the vampire cat, and the prince lived happily ever after. The end. Boring really.'

But Lottie didn't care about the prince. 'What about Aoi Tōyō?' she asked, perplexed.

Both Miko and Rio looked at her with an expression that Lottie didn't understand.

Miko turned back to her sewing, answering in a flat voice, 'She doesn't get a happy ending.'

9

'Japan is the safest place in the whole world.'

Haru's words were followed with a reassuring pat on Jamie's back, and Lottie watched curiously as Jamie tensed. It seemed something had happened; whatever charms Haru had placed over their Partizan were apparently broken.

'Can they not order what they need to be sent to the school?' Jamie asked, scowling at Lottie like this was somehow entirely her fault.

'It will take too long,' said Lottie, 'and we can't afford to waste any time finishing our vampire-feline-maiden-monster costumes.' It wasn't a lie, but it wasn't quite true either.

'Yes, and also . . .' Ellie bustled past Jamie, making for the car. 'I need to get out of this school for a while or I will literally explode.'

Jamie turned his sour look on Ellie. 'You never have this problem at Rosewood.'

'That's because Rosewood doesn't have any *queens of the school* that I'm stuck in a room with.'

Lottie was still trying to figure out Sayuri, and the little crumb of information about her parents that Miko had given her only made her more curious. All she knew for sure was that Ellie's aversion to her was not going to help anyone.

Lottie had to admit it didn't feel entirely safe to leave the school grounds, but Jamie didn't understand how important this was for Ellie. Just thinking about how scared Ellie had been to leave the palace made her realize that. To see Ellie now, almost back to her old self, wanting to get out into the world . . . it could only be a step in the right direction.

It had been Rio's suggestion, when Miko and Lottie had realized they didn't have any black platform shoes in his size, that she should use this as a chance to see Tokyo.

'Jamie would never let me,' Lottie had told them solemnly.

'Jamie? Surely he has to do whatever his master wants.' Rio had raised one of his fluffy caterpillar eyebrows.

'Haru can take them, but then Jamie has to go,' Miko had advised, and something passed invisibly between the blue pixie and her red-haired muse, something that left Lottie both achingly nosy and inexplicably nervous. Yet here she was heading off to Tokyo's fashion district with Jamie, Ellie and Haru.

The moment they set foot in Harajuku the world spun into a rainbow blur. Tightly packed with girls and boys in colourful outfits, the streets had a sticky-sweet feeling like they were walking through a world made of cake decorations.

'Is that guy wearing a real Vivienne Westwood shirt?' Ellie's eyes were practically bulging as she stared at a bleach-haired boy in ripped clothes held together with safety pins.

'Since when do you care about designer fashion?' Lottie teased.

Ellie's hands shot up in defence. 'Vivienne Westwood was an architect of the punk and New Romantic fashion movement, and I pay my respects where they're due.'

Haru was smiling happily, guiding them along and pointing out different boutiques and food vendors. Before Lottie knew it, they were eyeing up vintage Disney dungarees in shop windows while gorging on rainbow candyfloss. It was almost as though they were actually on holiday.

A daisy-themed paper fan with a golden handle caught Lottie's attention. It made her wonder what her mother would have made of all this, an ache spreading through her chest at the harsh realization of how long she'd gone without thinking about her. Her hand hovered over the tiara in her bag, wanting to stroke it.

'Enough,' Jamie snapped, making Lottie jump. 'We have your shoes. Now let's go back to Takeshin.' His whole body was tense. 'It's too crowded. It's unsafe.' Along with his black shirt and jeans, he sported a pair of dark sunglasses, looking remarkably like a candidate for *Men in Black*.

'Jamie!' Ellie growled back at him, a storm in her eyes growing. 'You don't speak to Lottie like that. Ever.' The edge in her voice was bitter and sharp like biting into coffee grounds that she wanted to spit out immediately.

This was not the familiar play biting of a wolf pack she was used to, but real anger, human anger, and it made Lottie nervous.

'People are staring,' Lottie whispered, and relief washed over her when Haru intervened, holding a glossy magazine titled *Popteen* with a pretty pouting model on the cover, seemingly unaware of the tension.

'Jamie,' he began, 'your princess and her friend are in this magazine.'

Stunned by that news, they broke their angry gaze and fanned out to see that Lottie and Ellie really were in the magazine. There were three photographs, two where Lottie looked like the perfect princess, and one of her and Ellie arriving in Japan three weeks ago, baseball cap and sunglasses barely covering her tangle of hair. The images were surrounded by characters she couldn't read.

'What does it say?' Lottie asked Haru, her voice hard when she expected it to be shaky.

He gave her an apologetic look. 'It says you are in Japan and . . .' He paused.

'Tell me.'

'It says the princess and her *bad influence* have flown to Japan to cause trouble in a whole new country.'

Lottie stared at Ellie. A twisted look like she'd eaten something sour rested on her princess's face, and she rubbed at her forehead like she was trying to erase the bad thoughts. Lottie could handle people talking about her, but not Ellie, no matter what.

'I see.' She plastered a smile on her face. *Be kind, be brave, be unstoppable. Please, please, be brave.* 'What nonsense. Best we just ignore it.' She took the magazine from Haru and placed it back on the shelf.

Haru beamed at her. 'An amazing attitude,' he said, but Ellie and Jamie were not so easily convinced, their eyes narrowing like wolves.

'Jamie's right, though; we should head back soon.' Lottie made to leave the shop, indicating they were to follow.

If only she'd stayed inside.

They heard it first. It was a distant electric hum that grew louder and louder, turning into a piercing, screeching symphony of engines and wheels. Then came the smell: fuel and fire and devilish brimstone. Everyone started running to the pavement, desperate to catch a glimpse of the legend. A shriek of wheels, and there they were, a flash of magenta weaving between the traffic. The Pink Demon.

The glow on Ellie's face was undeniable. Her eyes were lit up with the thrill of it.

The motorcyclists, three of them, skidded to a halt, turning back on themselves and creating an impenetrable wall at the far end of the street. In the centre, blinding in the white sun, the Pink Demon held up her weapon, the decorated baseball bat pointing at Lottie and her group. There was menace in the action, and it felt strangely like a warning. Despite the helmet, Lottie was sure the demon was staring her right in the eye.

'Strange. She's never done that before.' Haru sounded more curious than worried. 'Usually she vanishes after an appearance.'

The words sent a chill up Lottie's spine. 'Why are they staring at us?' she mumbled weakly.

'I don't know, and we're not sticking around to find out. Come on,' Jamie said, grabbing both his princess and her Portman and steering them away.

'*Briktah*, Jamie!' cried Ellie. 'Hey, let go! I –'

Jamie yanked at Ellie and she jerked forward reluctantly, stunned by the tightness and strength of his grip.

'I won't take any risks.' He pulled her close, but Lottie could hear his furious murmur. 'Think about your little *sessa*.'

Ellie's eyes snapped into focus over Lottie.

They fast-walked up the street, tracing their steps back to where the car was parked, people still rushing with their phones out to get a shot of the *Pinku Oni-chan*. It wasn't until they got there that it became clear they were being followed.

One of the white-helmeted bikers with a navy blazer suit and cobalt bike sped round the corner, appearing like a clap of thunder on the tarmac. The telltale sound of engines purring let them know the other riders would soon follow.

Something deadly sparked in Haru, and the Partizan began to morph. His deep brown eyes turned dark, shadows behind his gaze. It was like the surface of the earth had cracked, revealing a bubbling and dangerous lava.

'Stay close to me.' Haru's voice was no longer a happy summer breeze, but a fiery pit, crackling and intense.

Lottie looked at him, searching for that soft boy from moments ago, but he was nowhere to be seen and it scared her. It was a fear she'd only felt twice before, when Saskia had tried to kidnap her, and at the Tompkins Manor sabotage. It was a feeling of complete helplessness, and her whole body shook, unable to forget the utterly horrifying memories of when Leviathan had got her, had got *them*. A hand round her arm tried to pull her across the road to the car, but she couldn't move. She was frozen with the panic of being at their mercy once more.

'I can't,' Lottie whimpered, legs buckling. She was disgusted with herself for being so weak but fear overwhelmed her. It was almost as though she could smell Leviathan, a pungent smoke snaking into their lives to suffocate them.

A snarl like a wolf registered in her ear, followed by calm warm breath as she was lifted from the ground. She looked up and saw the world rushing past, the candy-coloured streets of Harajuku a blur behind two hazel eyes.

Jamie was carrying her. No, not just carrying her, but running with her, as if she weighed no more than a kitten.

'I won't let it happen again,' Jamie muttered, and for a split second she really truly felt safe.

Ellie helped Lottie into the car, while Jamie made for the driver's seat.

'It's going to be OK, Lottie,' Ellie said soothingly. 'There's nothing to be afraid of. They're not even moving – they're just . . .' Ellie trailed off at the sound of engines revving assertively. 'They're just watching us.'

Lottie sat up, the world still a strange blur of fear, and through the back window of the moving car she could see them: four of them now. Pink, yellow, purple and blue, flowers on the horizon, and they weren't moving. They slowly grew smaller as the car crawled away from them. But neither did they turn their bikes round. They stayed frozen in place, watching them, until they had turned the corner.

No matter how far away they got, Lottie still felt the presence of Leviathan, as if a shard had punctured the car and driven itself into her heart.

10

'We have no choice but to assume they are part of Leviathan.'

Jamie was pacing up and down the decking outside the paper door of their room.

It had been several hours since their encounter with the Pink Demon and Lottie couldn't get the image out of her head. The way she had torn through the city like a hurricane, Ellie's fascination with her, how her gang had just watched them, and watched them, and watched them . . .

'We don't know they were looking at us specifically, but why are they riding around on motorbikes?' Ellie lay back on her futon in the bright topaz light that leaked through the paper, playing devil's advocate.

'Maybe they know we're in Japan. Maybe they're looking for us?'

'Can't be. The news said they've been popping up since before we got here.'

'I know, but . . .' Lottie winced, looking out over the pond, still unsettled that Leviathan were nearby. 'I just think we need to remember to be careful. They have the Hamelin Formula – goodness knows what they're planning to do with it. It's safe to assume their lackies Julius and Ingrid could be out for revenge after we escaped them.'

Saying their names conjured up the deadly and furious duo, Ingrid's round feline face and Julius's Southern twang.

'Lottie's right.' Both girls turned at Jamie's voice.

'I am?' Lottie practically choked, not sure if she'd heard him right, and he met her confused expression with no humour. It had been so long since he'd agreed with her. 'Yes. I am,' she said quickly. 'We can't take any risks. Just because we're in another country doesn't mean we're safe.'

'We can't throw accusations around, though,' Ellie said. 'We have no proof at all that the Pink Demon – I mean, that those bikes were after us. They made no attempt to follow us.'

Jamie was firm, unflinching. 'Haru was also disturbed by them. It's a Partizan's instinct to sense danger and we both felt it.'

'Where is Haru anyway?' Ellie asked, rubbing the back of her head.

'He's gone to alert Sayuri to a potential threat.'

There was a gentleness in Jamie's voice when he spoke of Haru, and Lottie wondered if seeing him switch into Partizan mode had warmed him to him again. It had had the opposite effect on her; she'd never be able to look at Haru in quite the same way again.

'You're not going to bring the *queen* into this, are you?'

'Is that *all* you're worried about?' Lottie asked, not hiding her irritation. 'We might have had a run-in with Leviathan. You could . . . *We* could have been in danger and you're worried about Sayuri?'

Lottie wanted to be kind, she really did, but right now she was simply too tired.

Silence, sour and full of simmering frustration, filled the air, until finally Ellie let out a long sigh.

'I'm just saying.' She stood up. 'We shouldn't panic. There's no point in ruining our trip because of paranoia. This is meant to be our respite, remember?'

'Need I remind you this isn't a holiday, Ellie?' Lottie flinched at Jamie's words, knowing they'd only annoy Ellie even more.

'The whole reason we're here in the first place is because of Leviathan.' Sure enough the comforting smile Ellie had put on for Lottie turned into a snarl. 'Yes, Jamie, I'm fully aware this is all my fault, and none of us would even be in this mess if you didn't work for my fam—'

The paper door slid open with hasty efficiency, cutting Ellie off and revealing Sayuri in a spectacular blaze of white, bathed in the calming scent of lilies. Miko stood just behind her, the dusky evening light making her hair look like a purple shade of poison.

'Are you all OK?' Sayuri asked. She was dressed in a dazzling white robe that floated behind her, ghostly and graceful.

'We're fine,' Ellie said.

'And Haru. How was he?'

'Very helpful, a model Partizan.' Jamie relayed to her how calm he'd been and even added how good a tour guide he was.

A pensive look overtook Sayuri.

'Is something wrong?' Lottie couldn't stop herself asking.

Sayuri's face became a perfect mask of calm once more. 'I am quite fine. I think you should get an early night tonight.'

Lottie nodded, relieved to have an end to the discussion. Until all hell broke loose.

'Would you shut up?'

Lottie's mouth hung open. She could hardly believe what she'd just heard.

'I am so sick of you walking around here like you're perfect.' Ellie spat each word like acid. 'I can see right through you and you're a total fake.'

'Ellie!' Lottie and Jamie gasped in unison but Ellie gave them a sharp look that stopped them in their tracks.

'May I suggest we discuss what has upset you in the morning, once you've calmed down?' Sayuri seemed completely unfazed by the outburst.

'Upset me?' The venom was undeniable and Lottie realized there was more behind Ellie's anger than just Sayuri. 'How could you upset me when you never do anything wrong, ever?'

'Ellie, you need to calm down.' Lottie grabbed her arm, intending to soften her fury, but all it did was change direction.

'How can I calm down when we're completely trapped?' She turned suddenly, all her rage thundering in a whirling storm. 'Don't you see? We're stuck here, we're stuck, and you're stuck because of me. The cage is bigger and looks different but we're still trapped, still as helpless as we always were, and it's all my fault, and I *HATE* it!'

'Leave.'

Lottie blinked, for a moment unsure who'd spoken.

'I said, *leave*,' Sayuri repeated. 'I'm moving you both to a room away from Miko and me. I think you'd both benefit from spending some time alone.'

'Oh, great. The perfect queen thinks she knows how to fix everything. We're saved,' Ellie drawled sarcastically.

'I said, LEAVE!'

Ellie reared up, clearly preparing to make another snide comment, when a single salty tear escaped down Lottie's cheek.

She squeezed her fists together painfully. 'Let's just go, Ellie.' She was so tired.

Ellie couldn't even look her in the eye, her gaze landing on Jamie who shot her such an intensely profound look of disappointment that even Lottie could feel the burn of it.

'Fine, we'll go,' she said.

Jamie helped them move their belongings. Everyone in the dorms watched in silent curiosity while they dragged their slippered feet through the wooden corridors, to the tiny spare room that had previously been occupied by thirty or so hand-painted paper lanterns. It was stuffy and considerably less elegant than their last room but Lottie didn't have the energy to care any more. Anastacia and Lola poked their heads in, but Lottie shook her head, not wanting to explain.

'Will you two be OK?' Jamie whispered to her through the doorway, moving the last lot of luggage. It was almost nice to see him show concern again.

'I'll be fine.' She smiled, not caring how fake it looked. 'I always am.' Although she couldn't speak for Ellie.

Jamie nodded and she watched him walk down the gloomy path, a new symphony of night-time creatures chirruping in the moonlight.

The moment he was gone, Lottie changed into the oversized Hello Kitty nightie and shorts she'd bought in Harajuku and climbed on to her futon. Ellie did the same and then they lay there in silence, staring at the ceiling, until one of them caved.

'Ellie,' Lottie began, the shape of her friend's name a foreign object in her mouth. 'You know it's not your fault, right?'

'That's easy for you to say.'

The words felt like a punch in the gut, and she turned to look at her princess. Ellie rolled on to her side to face her. 'I shouldn't have said all that stuff. I just got so angry when I saw us in the magazine. I feel so useless, and weak.'

But Lottie wasn't upset about Ellie's outburst; she was upset about everything surrounding it. 'I don't care about that; I'm happy you said it. I just . . . I wish you'd be honest with me.'

It wasn't until she finished speaking that Lottie realized she was thinking about the kiss again, still confused by what it meant.

'Well, maybe the media's right . . .' Ellie said dully.

'What?'

'About me. I'm a bad influence. You wouldn't even be here if not for being my Portman, and that grade. If Leviathan –'

'I'd rather it was Leviathan. I still worry sometimes that it was just a stupid mistake I made.'

'Maybe the stupid mistake was you becoming my Portman in the first place.'

'Ellie!' Lottie growled, a sound she was not used to making, but she couldn't help it. 'How can you say that? How could you say something so cruel? I thought . . . and that kiss, and everything. What's wrong with you?'

The words came tumbling out of her, like coughing up barbed wire, and she couldn't stop them. Why would Ellie want her around if that's how she felt? After everything they'd been through together, for her to turn round and say something so ridiculous.

'What?' Ellie spluttered.

This was too much. Lottie scrambled off her futon and stormed up to the paper screen where her trainers lay, slipping them on.

'I'm going for a run. I'll see you later.'

'Lottie, wait. I didn't mean it like that. I –'

But in one violent bang of the door she shut Ellie out, and off she went to join the insects in the night and scream.

11

The late-night air was hot and oily, leaving a sheen of sticky sweat all over Lottie's skin. Her clothes clung to her body with gummy adhesion and the peel-thin sliver of the moon provided little illumination on the tar-black paths. She'd run up the decking, all around the giant pond and off down one of the walkways leading closer to the bamboo forest. Finally her feet slowed, and she found herself at the cat shrine, squinting stone grins watching her curiously. Her blood must have been particularly tasty because itchy pink lumps were blooming all over her legs and arms from mosquito bites.

'And I suppose the vampire cat of Nabeshima will be after my blood too?' Lottie huffed up at one of the stone statues, leaning her hands on her knees while she caught her breath. 'I'm afraid she'll have to be quick, or the mosquitos will take it all.' She tried to smile at the cat, feeling stupid and lonely in the silence that followed.

The few lights left on in the dorms were a haze in the night, the faint glow of the moon dipping behind a cloud, leaving Lottie submerged in darkness. It was not just physical darkness, but the dark inside her mind of unknowing and uncertainty.

There was too much going on inside her head: Leviathan, Jamie, Ellie, Sayuri. Nothing felt sturdy; even her own view of herself had started to feel warped and confusing.

Bad influence. How could Ellie say something so stupid?

'What do I do?' she asked the statues. 'Where do I even start?'

Lottie knew the questions were pointless, but what she hadn't expected was to get a reply.

Out of the shadows emerged the largest black cat Lottie had ever seen. Its eyes glowed yellow like a witch's familiar and it walked fluidly as though it had taken shape from the dark itself.

Lottie watched as the cat sat at her feet. *The vampire cat of Nabeshima.*

That was Lottie's first thought, and if she really were about to get strangled to death and have her blood and skin stolen, then it was her fault for suggesting it to the stone cats in the first place. The thought sent a shiver down her back that made her want to retreat slowly and then bolt all the way to the safety of the dorm. Yet the cat merely sat there watching her, its tail gliding left and right, left and right.

You should never ignore these things.

Miko's words, but the idea of following this cat anywhere in the middle of the night was terrifying.

Lottie's gaze fixed on the cat's swishing tail. What would Liliana have done? Had she been here in Japan? Had she felt the same worries and uncertainties?

If she had, then she'd most certainly braved them, and if she hadn't, Lottie never would have met Ellie and Jamie and all her friends from Rosewood and Takeshin in the first place.

'OK then. Show me the way.'

The big black cat continued to stare at her, unmoving, and embarrassment crawled up her spine as she realized she was talking to a cat. Just as she was getting ready to give up and walk back to the dorm the cat stood up, stretching out its long back with a little 'mrrow'. Its feet made gentle padding sounds until at last it began slinking into the darkness.

The sound of the cicadas got louder as she followed Vampy – the name she'd christened him with in her mind – along some of the smaller scenic pathways that gave the best view of the surrounding bamboo.

They paused briefly on their journey, stopping by a small wood-panelled building. Lottie nearly jumped out of her skin when she looked up at a golden woman pointing a sword directly at her. Only it wasn't a woman at all, but a statue: Kou Fujiwara watching them as they passed her museum, cast in bronze, her blade humming with quiet warning. Without a second thought, Lottie bowed to the statue, before continuing up the path to follow Vampy. Babbling water gushed beneath her feet as she crossed over a tiny wooden bridge near the back of the theatre, leading up to a set of mud and root steps in an area of the school she had yet to explore. It soon became clear why she'd never ventured this far, because when she reached the top she was met with nothing but dense bamboo held off by frayed green net.

The forest in front of her grew thick and large, fog appearing out of nowhere. The noises of the insects seemed to grow louder and wilder at the edge of these trees, the netting scarcely holding back the enchanting melody that echoed from within. Lottie stared down at Vampy, head tilted as if asking the big black cat whether she was supposed to be here, and in response the cat dipped under the netting and vanished into the mystery of the woods.

Lottie stared into the milky darkness where the cat had disappeared, and she felt in the shiver of her skin that the forest was staring back. She was sure she had reached the end, that the bamboo trees could not be penetrated, when two glowing yellow bulbs shone out from the shadows, beckoning her to follow further. She hesitated, but only for a second before getting down on her knees, not caring that her nightdress would be muddied, and crawled into the forest. Everything turned black again, the trees so tall and dense that they blocked out all light. But when she stood up the darkness vanished, replaced with tiny glowing orbs, fireflies that danced around her in a glittering flurry. The forest created its own light and even the moon had a different luminosity here, as if the sparks of its light were caught inside the moss and creatures, giving the world a cloudy, elegant shimmer like the surface of a pearl. The atmosphere felt familiar and new all at once. It felt like the Rose Wood.

The yellow eyes of Vampy continued to shine out, a lantern on a path, guiding her forward. Lottie did not notice, but all her thoughts and worries had disappeared, left behind her.

A prickle of fear tickled her neck then vanished. She felt like she was being watched, yet felt entirely alone. And all the while she kept the image of Liliana in her mind. Brave, relentless, a pioneer. If Lottie was going to make even half the positive impact she had on the world, then she needed to be just as unstoppable. Then Vampy vanished, fading into the moss behind an outcrop of bamboo. Lottie followed, but those glowing yellow orbs were nowhere to be seen. She was completely alone, and now the fear crept up again and there was nothing to push it back.

Turning round, all she saw was repeating patterns, the glowing fireflies dancing in the same image over and over. She turned round again in the hope that the black cat might have reappeared, but all she succeeded in doing was further disorientating herself.

'I'm lost,' she whispered into the dark. She was Gretel in the woods, her trail of breadcrumbs vanished with no way of knowing how to get home. If she was not careful, she might get eaten by a witch . . . or a vampire cat. Even the night-time sounds of the tiny creatures appeared to have been silenced. Lottie suddenly realized how stupid she'd been. Alone, in her nightdress and trainers, with muddy legs and mosquito bites.

She remembered the great big oak tree from the Rose Wood, so old and thick that you could imagine setting up a home inside its trunk. It was where Lottie had curled up to cry on her own, and it was where Lola had run to when she was upset about her father. The tree was like a beacon and a mother, calling out and cradling all those that needed comfort, its long branches a set of soothing arms. If Rosewood and Takeshin were really linked, then maybe there was something like that here too . . .

The fog parted on a small clearing, a perfect circle of green bamboo trees. Right in the centre was a tree, tall and fat, and with such peculiar and fascinating bumps that it looked like a giant woman emerging from the ground. Along the bottom grew silver vine in abundance, the little white flowers like patterned lace.

'Mrroow!'

Lottie's eyes lit up as Vampy reappeared from behind the tree.

'There you are!' She grinned at the black cat, walking over to it. It was so dark she could hardly see a thing, but as she leaned down to stroke Vampy a firefly illuminated the tree, revealing marks on the trunk, browned and white in the centre, carved in thick to last for centuries.

Lottie had seen this sigil before in a book and in a diary. Lili's diary.

It was a lily with two slivers of a semicircle on either side. The crest of the Mayfutts. Her ancestors, and Liliana's. But what was it doing all the way out here in Japan?

She straightened up sharply. One thought sprang into her head, as bright as the fireflies around her.

The answer to all her questions lay in that diary. She needed the diary she'd left behind at Rosewood – and she knew exactly who could help.

12

In Covent Garden, England, Binah Fae was watching the sun rise from the roof garden of her parents' penthouse. The little green nook looked down over the sun-soaked streets, trucks beeped in familiar melodies, while dustmen, bakers and business owners carried out their early-morning duties across the great city.

Wrapped in a canary-yellow robe, Binah liked to get up extra early during the summer holidays to water her plants and watch London wake up with a nice cup of camomile tea and a chapati smothered in strawberry jam. She'd read once that one of her idols, Oprah Winfrey, tried to get up every day between half five and half six to experience the day to its fullest. Even with the time difference she liked to think they were connected by their early mornings.

'Looks like it's nearly time to give you a haircut,' she whispered to the philadelphus flowers, pouring them their breakfast of water and plant food.

She'd also read once that plants grew better if you talked to them, and even though there was no clear science to back it up sometimes you just had to trust your instincts. Then she heard the buzzing from her phone.

Calls at this time were certainly not a regular part of her morning routine, but one look at the number and she knew all her plans were likely about to go up in flames.

'Lottie!' She slid the Facetime button to reveal sun-reddened cheeks and frizzy blonde curls.

Lottie looked relieved. 'You're awake?'

'Yes. Luckily for you I'm an early riser.' Binah could see something had happened. 'What's wrong?'

'Nothing,' her friend replied much too quickly. 'It's just, well, actually . . .'

'Why are you whispering?' Binah leaned down close to the screen, finding the whisper to be infectious.

'I don't want anyone eavesdropping.' Lottie looked around nervously before continuing. 'Listen, I need your help –'

'Where's Ellie?'

Lottie blinked, something fluttered past her head, which appeared to be a dragonfly, and the silence spoke far louder than words.

'Tell me. What's happened?' Binah was nervous now.

'We had a little falling-out the other night.' She sounded distant and melancholy. Shaking her head, Lottie suddenly snapped to efficiency. 'But that's not why I'm calling. Listen, this is going to sound super weird, so hear me out.' She took a deep breath and began talking in a rush. 'I found the crest of the Mayfutts carved into a tree in the Kiri Shinrin – the woods surrounding Takeshin – and I just have this feeling that it might give me a clue to the secret treasure hidden in the school.'

'Secret treasure? How delightful.' It was rare that Binah was confronted with a mystery she was unfamiliar with, and her mouth watered at the prospect.

Lottie gave a wry smile. 'Yeah, I thought you'd say that.'

A truck in the distant London streets made a great honking noise.

Binah shook her head clear. 'And you're sure it was Liliana's crest?' she asked slowly.

'I'm positive. I know that symbol like it's my own face.'

Ever since Binah was a little girl she'd had a knack for puzzles. She'd learned from a young age that puzzles are not about connections but about patterns, and once you learn to spot patterns you see them everywhere.

'You want me to get the diary from Lili's study at Rosewood,' Binah said, this latest puzzle already settling into place in her mind.

'I . . . yes!' Lottie's eyebrows shot up in surprise, but Binah was used to people being surprised by her. In fact, she even found it amusing. 'Please,' Lottie added quickly, 'if it's even possible.'

Taking a small sip of her honeyed tea, Binah tried to contain her delight. The very idea that the mysteries of Rosewood could stem all the way to Japan was as sweet as the tea in her mouth.

She began tapping her teacup. 'Breaking into Rosewood is, as I'm sure you know, highly illegal. I'll have to do some research, and I'll need help, but I'll see what I can do.' She spoke calmly, ignoring how her heart thumped. But it was not with fear. She was excited.

The grin on Lottie's face lit up the whole screen, and the glow of the sun seemed to surge around her.

'Will you tell Ellie?'

'I want to,' Lottie admitted after a long pause. 'I think we did the right thing by coming here, but . . . it's complicated.

She thinks my failing grade is her fault, still refusing to realize we're a team, that I *want* to be there for her. It's like she's pushing me away.'

Another pattern.

'Lottie,' Binah said, seeing the story unfold in her head, 'I can't pretend to know what you're feeling, or what happened, but if Ellie wants to share in this mystery, she needs to share something of herself first, and she has to figure it out herself. She can't always rely on you to guide her.'

The patterns were so obvious, and they revealed a puzzle with one clear solution. She could see it in her mind as a garden. Lottie was a rose, straightforward, valiant, blooming clearly, with a scent it shared with the world, both recognizable and comforting. Ellie was more difficult, a western underground orchid that required digging through the ground to reveal its sweet fragrant flowers. But they were there just the same.

So here was the puzzle and she shared it with Lottie: 'If there are roses in the garden, how can you encourage the orchid, which has spent its whole life hidden away, that it is worthy of the rose?'

'I don't think I understand,' Lottie said eventually.

Smiling through the screen, Binah took one final sip of tea. 'I'm saying,' she offered calmly, 'if you and Ellie want to get past this, she needs to stop blaming herself for everything bad that happens.'

'But what if she can't? What if she keeps pushing me away?'

'Then I guess we'll all just have to hold on tight.'

13

Every time Lottie thought no one was looking, she'd check her phone. *What's she waiting for?* Ellie wondered.

Lottie was still giving her the silent treatment, barely exchanging more than a few words when necessary. It was like she expected something of her, and it wasn't even angry, it was hopeful, and it only made Ellie feel like she was letting her down even more.

Saskia laughed after a slurp of her ramen. 'That's probably why she won't speak to you. She wants you to figure out how to fix it on your own. Ask Anastacia.'

Saskia's skin had grown even darker in the Japanese sun, glowing gold and radiant, but Ellie's Maravish genes simply gave her a pinkish brown stripe across her nose and cheeks that made her feel like a little kid.

'It's true,' Anastacia replied, breezing over to the table and taking a seat by her girlfriend. 'I'm a terrible communicator.' Chestnut hair billowed behind her with a dismissive swish of her hand, but Ellie was sure that wasn't it. Lottie was the best communicator she knew.

On the other side of the room Rio made a comment and everyone laughed. Even Lottie and Jamie had the shadow of a smile over their lips, and the two of them looked at one another, some kind of unknowable understanding passing between them, and it made Ellie feel like spitting her food back on to the plate in disgust.

Why did it bother her so much? To see Jamie talking to Lottie again?

It was like she was staring at the happy ending, an alternate dimension where neither of them had ever worked for her family and they could be happy and live normal lives without her.

'You should ask Micky. Ever since he and Percy started dating they're as perfect as chocolate and strawberries,' Lola trilled.

'We don't have that problem,' Micky replied casually, sticking his third chocolate biscuit in his mouth.

'See? Perfect.' Lola giggled, and Micky stuck his tongue out playfully back at her.

'No.' He smiled, his blue eyes turning dozy and enchanted as a pink blush crept over his cheeks that reminded Ellie of Lottie. 'Because Percy always knows exactly what to do. We couldn't talk when we met as kids so we learned how to read each other in different ways.' Micky spoke so candidly, with not an inch of irony or doubt about his boyfriend, that it made Ellie feel awkward. She could never be so open with her emotions.

'Urgh, sometimes I feel like I barely know Lottie at all,' Ellie groaned, planting her forehead on the table with a painful thump. It was too hot in Japan and their new tiny 'time-out' room only made her feel more sticky and out of place.

This is Sayuri's fault, she thought, but she didn't really believe it.

'Wow, being in love sure sounds exhausting.'

Ellie's head shot up so fast at Lola's words that the world started spinning. She couldn't be in love with Lottie; she didn't deserve her.

'Rosewood students.' Ellie nearly jumped out of her skin as Haru's breathy voice blew around her. 'My apologies, I did not mean to startle you.'

He'd appeared in front of them, dressed a little more sharply than usual, with fitted trousers and a tank top, but his hair was as fluffy as ever.

'Not at all,' Ellie said, trying to compose herself.

'If you would all please come with me to Chiba Sensei's office. We have a gift for you.'

Nodding reluctantly, Ellie got to her feet. Right now she didn't feel worthy of a gift.

Chiba Sensei's office was located on the northern side of the pond by the boys' dormitory and nestled beside Kou Fujiwara's museum with its bronze statue of the founder outside brandishing a deadly sword, challenging all who entered her domain. Ellie felt her watching them on their way past, the blade aimed directly at her heart.

As soon as they got to the office, the refreshing scent of sandalwood incense hit them like a bolt of energy. The room was only just large enough to fit all the Rosewood students, with Haru and Sayuri perched at either side of the headmaster behind his desk. Modestly decorated, with a simple *tatami* mat and a sliding door that looked out over a small zen garden, the room felt ornamental, like they'd walked into an expensive doll's house and must not touch a thing.

Lips curving in what was almost a smile, the headmaster stepped forward while Haru and Sayuri bowed in respect.

'I have made some very special arrangements for you all. A chance to experience a truly wonderful piece of Japanese culture.'

It was hard to concentrate after Lola's bombshell statement. Ellie just wanted to get out of the headmaster's office; the tight space, the ceremony of it all, was like being back at the palace. And then it came, the worst possible gift they could ever have received.

'Haru has brought it to my attention that one of you is celebrating a birthday this weekend, the twenty-sixth of July.'

Oh no.

Haru shot his happy-go-lucky smile directly at Jamie, with no idea of the storm that would follow.

'Every year Takeshin sponsors the *Aka Taiyo Matsuri*, a festival in Tokyo, and I have arranged for you to attend in celebration of your Partizan's birthday.'

Oh no! Oh no! Oh no!

There was only one rule Jamie demanded. Do not celebrate his birthday, ever. And, even with their growing distance, she knew better than to break that rule.

Jamie's presence in the room felt like a growing mass of darkness. She didn't dare look at him.

Doing better than she was, Lottie held face, armed with a perfectly pleasant smile. 'Chiba Sensei,' she said with not even a quiver. 'This is indeed a wonderful gesture, but I'm afraid . . .' She trailed off, distracted by what she could see just beyond the headmaster . . . His granddaughter.

Sayuri shook her head in warning, and with one quick motion of her fingers gestured for them to bow.

It appeared this was an offer they were not allowed to refuse.

'But we will need extra security,' Lottie quickly said, bowing as Sayuri had instructed. 'Would we be allowed to borrow Haru?'

Damn, she was so smart.

How did Lottie think of these things? How was she such a good diplomat? How did she stay so calm when everything was such chaos? And how had Ellie messed everything up so badly?

Bad influence. The words pounded against her skull like a fever.

'Ah, yes.' Chiba Sensei nodded. 'I know you have security concerns, but Hinamori-san has assured me that the motorbiking menace has recently been apprehended and will be nothing to worry about. Nevertheless,' he continued, and Ellie strained to listen, hardly believing that fiery force could have been caught and that they would have heard nothing about it, 'he will escort you for peace of mind.'

'An excellent idea,' Haru chimed in.

Biting her cheek, Ellie turned her head just enough to see Jamie.

Nothing. His face was entirely blank, a cold wet lump of clay with no emotion or purpose. She wanted to reach over to him to push his nothingness into something, anything, dig deep to find him at the centre. But once again all she could think was that this was somehow her fault.

Bowing low, he spoke in a monotone: 'Thank you.'

'This is a nightmare,' Ellie groaned.

Saskia pinched Ellie hard on the arm.

'Ouch, what the hell is your problem?'

'See? Not a nightmare.'

Laughing to herself as if she were the funniest person in the world, Saskia ate a spoonful of her vanilla pudding.

Jamie and Lottie had swiftly vanished back to the dining hall, but Ellie couldn't bear facing their solemn expressions, opting to take her dessert out to the decking by the koi pond, the sun so hot she thought it might melt her face off. Much to her irritation, Saskia had decided to follow.

'You don't understand. This festival is a curse. I can feel it. Jamie hates his birthday, there's a possible threat out there, and with this Lottie thing it's just . . .' Her words dried up and another groan escaped her. 'What am I supposed to do? This is all my stupid fault.'

'You're completely wrong.'

'What?'

'You're wrong,' Saskia reiterated. 'This festival is a blessing. Listen, you have until this weekend to figure out how to make it up to Lottie, and you'd better make it good.'

The smell of the vanilla pudding drowned out everything else, Saskia's golden spoon swirling in the pot.

'Ellie. You need to be honest with your feelings, from one gay girl to another. That's all Lottie wants. She wants you to drop your ego and be honest. Tell her what's bothering you, instead of bottling it all up and pushing her away.'

'You have no idea what you're talking about.' Ellie felt her defences come up, an anger that she didn't understand rising like a hurricane through her body, but Saskia calmly waved it away. 'No one would be here in this mess, if not for me. I did this.'

'Do you really believe that? Do you think Lottie believes that?'

A particularly fat koi, gold and crimson, bobbed out of the muddy water, plopping upward ungracefully, and Ellie was sure she could smell it: salt and mud. It was gross. As quickly as it appeared, the fish vanished back into the murk.

'I don't even know what I believe any more,' Ellie admitted. 'I need to think, but,' she continued, staring at the koi as they moved around in circles, 'if I'm going to fix this, I need to do it properly. And that means . . .' She glanced at Saskia. 'I need you to do something for me first.'

14

'Would you like one?' Haru pointed at a curious fish-shaped cake, with pretty scale patterns across it. There must have been hundreds of them, from rows and rows of street-food vendors with bright calligraphed banners, the salty-sweet smells filling the evening air. 'They're *taiyaki*, with a sweet filling.'

'Yes, that would be nice, thank you,' Lottie replied, mirroring Haru's breezy smile, although she wasn't sure how on earth she could eat anything with her *yukata* tied so tight.

Miko had insisted they all wear the summery cotton kimonos if they were going to the *matsuri*, even if none of them actually wanted to be there. Hers was a pink-and-cream fabric with plump red cherries that made her feel like a summer pudding. It didn't match her tiara at all, but she was wearing it anyway, needing to feel like herself again.

The boys were also wearing *yukatas* in a dark blue and green material, which made Haru look light and comfortable while Jamie looked like a formidable warrior. Lottie wondered where they were keeping their weapons.

'Me too. Anastacia?' Saskia said, not even looking at Haru.

'Yes please.'

115

'Us too, please,' the twins said in unison.

Lottie was sure she saw Haru's lips twitch. It had been rude for Saskia to assume he was offering her one as well. Ellie didn't respond. She seemed nervous, fidgeting with the sash on her star-patterned *yukata*, though Lottie quickly looked away again.

It had been a struggle, but she was sticking by Binah's advice and waiting for Ellie to open up to her first. She'd quickly come to realize it was very, very hard. But, miraculously, Jamie was talking to her again. Kind of.

She smiled over at him in an apologetic way, knowing he must hate this situation more than anyone, and he nodded back to let her know it was OK, more of an interaction than she could ever have dreamed of just a week ago.

'My pleasure,' replied Haru. 'And Jamie-kun? As it is your birthday?'

Jamie seemed to prickle at the offer. He had reluctantly agreed to accept the headmaster's offer on the very strict conditions that they were not to stay longer than an hour, and no one, under any circumstances, was to get him a gift, and this sweet treat was tilting dangerously close to the parameters of 'gift'.

'No, thank you.' His eyes darted around, constantly on the lookout, as if he expected an ambush at any moment. 'Will Sayuri be joining us?'

Pretty yen notes passed between Haru and the food vendor, and he began handing out the sticky filled cakes.

'She is with her friends,' Haru replied simply.

'You're mad!' Saskia chuckled. 'I wouldn't let Ani anywhere out of my sight in a place this crowded.'

116

'She is a smart girl,' he replied calmly, and it almost sounded like a jab.

Lottie felt bad for thinking it, but she was relieved that Miko and Sayuri were somewhere else; she didn't think her presence would help Ellie in any way.

'Look – the Ferris wheel!' Micky pointed to the glowing pink and emerald lights of the ride at the other end of the walkway. Behind it, red sky was giving way to moonlight, a cloudless backdrop for the swirling patterns. It was mesmerizing, like a spinning wheel that might send her into an eternal slumber.

'We're going on it,' Saskia proclaimed, marching them all forward.

There was no room for argument. Above them lanterns like floating flames criss-crossed in diagonal lines, blurring into a haze of red the closer they got to the Ferris wheel.

'I'm going with Micky.' Lola pulled her twin close to her side, their matching peach *yukatas* morphing into one. Miko had spent a long time looking for a matching pair, saying that most boys' kimono styles were too bland for Micky.

Saskia smirked, scrutinizing Ellie like she was trying to give her some kind of secret code. 'I'm with Ani.'

'Lottie.' Ellie spoke her name with such strong conviction that it was almost comical. 'Do you . . . Do you wanna come with me?'

Lottie felt the wolf at her chest burning as her cheeks turned pink and she smiled at Ellie's uncharacteristic bashfulness. She felt hope rise within, mad at herself for ever having thought that Ellie wouldn't be able to open up.

'Yes, of course. I'd love to.' Lottie beamed, and being able to smile at her again was so sweet it made her teeth ache.

117

'Great.' Ellie grinned back, and it almost looked like she was blushing.

The only two left were Haru and Jamie. She watched as Jamie's body seemed to recoil in on itself, muscles retreating beneath the swathes of dark fabric like he wanted to disappear into the night.

'Why don't you two go together?' Lottie asked.

Haru's eyes lit up, but one look at Jamie and he shrugged. 'I would like that very much, but I think Jamie would be happier if we stayed here to keep watch.'

There was no room for debate; she could see as clearly as the gold flecks in his eyes that Jamie would not be leaving the ground. She was only thankful that at least he had Haru with him.

Each side of the Ferris-wheel compartments was covered in large sheets of coloured paper, shining bright against the dark sky from the LED lights underneath like glowing clouds. Sat cosily by Ellie's side, Lottie at once felt shy, something she hadn't felt around Ellie for a long time.

'Are you comfortable?' Ellie asked, a little awkward, as the wheel creaked into motion.

'I'm OK. I'm just getting used to wearing this *yukata*,' said Lottie, straightening her sleeves. 'They're so pretty. I can't believe you agreed to wear one!'

'I didn't want to incur any more of Miko's rage and . . .' Ellie hesitated, looking out of the side as the festival below got smaller. 'I thought it'd make you happy, and I definitely owe you.'

Lottie gulped. Was Ellie about to actually open up?

'Lottie, listen, I . . . well, I shouldn't have been so rude to Sayuri. I don't wanna be a mean person. I won't do it any more.'

The sinking feeling in Lottie's stomach was instantaneous, pulling her down the higher they climbed. Was that all Ellie was going to say?

'Yes, well –'

'No, wait, there's more I need to say.' Ellie pushed her hand back through her ebony hair, the silver light shining off it like a halo, and Lottie couldn't help noticing how long it had grown.

'Ellie, your hair.'

'What?' She looked up at her, confused.

'It's so long now. It's almost past your chin.'

Ellie grabbed a strand, trying to look at it. Failing, she dropped it, and their eyes met like magnets, dark and light facing head-on.

'Lottie, what I meant to say is, I'm sorry.' A powerful breeze caught up with them, blowing Ellie's hair around her head, but she didn't flinch. 'I'm sorry you have to deal with this media stuff, I'm sorry you have to deal with Leviathan, and mostly I'm sorry you have to deal with me.'

'Ellie, that's not –'

'No, listen.' She cut her off, a storm brewing behind her eyes. 'Being my Portman has put us both through hell, but I'm so thankful to have you. It's hard seeing you constantly put yourself in danger for me. I never want to be the reason you're hurt. You're the most important thing in the whole world to me, and until we're safe and we really can be free, I have to trust that you know what you're doing and stop blaming myself. Until then, until I know what I'm feeling, I can't play with your emotions.'

It took Lottie a moment to realize she'd stopped breathing and when she finally took a deep breath she saw they'd reached the top. Tears brimmed in her eyes, making the world turn blurry.

'Ah, geez, I made you cry. I'm sorry.' Ellie began fiddling with her sash again and pulled out a paper fan. 'I got this for you, to apologize. I had Saskia and Anastacia pick it up from town.'

Lottie didn't think she could possibly feel any more overwhelmed, but when she looked down at the gift her whole heart lit up, spreading warmth through her body like sunshine. It was the daisy paper fan she'd seen in Harajuku, the one that reminded her of her mother, Marguerite.

'I saw you looking at it and it made me think of your mum and –'

Lottie wrapped her arms round Ellie, enveloping her in the cotton of her *yukata*. She squeezed her tight enough that they might melt together, and in return she felt Ellie's arms fold round her back. They were complete. Beams of twinkling embers from the glittering festival below surrounded them in their colourful cloud as they floated into the moonlit sky.

'Thank you,' Lottie whispered. 'And please always remember that nothing that's happened to us is your fault. None of it.'

Machinery creaked around them and they slowly began to descend back to earth, the lights and scents of the festival washing over them.

'I'll try to remember,' Ellie replied, the two of them squeezing each other once more before pulling apart. 'Now, did you have something you wanted to tell me?' Ellie asked. 'I feel like you've been about ready to burst.'

Lottie had almost forgotten about her discovery in the forest.

'I found something,' she said. 'When I ran away, that night we had an argument. It was the strangest thing. In the forest I found a carving in a trunk of bamboo that was so big it looked like it should have split the ground in two.' Lottie looked up, checking Ellie was following, and found her eyes glimmering. 'It was Liliana's crest, a lily. But it doesn't make any sense.'

'Why?'

'Because Liliana was alive during the *Sakoku* period in Japan, when their borders were closed to the rest of the world, so . . .' She mulled over the image in her head again – all the questions it raised. 'How did she get here? And why? What's the connection between Takeshin and Rosewood? I can't stop thinking it's a clue to the hidden treasure.'

'How can I help?' Ellie asked, a grin spreading over her face.

'Well, actually, I've already asked Binah if she can get Liliana's diary to us.'

'So that's why you keep checking your phone!' Laughing, Ellie stared up at the sky as if she'd just solved her own personal puzzle, before turning back to hold out her hand for Lottie to take. She looked like Ellie again, gallant and handsome in a moonlit frame. 'Another mystery for us to solve together.'

With a creak of metal, they reached the ground where Saskia, Anastacia and the twins were waiting for them. But they didn't see the happy faces they'd been expecting. Something was wrong. Badly wrong.

'Do you guys know where Jamie and Haru went?' Anastacia asked, and all thoughts of Liliana and the hidden treasure vanished.

121

'They're not here? They said they'd be waiting.' Ellie marched forward to Saskia who looked equally as confused.

It was impossible for Jamie to have wandered off. He would never allow himself to be anything other than professional. Even the twins were fidgeting uncomfortably, squeezing each other's hands like nervous children.

Lottie felt her heart rate quicken. She could see that Lola and Micky were frightened, flashbacks to the Tompkins Manor scraping at their brains. Whatever had happened here, she couldn't allow them to remain and risk more trauma.

Be brave, be kind, she told herself. *Act how you would want someone else to in this situation.*

'I'm sure it's fine.' She tried to sound as reassuring as possible, even though there was dread in the pit of her stomach. 'You two should go back to the school. We'll go and find them; they're probably not far away.'

The twins nodded, before hurrying off into the crowd.

Lottie glanced at the others, the sounds of the festival expanding around them until it felt like a haze of chaos. The only Partizan left in their group let out a long whistle, looking out over the masses of people.

'This is bad,' Saskia said, shaking her head. 'Very, very bad.'

15

There were too many people. Everywhere they looked bright colours and sticky smells and people, people, people. It had turned from enchanting to dizzying and Lottie could hardly move in her *yukata*, not used to walking in *geta*, traditional wooden sandals. She'd tried calling Jamie on his phone but there was no response, so she'd left one simple message: '*Jamie, please come back.*'

'They have to be here somewhere,' Saskia said. 'Jamie wouldn't just leave unless –'

She stopped herself mid-sentence. Jamie wouldn't leave unless there was a threat, unless Leviathan were here.

'Anastacia, stay close to me.' Saskia no longer tried to blend in with the crowd. Her sash had come loose, and she pulled off her *yukata* to reveal a navy catsuit. Lottie should have realized Saskia would be just as prepared as any other Partizan. Prickles of fear brushed Lottie's skin. This was the Saskia who'd kidnapped her, the one who'd taken Julius's eye out; she was formidable and deadly. Could they really trust her?

'Someone's coming,' Saskia said, pulling Anastacia behind her.

'HARU!' Lottie called.

The Japanese Partizan appeared through the crowd, running full speed and with a dark, terrified expression that made Lottie feel sick.

'Jamie!' Placing his hands on Saskia's shoulders he gasped for breath. 'Jamie saw someone from Leviathan here at the festival. He went after them but I lost him. He disappeared so fast.'

It was impossible to take in anything after the word 'Leviathan'. All of Lottie's worst fears had followed them to Japan. They were not safe anywhere. Leviathan were a virus that was spreading around the world, and she was a host. Worst of all, now they might have Jamie! The stupidity of her own self-absorbed concerns slapped her in the face. They'd left Jamie behind. *They'd* done this. Ellie and Lottie had lost their Partizan.

'The motorbikes,' Lottie said, fighting back tears. 'It has to have been them.'

'We don't know that,' Ellie protested, and everyone stared at her, unbelieving.

'I know which way he went.' All eyes focused on Haru, his words lingering. He didn't realize how loaded they were.

Ellie was the first to speak. 'I'm going after him.'

'But, Ellie!' Lottie felt horror at what she knew she had to say, and she leaned in to whisper in Ellie's ear. 'Our job is to keep you safe. What if you get hurt?'

Everyone's gaze was on them, and they turned for a little more privacy. Haru seemed to be the only one oblivious to the problem.

'I can't leave Jamie behind,' Ellie whispered quickly. 'He can hate me as much as he wants, but I have to go after him.

We shouldn't have left him!' A furious storm grew at the back of her eyes and Lottie knew she felt the same guilt. 'I'm giving you permission to do the irresponsible thing.'

Lottie grabbed Ellie's hand like it was a weapon, and, turning back to the others, she said, 'Show us the way.'

They were going to find Jamie together.

Haru didn't miss a beat. They followed him into the crowd, weaving between the happy festivalgoers. They were ghosts, flying past everyone in the real world. But it was impossible to keep up with Haru, and Lottie kept tripping over her sandals, relying on Ellie's strength to hold her up.

'Here!' Haru called eventually, turning round on the spot. 'I lost him here.'

They were at the edge of the festival. Stone steps led down to alleyways that gave way to exposed streets, and the glowing neon lights of the city reflected in wet patches on the pavement.

None of them said a word as they descended, the dizzy decadence of the festival melting away behind them. The alleyways were alive with fingers of shadows wrapping round their skin, enveloping them in darkness. Lottie could feel Haru behind her. It made her feel both nervous and brave, like having a great beast at her back. One step into the alley and the world turned cold, nothing but dank wall and dripping gutter. Saskia stopped them in the middle, halfway between the street and the safety of the festival. 'OK, I think –'

'Argh!'

'Haru?' Lottie turned to where Haru had been, to be confronted with . . . nothing. Only darkness greeted her. He'd vanished.

'What was that?' Saskia asked, her voice as cold as the wall they were pushed against. 'Where's Haru?'

'He's gone,' Lottie whimpered, unable to stop from shaking.

'Then we need to get out of here.' Saskia grabbed Anastacia and signalled for them to follow her, all of them hurrying down the alley. They emerged into the gleaming lights. It was the end of a street, grey wall on one side and a turning on to the road on the other, with another tiny alley opposite them as skinny as a crack in the floor.

'Wait!' Lottie jerked away from Ellie, who was pulling her hard towards the open street. 'This feels wrong.'

Saskia, their only remaining Partizan, nodded, narrowing her eyes. 'I agree. We need to –'

'No!' The storm in Ellie was simmering, electricity leaking into the air. 'You . . .' she growled, her teeth glinting like fangs. 'You persuaded me to come to the festival. You said it was a blessing.' Her ebony eyes sparked. 'Is this your plan, Saskia? After all this, we thought you'd changed and you've led us right back to Leviathan.'

'How dare you?' It wasn't Saskia, but Anastacia who stepped forward. 'Saskia's protecting us. She was brainwashed. She's a victim.'

'Why don't you let her speak for herself?' Ellie barked.

All eyes turned on Saskia, and they waited. Nothing. She didn't respond, just stood there, head bowed.

'Saskia?' Lottie asked, trembling, the air around them feeling cold. 'Saskia, what's –'

The sound that followed was like nothing Lottie had ever heard. A metallic whizz so close to her that she swore she felt the metal graze the down on her face. Saskia reacted before any of them even knew what was happening, pulling the fan out of the back of Anastacia's *yukata*, and catching the knife between the patterned paper, moments before it hit her right between the eyes.

'It's not me,' she said calmly, pocketing the knife. 'But you were right to be suspicious.'

Everything turned blinding white from car headlights blinking on at the top of the street. Lottie had to cover her eyes with her arm as she faced the vehicle. Leaning against the door of the shiny black car was a mountain of a man with an eyepatch and a cowboy hat.

Julius.

'You can all make this easier for yourselves and hand over the princess now,' he drawled. His voice sent shivers up Lottie's spine. 'Or if you'd rather, I can take that eye you owe me, Saskia.' He waited for a moment. 'Come now. Let's not make this harder than it needs to be.'

Lottie desperately willed her heart rate to slow down, her whole body going into a strange moment of calm, and then she heard a sound . . . a noise she'd heard once before.

A low electric hum sent shivers through the ground. It grew louder, like an approaching storm, roaring, pounding and pulsing through the night. It growled in the moonlight, wheels screeching like a beast, and then she appeared. The Pink Demon.

Spray from the puddles billowed around her like a shield, pleated trousers flying at her side, her motorbike thundering beneath her legs.

Four mystery bikers, blue, yellow, pink and purple, cut off Julius's car, bats raised, daring him to move forward.

'I *knew* they weren't with Leviathan!' Ellie practically squealed.

But they weren't safe yet.

Julius scrambled into his car, revving the engine, the fury in the sound cracking the air. One of the bikers turned to them and nodded their helmet, tapping the back of the bike.

'Everyone get on!' Saskia called.

'Really?' Anastacia spluttered.

'It's either them or Leviathan – your choice.'

Lottie didn't need to be asked twice. Ellie helped Lottie scramble on to the back of the blue bike, and then, with eyes ablaze, she ran to saddle up with the Pink Demon.

'Let's go!' Ellie screamed.

Lottie clutched her hands round the waist of the helmeted figure, the ground trembling. As they tore away, it was impossible to stop the tears that streaked down her cheeks. She glanced over her shoulder once more as they weaved between traffic.

Jamie was still missing.

Jamie was lost somewhere and he was still so vulnerable.

She just had to hope this mysterious gang could help them.

'I don't know who you are,' she called against the wind as they powered on through the city. 'But I trust you.'

16

Lightning. It felt like lightning cracking beneath her, tearing the ground in two, ripping away at the world. Ellie had never felt anything like it, hoots of laughter and ecstasy pouring out of her. One moment she'd been so scared – scared for Lottie and everything she'd got her into, scared for Jamie and everything he had to bear – but now she was elated, flying through the moonlight, neon lights making comet trails around her.

'I'm free!' she roared, the rev of the engine beneath her drowning out her words.

They weren't true anyway. Nipping at their heels were two oily black cars, thin and close to the road, like ink seeping towards them. They glided round every corner, stormed down every road, just at their tails, yet never quite close enough.

The Pink Demon made a juddering, violent turn into a smaller alley, wheels screeching. Signals flew out from her leather-gloved hands, splitting them and the purple rider off from the rest of the group who sped down the main road.

Who were these people? Why were they helping them? Ellie couldn't explain it but she felt a deep connection to them, like tree roots intertwining beneath the ground.

'Who are you?' she bellowed, but the mysterious biker simply raised her hand.

Electric signs in kaleidoscope patterns whirled above their heads, bubblegum kanji that floated and disappeared as they zoomed beneath. It felt like a garden of lights growing and glowing out of the buildings, twisting their neon vines over the city. People screamed as they tore through the streets, cameras flashing. Ellie loosened her robe and pulled it up over her head to hide her face.

They were out of sight for barely a second before their dark shadow followed them, but there was only one this time. The two cars had had to separate to keep up with both halves of the gang. The demon made another signal and the bikes split, abruptly spinning out to face the traffic. Ellie didn't even realize she was screaming until the sound turned to manic laughter. Vehicles were coming head-on at them, barrelling down the road and dipping in and out to avoid them, and just when Ellie thought they'd zip past the black car and back to the other motorbikes they dipped again to meet their pursuer. The black car inched between them, a bike on each side, and Ellie could see Julius through the glass, his one furious eye burning with rage. He was so close that she could reach in and touch him if the window was open. Grinning, like he'd won, he prepared to pull the steering wheel aggressively and crash into them. Ellie tried to scream, to warn them, but it didn't matter. The Pink Demon and her purple accomplice began an intricate and brutal dance, pulling out their bats and smashing the wing mirrors. Shards of glass glittered around them, reflecting the colours of the city like chemical confetti. The purple rider made a final bash at the window, blowing it through, and it was as if the wind gushed into and round the car. Julius lost his grip as the shards hit him, the car skidding.

There was no time for celebration. Julius was already righting himself, but it was too late for him – the bikes took off down a narrow paved street that was certainly not for vehicles. People dived out of the way, squeezing themselves against the stone walls. Yet they had nothing to fear; the Pink Demon and her purple rider were effortlessly capable, leaving all around them untouched, not a scratch or a scrape on the city or a person.

'Anastacia!' Ellie shouted, the motorbikes drawing closer together again. 'How are you holding up?'

Anastacia turned, white-faced with terror in her eyes.

'*Aidez-moi!* GET ME OFF THIS THING!' she screeched, a death grip on the rider. Ellie was sure she heard the biker laugh before the engine revved and they sped off back to the main road, Anastacia screaming at the sudden movement.

They met with the others just as a distant howl of sirens began to echo through the night, all of them disappearing down a dark street with a concrete wall, far away from the chaos of the city. The blue one pulled something out of her jacket, and, pressing a button, the concrete wall began to lift, yellow light pouring over them to reveal a decaying white, blue and green room the size of a swimming pool. It *was* a swimming pool, but old, mildewed and dank, a perfect place to hide demon motorbikes.

They pulled in and stopped, humming engines sending reverberations through the tiled floor.

'*Dieu merci!*' Anastacia wailed, clambering off the bike. 'I am never, *ever* getting on a motorbike again.'

'Where are we?' Saskia asked, running over to assist Anastacia while the concrete door moved back into place.

The last one off was Lottie, her face a wet mess, cheeks bright red, and eyes to match.

'We need to find Jamie,' she said. 'We have to find him!' She clung on to Ellie who cradled her gently, the two of them falling into one another.

Up close now she could see the four in a circle on each of the bikes like a brand. Her heart pounded. A petrol fire burning in her chest spread through her with anticipation.

She focused on the Pink Demon, whose gloved hands were reaching up.

The fluorescent magenta helmet came away and silky black hair poured out from underneath it. Pale white skin, soft pink lips and dark eyes that blazed like burning oil.

It took a while for Ellie's brain to believe what her eyes were seeing. She practically choked. 'You?'

Sayuri Chiba casually held her helmet between her arm and torso, one leg resting against the bright pink metal of her steed, and it was clear she'd done it a million times before. The engine purred now, waiting in anticipation for Sayuri to ride it through the glowing city.

'I thought,' she said with a lazy smile, 'you might need a ride.'

PART TWO

森林浴

Shinrin-yoku

Japanese phrase: 'Forest bath – the act of
finding clarity and wellness within the woods'

17

Jamie Volk had been trained to become a perfect machine, picking up on every detail, alert to every danger. So how had he allowed himself, once again, to be trapped?

He'd been so filled with animal rage, childish resentment and petty emotion that he'd abandoned his instincts, letting them crumble under the weight of his own vendetta, his own desire to escape, and now he was alone, the twinkling lights of the city beneath him. Alone with their greatest enemy.

It was just as Lottie and Ellie had reached the top of the Ferris wheel, and Jamie saw from the ground how they'd embraced, intertwined again. Whatever had pushed Lottie away from Ellie had been resolved, and the solidarity that he'd rediscovered with the Portman was over. Then Haru had spotted her. Ingrid. Haru had told Jamie someone suspicious was watching them from the shadows of a festival game, small, freckles, hair like oil. Jamie knew it was her before he even looked, and he was thankful.

He saw her catlike grin, and a wave of adrenalin washed over him. It was a chance to get away, something to give him purpose again, but most of all a chance to get revenge.

Jamie heard Haru saying he'd look out for the others and take them home if he wanted to go after her. There was a split second when he wondered if he could trust Haru, whether he could trust anyone, and he allowed himself one lingering look at his fellow Partizan, the sweet smiling feathery laugh of a boy who'd been so relentlessly nice to him – and he nodded.

He hadn't even considered how strange it was that Ingrid was here in Japan. He'd just taken off, like a feral dog. Ingrid's face had torn into a jaw-splitting smile as the pursuit began, and they ran, knocking people down without caring. Glad he hadn't worn the sandals everyone else had, he could have run forever through the city, getting further and further from the festival, until she dipped into a building.

A *trap!* a voice in his head screamed, but he ignored it, storming up the stairs behind her, the click-click-clicking of her shoes a constant taunt.

He followed her up to the roof, darkness greeting him as he barrelled through the metal door behind her, sure he would be confronted by an army ready to take him out. So when it was only Ingrid he was almost disappointed.

She looked around, her bleach-white skin light in the dark. It was as if she expected something, but nothing came. It was just her and him alone on the roof.

Easy, he thought.

He charged at her with a force built up from deep within, all the anger and humiliation, all the self-doubt and regret. The catlike eyes narrowed into slits as he threw out a kick at her face.

She stumbled backwards out of his way and knives appeared in her hands so fast it was as if they came from thin air. Black spider blades, the same ones she'd had at the Tompkins Manor, when she'd subdued him. The sting of the memory was enough to set him ablaze again, pulling his own knives out, which had been hidden in his robe.

Metallic clangs echoed around them with each strike, a barrage of blows bearing down on her. She snarled and growled, but with each attack she was pushed further backwards until she was up against the door.

'Such a perfect Partizan,' she teased. But in her callous attempt at a jab she left herself open. He dropped his own knife and effortlessly stepped out of the way of hers. She tripped forward and he grabbed her wrist, which was tiny in his hand, like a twig. Then he seized her other hand and squeezed, his grip getting stronger and tighter until she dropped both knives. Her eyes were filled with horror; she was no longer the prowling, smirking cat, but a mewling kitten.

'Stop, please.' But he didn't; he squeezed harder until he felt the bones beneath her skin grinding and creaking from the pressure, ready to crack.

'Someone help me!'

But he could hardly hear her. His face twisted like a monster, intent on nothing but revenge as she cowered beneath him.

A single tear rolled down her cheek and one last mew of pain. She was so weak, so easy to subdue, so very pathetic. The only reason she'd beaten him before was because they had Lottie, but here, now, he had nothing to lose except . . .

The thought struck him so hard that he abruptly let go.

This was most certainly a trap, but maybe not how he'd anticipated.

Ingrid made for her knives, her head coming into contact with Jamie's knee as he half-heartedly bashed her nose. Blood spooled out from her face on to the ground below, down his robe and the white of Ingrid's shirt. She tried to right herself, but he pushed her down, grabbing the knives for himself. He had to go back and find the others.

'Well, it looks like you've won.'

Jamie went rigid at the sound of a new person. It was a man's voice, calm and low, with a dizzying edge like a snake's hiss. It was a voice that could hypnotize you.

He turned to greet his new assailant and found that there was more than one. Three to be exact, covered with animal masks and hoods. In a strange fever dream a rabbit, a bird and a goat were dressed in black like undertakers, demons ready to guide him to the afterlife. Their masks were split below their noses, creating dark, twisted versions of animals with human mouths. It was the goat who'd spoken; he was taller than the others by at least a head and his mask extended upward in two sharp horns like the devil himself.

Ingrid's face became elated as she saw the new arrivals.

'Master! You came!' she cried, rising to her knees, before hobbling to the safety of her black-clad comrades. The rabbit extended its cloak, welcoming her into its shadows.

The Master of Leviathan. The man that had tormented them for the last two years.

Jamie knew he was vastly outnumbered, that only a fool would attempt to fight his way through what he assumed were three trained fighters, but Jamie was feeling very foolish that night.

He took a deep breath and his shoulders relaxed, eyes focusing. He took one final look at the moon and thought how much it looked like a boat in the sky, just as it floated behind a cloud, submerging them in darkness. He let out the breath, let the rage consume him, falling into a fighting stance.

The goat cackled, a wide-jawed laugh that revealed a perfect set of white teeth. 'Such aggression . . .' His words were thick with humour, unafraid.

The mocking half-smile made Jamie both furious and confused.

'We don't want to fight you, although I'm sure it would be fascinating to see.'

Jamie was standing on a knife's edge; one misstep and he would fall. 'What do you want?' he demanded, still holding his stance.

'I simply came to wish you a happy birthday.' The goat raised his arms invitingly, but the words had Jamie frozen. They caught in his nose, oily and foul, reaching down his throat, and into his blood, coursing through his body in greasy panic. Jamie willed his heartbeat to slow.

Saskia had told them he was the top of their list and, if he could just keep steady, maybe he would find out why.

'And once you've done your talking –' He felt his head cock to the side, amazed by how easy it was to talk to this strange devil man – 'can I leave?'

'So long as you do us no harm, although it seems a shame when you are finally in our home.' The Goat Man smiled again, the split below his mask like the call of an abyss. It felt familiar, disarmingly so, but the most important thing was that Jamie had gained new information.

'Home' . . . *Leviathan are based in Japan.*

Despite everything his body screamed at him to do, Jamie dropped his stance, placing the knives away in his robe in a show of passivity, but in such a way that he knew he could reach them easily at a moment's notice. 'OK. Talk.'

Ingrid remained hidden, wrapped in the cloak of the rabbit, but the shiver of the fabric was a dead giveaway; she was trembling with fear.

'Are you happy, being a Partizan?' The question came so abruptly it might have knocked a lesser person, but Jamie answered without hesitation.

'Yes. It is my vocation.'

The rabbit sneered at his response until silenced by the goat-masked leader.

'And your master. Does she feel the same way?'

The moon boat in the sky reappeared, illuminating the masked creatures and casting shadows along the concrete floor. Jamie didn't want to answer; he didn't want to think about this. Ellie didn't want him to be her Partizan – she didn't keep it a secret – but he wanted to keep them safe, Lottie and his princess, and if he couldn't do that, he was useless.

'No.' It took all his willpower not to look away as he spoke. 'But it's not her choice. She needs protecting from people like you.' Jamie blinked. It was not Ellie he conjured in his mind; it was Lottie – which infuriated him.

'We mean no harm.'

'Kidnapping and brainwashing seem pretty harmful to me.'

'That is not what we do –'

'The rabbit and the bird, did you kidnap and brainwash them too?'

The masked figures switched into a defensive pose, shadows that morphed around the Goat Man.

'Now, now.' The devil gestured with his hands again. 'He is only playing.'

A slimy feeling, like being washed with dirt, spread over Jamie at the insinuation. It made him feel as if he were being mocked for taking this situation so seriously.

'These are my children,' the goat said grandly, posturing proudly in a way that had an instant effect on his two masked marionettes. 'Everyone who joins me does so of their own accord and we welcome them to their new home graciously.'

'Why are you collecting children?' Jamie asked, matching his casual tone. 'Seems a little creepy.' If he was going to treat him like a petulant child, then he was going to act like one.

The Goat Man laughed again, but there was an edge to it now, and Jamie could practically smell his irritation. 'I lost a child once.' He spoke brusquely, not masking his anger. 'That little baby had his whole life ripped away from him.' There was a dripping, bloody feeling in the air, the memory clearly still raw. 'So I became a father to the world. I want to make sure the children of today have a future. One that they choose, not one chosen for them.' He tilted his head as if he and Jamie were familiar, dropping his bone-chilling tone with ease as that enraging half-smile spread back to his lips. 'Maybe soon you shall join us too and choose your own future?'

It took Jamie a moment to understand what he'd just heard. A siren wailed in the distance. It wasn't until a metallic taste spread over his tongue that he realized he'd bitten his cheek.

'I would never join you.' But, even as he said this, comprehension spread through him, blossoming like a wound in his chest. This man was charming and dangerous, an anger in him that matched his own, and he could see how easy it would be to fall for it.

It's all a lie, he told himself, but the fact he even needed the reminder sent white-hot rage through him. How dare they force these questions on him?

A buzzing in his left pocket caught him off guard, a pesky distraction tickling his leg. His phone. He knew it was Lottie, but he couldn't answer. With a flash he reached into his *yukata*, grasping one of Ingrid's knives, and threw it at the shoulder of the Goat Man.

The bird registered the move, throwing out a cloaked arm to deflect the lethal weapon, and Jamie realized the cloak was padded armour, an intricate mesh to protect them. The knife ricocheted off the bird's extended hand, but the force sent it flying into the bird-masked figure.

The Goat Man gave no second look to the bird who now clutched his bleeding stomach. His mouth turned downward in a despondent frown. 'How disappointing.'

The rabbit came at Jamie fast. Its mask was a hair's breadth from his face. Diving out of the way, Jamie felt his foot meet with the edge of the rooftop, the world below swirling.

The roof door was blocked off by Leviathan; the only way out was down.

'Quick, isn't he?' the Goat Man called with a laugh. 'We made a deal, Jamie. *So long as you do us no harm.* I think it's clear you broke that rule and, if I didn't know any better, I'd think you wanted to come with us.'

It was surely intended as a distraction and, sensing as much, Jamie pulled Ingrid's other knife from his robe, holding it out defensively. 'One step closer and I'll jump.' He could feel the ledge, a purgatory between the humiliation of capture and the relief of escape. Below he could see a pile of garbage bags, a place to cushion the fall, but he could not let them see it on his face.

Still clutching his stomach, the bird looked up at him through the mask, and it was the strangest thing, as if his eyes were like beacons, beseeching him not to do it.

The Goat Man held up his hand in a false truce. 'There's no need for –'

'That's mine!' Ingrid screamed, rushing forward as the others turned to her.

'Ingrid! No!' the rabbit screeched at her.

She came up slow and clumsy. With one quick swipe Jamie was falling.

It was so easy, a floating sense of acceptance, the wind whistling past in a soothing welcome, the descent singing like a lullaby. If he chose, he could have simply let go, let himself meet the ground in one final sigh, but that was not his plan.

Pushing hard off the brick wall, he landed in a brace position over the pile of rubbish, the stench thick and grotesque as the air rushed out of his lungs, his bones shaking.

As he hit the ground, his face raised to the sky, and the world slid out of focus as the clouds opened and it began to rain.

18

'This is certainly a surprise.' Deep gasps racked Saskia, her hands on her hips. It wasn't exhaustion; she was relieved.

Dishevelled and confused, the Rosewood students struggled to make sense of what was in front of them.

'OK,' Anastacia declared, trying her best to tame her wild mane of hair after the motorbike restyling they'd all received. 'Can we agree right now that I never have to touch a motorbike again?'

Peeling lemon and lime tiles surrounded them, the chipped ceramic spilling off the empty pool. The room felt too bright, shrinking Lottie's pupils and making her eyes sting, tears dripping down her wind-pinched cheeks. Ellie held her in the crook of her arm while she stared down their saviours.

Four familiar faces: Rio, Miko, Wei and their Pink Demon leader in all her ethereal glory. Sayuri.

Release, that's what she wanted to feel, but Lottie could only think of Jamie, how careless they'd been with him, that he was all alone.

'Jamie still hasn't answered. We have to find him,' she said again, sniffing hard. 'We shouldn't have left him alone. I'm so stupid. We should have helped him, not left him. I'm so –'

'Your Partizan can fend for himself.' Sayuri's voice was unrecognizable – fiery and intense. 'We have more pressing matters at hand.'

'Haru too,' Lottie began. Her worry was so sharp she could taste it in the back of her throat, salty and bitter. 'Haru's in trouble. We have to go after them.'

A sour smirk tore across Rio's face, Miko by his side tutting.

'Haru is part of Leviathan,' Sayuri said calmly, no emotion to be found in the terrible statement.

A pressure was building in the air, a static intensity, and in the distance came a low rumble.

Saskia's eyes sparked with fury. 'What? How long have you known this?'

Haru, the friendly boy whose smile radiated warmth, the boy who'd even charmed Jamie, someone he trusted. It was too horrible; Lottie couldn't make sense of it. She was ready to believe it was a lie until slowly the memories slotted into place. How scary Haru had been when he'd switched into fighting mode, how oddly he'd reacted to Saskia, how annoyed Sayuri had been to find Lottie and the twins alone with him in the library. And, the most menacing of all, his favouritism for Jamie.

'He led us into that trap,' Lottie said quietly, her tears drying with the realization.

A murmur of agreement came from Sayuri. 'I have known he was part of that despicable group for over half a year, although it is unclear exactly when he joined them or how they got to him.'

At her side, Lottie felt Ellie tense.

'How could you let this happen?' she growled. 'How could you let us spend all that time with him and not tell us?'

'We've been following you,' Rio replied casually, fixing his hair in the reflection of his helmet. 'Waiting to see what Leviathan would do.'

Ellie marched forward. 'What? *Why*? Are you insane? Why didn't you just tell someone when you –'

'Ellie.' Anastacia's voice came out cold and with clear warning. 'You know it's not that simple.'

'*Chigau yō.*' Miko spoke this time, narrowing her eyes with contempt. 'We know about your case and we are not like you. Sentimental!' The word had the venom of a curse.

Lottie had to do something. 'How do you know about Leviathan?' she asked, gulping back her emotion.

Sayuri and Wei, who had both remained quiet, turned to each other. Lottie had seen Ellie and Jamie share similar looks in the past.

Jamie, she thought again, her whole body aching with worry.

'Two years ago,' Sayuri began, 'I met a girl called Emelia Malouf. She came to one of our summer schools and became a dear friend to me.'

Lottie was sure she recognized the name.

'A year ago she was kidnapped and had her whole life torn apart by the people who came after you tonight.'

Murky images floated into Lottie's mind, a furious girl in a hijab with dark skin and even darker eyes, the girl who was kidnapped with Percy all that time ago.

'I remember her. From the Tompkins merger!' Lottie exclaimed.

Sayuri nodded. 'She took it upon herself to figure out what had been done to her long before you all came along. And the one connecting factor in everything Leviathan does is –'

'You,' Miko cut in, her little fang tooth protruding like a snarl, still ready for a fight, but Sayuri held up her hand to calm her.

'We are Banshee,' Sayuri announced, clear and precise as she extended her arms out to the other bikers.

'Banshee?' Lottie asked, fascinated by the fairy-tale connection.

'Banshee. There's four of us – *shi* – and we are inspired by the wailing spirits that warn of death: banshee. We are family. We look out for one another, protect each other,' Wei said, echoing their leader's commanding voice, glasses glinting in the harsh light. 'And that means we're going to stop whatever Leviathan are planning.'

It was hard to pinpoint what Lottie was feeling. She was in awe but it was tinged with something uncertain. A respect for this group of kids, none much older or younger than herself, who'd taken on a task so huge.

'We need to tell someone about Haru,' Ellie said.

'*You* won't be doing any such thing. This is not a recruitment mission. You're too much of a liability, and besides we can't,' Wei replied, entirely matter-of-fact. 'He's our eyes in Leviathan, not that he knows it.'

'Wei duplicated his phone number. It's how we knew about tonight,' Miko said, the lime-green lights giving her a sickly, turquoise glow.

'Wait.' Anastacia stepped forward to join Saskia. 'I don't understand. How does it all link back to us? Why are we a liability?'

'No, not all of you.' Miko rolled her eyes, before pointing at Lottie. 'Her.'

147

A sudden flash of white-hot lightning shot through the sky. The storm had broken.

'Me?'

'The princess of Maradova.' Miko's words reminded Lottie of a furious viper, spitting and writhing in warning.

'What do you mean?'

'We are not certain yet, Miko,' Wei continued. 'It's a theory Emelia's had for a while, that every person on their list somehow leads back to the princess. As far as we know Leviathan is smaller than they let on, no more than a couple of dozen members, so they pick them very carefully and with purpose. Purpose revolving around you.' He gestured at Lottie again. 'It's precisely why we've been watching you. We needed to be one hundred per cent sure none of you were with them.' He spoke casually. 'Everything's about making your life more difficult, manipulating you. The fact you're even here in Japan may very well have been their doing for all we know.'

'My grade,' Lottie breathed nervously, still sure she believed what they were saying. 'But how could they know we'd come here, Saskia?' She turned to the Partizan, terrified to even ask the question. 'Could the girl who gave us the information about Takeshin . . . ?'

'It's possible. If the Hamelin Formula works, there's no saying what they could be doing with it,' she replied.

It was a dreadful thought and, if it was true, had they also infiltrated the media? There was no one they could trust, not even the police.

'I don't understand; this all seems so . . . petty,' Lottie couldn't help saying it, her head spinning. All this time they'd been trying to uncover a huge world-wide conspiracy, the idea that it might all be about her – about Ellie, somehow made her even more afraid. It was a child-like fear, the kind you feel when the lights turn out and you need to check for a monster under your bed, only this monster is real, and it only has its eyes on you.

The four Takeshin students murmured between themselves, Rio's gaze lingering over Lottie with playful menace.

A pitter-patter began to tap away at the window, spindly fingers of rain against the glass. Jamie was out there, somewhere.

Through a haze of freshly building tears Lottie glanced at Ellie, and her heart stopped. Her princess's face was twisted with pain. It was all her worst nightmares come true, the possibility that it all led back to the princess of Maradova. That it was her fault.

'This is useful information,' Wei said at last. 'But it's only a theory.'

Ellie appeared to loosen slightly at his words, but Lottie could see the shadow lingering, the dark thoughts she'd worked so hard to pour light over creeping back in.

'Now we will be sending you back to school.'

Another flash of lightning illuminated the room.

'We still have to find Jamie,' Lottie pleaded, trying to shake off new Leviathan fears. 'And what do we do about Haru?'

'*You* will not be doing anything; while you're here at our school you're our responsibility. It's likely Haru will return and act like nothing happened,' Sayuri said.

'He's done things like this before.' Rio's smirk was laced with anger.

'We need you to continue to pretend you know nothing about Haru or us. No one can know; he's our most valuable

149

source of information. We will keep you safe, and we ask you to share any material you have on Leviathan,' Sayuri added.

'And will you tell us what you know?'

They turned on Anastacia so fast you could hear the air snap.

'No,' Sayuri said firmly. 'And you should stop hunting for Leviathan. If it's true that they want you here, for whatever reason, you need to stay out of their business, or you'll be playing right into their hands.' She looked at Lottie so sharply that Lottie felt it like a knife in her chest. 'We don't want you doing that again.'

Lottie felt the sob crawl up her throat. 'What about Jamie? What do we do about him?'

'You will go back to the school and hope that he returns. If he does not return, we will call the police and your parents. That is all that can be done.'

Lottie and Ellie turned to each other, the remnants of the festival still clinging to them: the acrid scent of fireworks, the sweet taste of the taiyaki, and their now-dishevelled yukatas.

Slowly Ellie blinked. 'Lottie, he's . . .' She didn't finish the sentence, but the word still hung in the air.

Jamie was gone, they'd lost him, and there was nothing they could do about it but have faith in him to find his way back.

'Now quickly, everyone,' Sayuri announced, glancing out of the window. 'We're in the eye of the storm.'

19

It was a relentlessly hot midsummer day in St Ives and tourists had hijacked the streets to guzzle overpriced ice cream and sizzle their skin in the stifling heat. It was hard enough to find things to do in the town during low season, but as soon as the summer holidays rolled around Ollie Moreno was virtually trapped in the prison of his house.

All his other friends had sensible parents, who'd get out of the town as fast as possible and rent their homes as holiday lets to make money off the seasonal tourist hellscape. But not Ollie's mum. Oh no. Manuela Moreno needed to 'mind the art gallery and get those tourists hooked on my work'. Artists and their egos.

He knew he wasn't doing himself any favours by lying on the white linen of his bedsheets, barely any natural light reaching him through the curtains, but he didn't have the energy to do anything else. He was sad. He knew it was stupid, yet he couldn't shake it.

Lottie was practically ignoring him, nothing but curt text replies to tell him she was busy. It was so unlike her, and she didn't even seem to realize, and, worst of all, he knew she was right. She *was* busy, and she *did* have more important things to worry about.

He wished it was only sadness he felt but there was more, a prickly feeling in his stomach that itched and bit at him. Jealousy.

It had been one of their childhood dreams to go to Japan together one day and go on adventures. To spend a week going to all the nerdy cafes and themed restaurants, then another week exploring the awe-inspiring sites, and now Lottie was there with her new princess best friend and that grumpy bodyguard, and he was just a stupid slug bothering her.

Rolling over, Ollie picked up the newspaper he'd thrown on the floor. There was one more thing troubling him. Lottie had been all over the news. There weren't many photos, only some grainy shots taken sneakily, but a collection was starting to build. The pictures of her at the summer ball the previous year, the pictures after the fencing tournament, and now this. It was inevitable that their old school friends would see her, but when they did something miraculous happened. Not a single one of them recognized her.

The closest call was a comment from Charlie saying how the princess reminded him of Lottie, resulting in hiccups of laughter from the girls, especially Kate.

'Can you imagine if that pink-faced airhead was the princess?'

'More likely she would turn into a pumpkin.'

They were mean and stupid. 'Ugly stepsisters' Ollie called them, but he didn't say anything. Lottie was going off, living a life he could never imagine, growing and blooming into someone new and whole, while he remained here, a mere sapling.

He grabbed his phone and typed out the silliest, most dramatic thing he could think of that might make Lottie laugh.

> RIP Ollie Moreno. Died from being left to
> melt by his ex-best friend in the world's
> worst hellhole tourist trap.

Before hitting send he quickly snapped a photo of himself lying against the bed, tongue drooping out of his mouth like he was dead.

There was no response, as expected, and he could practically hear Lottie groaning at how pathetic he was. He already felt stupid for sending it.

Defeated and bored, Ollie picked up a handful of jellybeans from his bedside table, throwing them in the air and catching them in his mouth. It was on the fifth bean, a candy-floss-flavoured one, that he said out loud, 'I want to grow.'

Swallowing it, his phone buzzed. It was a number he didn't recognize, but whoever it was certainly seemed to know him.

> Hello, Ollie.

Not a question, and yet it had an inquisitiveness to it, like whoever had sent it was testing the water.

> Umm, hello?

More typing, the little grey dots watching him in a strangely nerve-racking way.

> Ollie, this is Binah :D

All his worries vanished in a puff of curly brown hair and fairground smells, candy-floss and salted caramel like a day at the beach. His whole mind was overcome with her warm hickory-brown skin that glowed when she smiled, the smile that could melt the whole world, curious, warm and wise. This was what Ollie remembered when he read the name, even though he'd only met her once. He fumbled for a minute, not sure what to say.

> Everything OK?

More typing.

> We need your help with something but,
> before I add you to the team, I need to
> know . . . Will you do anything and
> everything for the sake of adventure?

Blinking at the message, he wondered if it was a prank. *But . . . if I were Lottie, would I take this as a sign?*
Yes, he replied.
Binah wrote back almost instantaneously.

> That is wonderful news. I'll add you to the
> chat, but no one else in there knows about
> Lottie's secret, so don't mention the war.

Ollie chuckled, but his laughter immediately stopped when he saw the name of the group chat he had been added to.

The chat colours were red, and there were two other people in the group, besides Binah – Percy and Raphael. And at the top of the phone screen, in big bold letters, the group name read:

OPERATION: BREAK INTO ROSEWOOD HALL.

20

Sleep refused to welcome Lottie, and she tossed and turned on the sinking futon. A storm like she'd never seen before raged beyond the screen door, the room quaking with each flurry of wind and rain. Everything rattled – the floor, the wall, the ceiling, her mind – and every time she felt her eyes get sleepy the world would bark at her to wake up again. And every bark sounded the same: a single name in her head, tormenting her. *Jamie.*

Her phone buzzed next to her pillow, and she fumbled to find it, praying for the sign she was waiting for.

The screen showed Ollie's name and a childish message she could barely decipher, with a photo of him pretending to be dead. Horrified and furious at the flippant words, she threw the phone to the floor, the screen cracking. Beside her, Ellie turned over, trapped in an unknowable nightmare, but asleep nonetheless.

'I'm sorry. It's my fault. I'm weak,' she mumbled.

Lottie wanted to wake her up, tell her she was wrong, only the real world seemed even worse. How could everything she'd been working towards have been destroyed in one night?

She wanted to run again, to say to hell with the storm and dance around in it, accepting all the fiery rage the universe had to offer.

Why the Princess of Maradova? Why would Ellie be at the centre of it all? But the thought only made her want to run even more, to run away from the very idea of it, because if it was true, she wasn't sure Ellie could handle it.

Her hands reached for her rain clothes, fingers curling round the yellow mac, but before she'd had a chance to consider putting them on, a mew came from the other side of the screen door. A towering black shadow was illuminated by a crack of lightning, a giant cat pawing desperately at the paper door.

The breath caught in her chest and she did not dare make a sound as the vampire cat flooded her mind, here to punish her for overlooking Jamie. But then she threw off her covers and went to welcome him in.

The screen rattled as she pulled it open, and the wind pounded in. With the wind came the desperate creature, the same oversized black cat from over a week ago, Vampy, yellow eyes wide with panic and fur drenched from the rain. She closed the door again and the cat dived into her arms, its heartbeat vibrating against her as she wrapped her arms round it, warming it.

'Now, now,' she whispered, careful not to wake Ellie. 'You're safe now.'

But Vampy refused to rest, diving out of her arms and landing on her rain clothes where it began to paw at the yellow material, before moving again to the door, scratching at the screen and leaving marks on the wood. It wanted to go out again.

Thunder growled, the room quaking at the furious weather, and she felt in that moment that something terrible was happening within the school.

'I will be kind, I will be brave, I will be unstoppable,' Lottie said, squeezing her eyes shut before reaching for her rain clothes and an umbrella.

The storm screamed at her when she stepped outside. A paper-thin river cascaded over the edges of the decking, the lake in the centre of the school growing and spraying its murky dark water upward.

Lottie stepped clumsily with the cat darting between her legs, careful not to lose her footing. She was cold, and her exposed skin stung from the biting fury of the storm. It nipped and snapped at her ankles, tangling her hair menacingly with each step she took, but she persisted.

The cat took her to the very edge of the forest again, the step path covered in mud and dripping debris. All-consuming darkness drifted from between the bamboo, the rain turning silent in the midst of the towering trees. Holding her breath, Lottie prepared for the cat to guide her back into the otherworld of the wood, but instead Vampy turned back, leading her to the narrow path to the overgrown back of the dojo where it vanished. Tangled weeds and tall wet grass clawed at her legs as she stepped into the clearing. Her feet stopped, frozen, as she saw the large dark figure skulking, a sword extending from his palms.

Miko's stories of the red-faced, long-nosed *tengu*, wielding *shakujō* and holding the power to stir up great winds, filled her mind. But this creature was no *yōkai*. It turned slowly, leaning on the wooden sword in its hand – not a blade, but a stick to hold itself up – and Lottie could see his face clearly.

Lightning cracked around them, illuminating his damaged, dirty state, and for a split second she thought he'd been attacked. He was soaked through, stumbling from the bamboo trees, hair stuck down to his face like slick oil, eyes gaunt. There was a flush on his cheeks, a dreamy look consuming him as if he were stuck in a fog, and he swayed.

'Lottie.' His voice was slurred, eyes not quite focusing. 'You need to get inside; you'll get sick.'

'Jamie!' She rushed forward, her tears melting into the rain, while the wind continued to whip at her flesh, but she didn't care – Jamie was in a much worse condition.

'Let me take you back to the dorm,' she pleaded, but his face remained passive, muddled.

'I need to keep you safe.' His foot caught on a patch of gorse and he tumbled into her.

Just over a year ago, Jamie had fallen into her arms and plummeted them both into an ice-cold pool. Now Lottie planted her feet firmly in the muddy ground and embraced his weight. His face brushed hers as she held him up, his skin scorching hers. He was sick and delirious, running a dangerously high fever.

'Let me go. I need to warn you all. They're coming,' Jamie growled, but the sound came out as a desperate plea. A moan seeped from his lips and he slowly sank into her arms, the full force of him nearly overwhelming her. She needed to get him out of the storm – now.

His weight was crushing. Every bone in her body screamed against the burden, telling her to let go, to drop down and give up. Conjuring images of Liliana, she roared, drawing up a strength she didn't know she had. Another flash and growl came from the sky, the bellow growing around her.

'I won't let him go again!' she shrieked into the storm, marching Jamie's slouched form towards the dojo. The entrance came into view and through the aching of her body she howled, kicking open the huge doors. The tempest swirled, blowing open her clothes and carrying her hat away. Long tangled hair whipped about, like coiling snakes on a gorgon.

Ignoring the cold and discomfort, her crying bones and muscles, Lottie gripped Jamie tighter, shouldering him on her back as she stumbled inside. The pain was unbearable, but she wouldn't let him fall hard, holding his slouching form close and gently placing him on a soft mat.

With his body splayed she could see the damage. There was a purple tinge to the skin on his ribs where the *yukata* lay open, bloody scratches on his face and left arm that he held painfully to himself, and he smelled sour, like he'd fallen in rubbish, his garment covered in grubby smears that made Lottie's nose sting.

'What happened to you?' She tried desperately not to cry.

'I fell.'

'You fell?'

'Yes, I fell, off the roof, and then it started to rain.' He winced, his breath catching before he continued, but he was hardly making sense. 'I walked back to the woods.'

He'd walked all the way back in this state?

Lottie rushed over to the closet and grabbed as many kendo robes as she could, placing them over Jamie and balling them up under his head like a pillow. 'I'm going to get help. Don't move.' She lay the last blanket over him.

When she stood up to leave, his hot fingers curled round her wrist, pulling her down. Blinking eyes stared up at her, dark circles building beneath them like bruises. Jamie looked entirely lost, like his worst nightmares were coming true in front of him, and she had no idea how to pull him out of it.

'Lottie, please,' he begged. 'Don't go.' It sent another stabbing pain through Lottie's heart. 'They'll get you!'

Something in his voice made Lottie pause, turning back to him with a creeping chill in her bones.

'Who, Jamie? Who will get me?'

'Leviathan.'

Lottie shook her head; he was delusional. 'Leviathan aren't here. You're safe in the school now.' She cringed at the lie but she needed to get help. Moving to prise off Jamie's fingers, Lottie yelped as his grip tightened painfully.

'No, the Goat Man.' His voice was rising, terrified. 'He's waiting for me, for us.'

'Jamie, that doesn't . . .' She trailed off. 'I need to get help.'

'No, Lottie, you need to run; you're good at running.' He jerked her towards him with all his remaining strength, nearly pulling her over. 'You have to run as fast as you can. Or he's going to steal your soul. He's going to take everything good about you and swallow it.'

'What? Jamie, please. You have to let go!' But his grip remained like a vice on her tiny wrist, bruises already forming underneath.

'You are good and he is evil. And he's going to eat you up if he finds you. I need to keep him away or he'll steal me too.'

'Jamie, you're hallucinating.' She yelped once more, his fingernails digging into her skin. 'There is no Goat Man, and

161

Leviathan aren't here; you've escaped them. You're sick and I need to get you well again.'

'No, he is Leviathan; the Goat Man is Leviathan.'

Lottie froze. A sickening dread built up in her, terrified of what he was going to say next.

'I met him on the roof.' Jamie's eyes were wide as he let go of her wrist, and then he spoke the words she prayed he wouldn't. 'I met the Master of Leviathan.'

Lightning crackled around the dojo, and with one final groan Jamie drifted into unconsciousness.

'Jamie?' She tried desperately to jolt him, but there was no response.

Panic started to crawl up her, her throat tightening, knowing she couldn't do this on her own. She needed someone. She needed help.

With another great crash the door blew open, and in its wake, hair billowing like black smoke, stood a girl in a white nightdress, illuminated in the light of the storm, a fat ginger cat at her feet. 'That's a very good Partizan you have,' she said.

'Sayuri!' Lottie screeched, relief flooding through her. 'Help me . . . please.'

21

'What's wrong with him?' Lottie was quick to jump out of her seat when the nurse finally emerged from Jamie's room.

She hadn't slept all night, the storm continuing to pound relentlessly against the windows like a beast trying to break in, only clearing as the sun began to rise. Beside her, leaning against the wall, was Sayuri, still and calm as the statue of Kou Fujiwara, while she translated the nurse's report.

'He has a cracked rib, sprained wrist and ankle, and a serious bout of flu delirium, but he will be fine. He had a bad fall.'

'Thank you,' Lottie replied. 'Can we see him?'

The nurse shook her head. 'Not yet.'

Jamie had fallen somehow from somewhere high – that much was clear. He was hurt badly, and worst of all he'd met the Master of Leviathan. All things that would never have happened if she hadn't been so preoccupied.

'Arigatō gozaimasu,' Sayuri added, bowing to the nurse.

It seemed impossible that they'd been in the same storm; Sayuri's hair had dried in pretty clumps of silky waves, her skin, though flushed, was still feather soft even after their lack of sleep, while Lottie was a mess, blistered cheeks, still caked in mud all the way up her legs, hair frozen in place like a wind-swept tangle of yarn. She caught a glimpse of herself in the window and was disturbed to find she could hardly recognize herself.

Getting Jamie to the school's infirmary had felt like an impossible task. They'd carried him together, Sayuri holding one arm and Lottie the other, the two of them battling the storm as one unstoppable force. And Sayuri was strong, stronger than Lottie could ever have anticipated. It was the strength of a leader. The strength of the Pink Demon.

It had been the strangest thing to see the look on her face when she'd found them.

That's a very good Partizan you have . . .

The words played over and over in Lottie's head, and the more she thought about it, the more she was sure there'd been a hint of regret, an edge that had Lottie wondering once more about the queen of the school, her family, what she wanted and why she'd had to become so strong.

'You should go and tell your friends,' Sayuri said. 'They'll be waking up soon, and I'm sure they'll want to hear that your Partizan has returned. I'll keep watch here.'

Lottie sensed that she shouldn't leave, an absurd thought that Jamie would be snatched away from her again, but she swallowed it down, knowing she did need to tell the others.

'I wanted to say, Banshee, if they change their minds . . . If *you* wanted to extend a hand . . . We could make a good team. Whatever Leviathan are doing here, I want to help stop them.'

'That will not be necessary,' Sayuri replied bluntly, turning away.

'You must have more info, something we might be able to decipher –'

'As a matter of fact –' Sayuri turned back sharply – 'we do, but we will not be sharing it with you. We'd rather you all just stay out of trouble.'

The words felt like a door being shut in her face. Lottie couldn't understand why Sayuri didn't want to work with them. They needed to find the Master of Leviathan, and to do that they needed all the information they could get.

Lottie tried to pull herself back together. 'Well. Thanks anyway, for everything, I mean it.'

She heard Sayuri's voice behind her, cold and final. 'Don't mention it.'

The storm had cooled the earth, a welcome chill that would soon evaporate under the heat of the sun, but Lottie was going to relish it for as long as she could. Anastacia, Saskia and Ellie had convened outside the infirmary, leaning over the decking of the pond and watching the fish, distracted and sobered by everything that had happened last night.

'This is all my fault.' Ellie sank low. 'I need to . . .' Her words vanished into nothing behind a black curtain of hair. It hurt to see all the work Lottie had put in to persuading Ellie not to blame herself crumbling away again, but right now they needed to think about Jamie.

'There's more,' Lottie added hesitantly, her eyes flicking to Saskia. 'When Jamie was delirious he said something.' She took a deep breath. 'He said he met the Master of Leviathan.'

'He met him?' Saskia's eyes lit up like a fire had been ignited inside her skull, and she nearly knocked over Anastacia to grab Lottie by the shoulders.

'Saskia!' Anastacia cried.

165

'Did he see his face? Did he mention me? Did he touch him?' Her fingers were trembling, a ghost inside her that she'd buried deep itching to get out. 'What did he say, Lottie?'

Ellie tried to pull Lottie back, both of them nervous seeing Saskia switch so suddenly. They'd heard the stories, the way she behaved when they tried to ask her about the Master, but they'd never seen it first-hand. It was awful.

Lottie couldn't help wondering what that man had done to these people – and what he would do to her or Jamie if he got the chance. The only thing she could cling to was that at least Ellie was safe, as long as she stayed a good Portman. She needed to stop getting caught up in personal stuff; there was too much at stake. Right now, if they were going to solve this and help Jamie, they needed to deal with Saskia first. It was time to start fighting back.

'Who was with him? Was it Ingrid?' Her fingers tightened on Lottie's shoulders. 'She's such a little sycophant!'

Lottie didn't flinch. 'Saskia . . .' She spoke calmly, grabbing the Partizan's wrist. 'You are not with Leviathan any more.'

'I know, I just –'

'Saskia.' She grabbed her other wrist and carefully removed her hands. 'That man never cared about you. He was only using you. But we care about you, Saskia. We don't care how useful or strong you are; we like you for *you*. That's never going to change.'

'I don't want to disappoint –'

'No, Saskia.' These were the words everyone needed to hear. 'We love you, Saskia, no matter what.'

Lottie scooped her up in an embrace, and the Partizan melted into it, her warm honey scent mingling with Lottie's rose scent. Every muscle melded against her, a map of Saskia's powerful Partizan body. A body that reminded her of Jamie.

'OK, you can get off me now,' Saskia mumbled, but Lottie could hear a lingering crack of emotion, even if she wouldn't show it. The Partizan pulled away. 'We should go and check if you're allowed to see Jamie yet,' she added, uncharacteristically bashful.

The sun was full and plump in the sky now, beating down on Saskia and turning her into a golden statue. Lottie caught sight of Ellie again. She looked twisted in an unnatural way like rotten tree roots.

'Thanks, Lottie,' Anastacia whispered.

Lottie smiled over at her, but again all she could think was that it wasn't enough, that she needed to help Jamie and Ellie before it was too late.

They made their way into the infirmary, the scent of lemons becoming more intense with each step down the corridor to Jamie's room where Sayuri was waiting, only her face was strained, her mask of patience slipping just enough for Lottie to notice.

'Sayuri, what's wrong?' Lottie asked as she approached Jamie's door, which was slid open. From beyond it voices drifted out. Voices she recognized.

She rushed so fast that she nearly slammed into the door frame. And there he was, propped up, half awake, his still-foggy gaze illuminated by the stripes of sunlight through the blinds. She wanted to run to him and throw her arms round his injured body, but there was no hope of that. Beside him was a sneaking bird of prey, waiting like a vulture to retrieve its pickings.

Haru was back.

22

'Haru.' His name was like poison on Lottie's lips. 'I'm so glad you're OK. What . . . what happened?'

'I got back last night.' He looked away, as if embarrassed, and she so easily could have believed him, if she hadn't known better. 'I don't remember what happened.'

How stupid did Leviathan think they were? It was pathetic.

'What happened to you guys?' Haru asked, and she could almost have believed he was genuinely concerned.

'We were rescued by strangers, but we never saw their faces.' Lottie didn't falter as the lie rolled off her tongue. Sayuri had told her to keep the story simple, leave Haru frustrated, and, by the way his lip twitched, it looked like it had worked.

'We're glad you're safe.' Jamie's voice was low, barely audible through his laboured breathing. But even in his weary, confused state, there was a hint of a smile, a smile of relief for Haru.

She was so angry and frustrated. And sad. Sad for Jamie, to see how much it meant to him that Haru had returned unharmed, and to know that she couldn't tell him for fear of putting them all in danger. Jamie was too fragile; it was impossible to tell what he'd do if he found out, and, most importantly, they'd promised Sayuri not to say anything.

'Haru, I would like a moment alone with my Partizan.' She didn't ask. She was telling him to get out. To her relief he didn't protest but sent one of his fake summer-breeze smiles to Jamie before making his way out.

They all stared at him. Anastacia, Ellie, Saskia, Lottie and Sayuri – five girls in a blockade against this creature that was sneaking around Takeshin.

'I'll see you guys in a minute,' Lottie said, sliding the door shut behind her. She caught Sayuri's eye, and this time she was sure of it. Sayuri was definitely worried.

Lottie took a seat, not daring to touch Jamie in case he recoiled. 'How are you feeling?'

Closing his eyes, Jamie turned a little, the pink flush still strong in his cheeks. 'Not good. Could you pass me some water?'

She picked up the plastic cup on the bedside table, holding it out to him, and his hands trembled as they went to take it. His fingers brushed against hers, feather soft and too warm, a furnace of sickness under his copper skin.

His sips were small, mouse-like, a strange juxtaposition with his huge body.

'Jamie . . . Do you remember anything about last night?'

Slowly, with no indication that he'd heard her, he handed back the cup, but as she went to take it he dropped it, his fingers curling round hers instead, squeezing tight.

'I remember it all,' he said at last, not letting go. 'How did you find me?'

Lottie gulped, knowing it would be impossible to explain, to tell him that she'd been led to him by the school, that

169

Takeshin had saved him. It was absurd, and the thought made her want to check her phone again to see if there was any word from Binah, until she remembered that she'd smashed her mobile in a fit of fury.

'You said . . .' she began, 'that you met him. You called him the Goat Man, the Master of Leviathan.'

Finally he let go of her hand. 'Yes, I did. He was wearing a mask. Ingrid was there . . . I think I took one of her knives . . .'

Lottie nodded. They'd found it in his robes when they got him to the infirmary. That black spider curling round the handle of the blade, an evil little thing.

The door slid open, a nurse appearing with an extra pillow and thermometer.

'I'll be back later, Jamie,' Lottie whispered, standing up. He needed to rest. 'I promise.' And she meant it.

Stepping out of the room, she was confronted by three faces. 'Guys!' She pushed them back, closing the door behind her gently. 'What are you doing?'

'So it's really true?' Ellie began, chewing her cheek. 'The Master really made a move on him?'

'Yes . . .' Lottie felt her voice fade away.

Sayuri was gone, only the memory of that look on her face remaining.

'Lottie –' Saskia cast a quick look at Anastacia, who nodded at her to continue – 'I want to help.'

'What? You've done plenty, Saskia. It's fine –'

Saskia cut her off. 'No. I want to help you figure out who the Master of Leviathan is. I'm ready.'

*

They waited five days until Jamie was well enough to go back to his own dorm. Armed with a pencil and sketchbook, Saskia and Lottie sat on each side of his bed, waiting for him to finish sipping some water.

He was sitting up with mountains of pillows behind him like a plush throne, decorative blankets with woven stories covering his legs. He was a little too big for the set-up, and his strong body and energy clearly didn't deal well with having to rest. The room was much like any of the other dorms, wood panelling and paper screens, raised platforms where the futons lay, but Jamie's room had the distinct smell of cinnamon. The screen had been pushed open to let a breeze through, giving a perfect view of the pond sparkling orange in the evening sun.

'OK!' Jamie sighed, cutting right to it as soon as he placed his water bottle back on the tray. 'What are we doing?'

'You and Saskia are going to piece together everything you can remember about the Master of Leviathan, and I'm going to try and sketch him,' Lottie said frankly, opening her rose-covered notebook to a blank page. 'We need to find out who he is before they use the Hamelin Formula for something awful.'

A harsh exhale hissed through Saskia's teeth, while Jamie simply looked accepting. The bruises under his eyes had almost completely faded, proof that he was fighting whatever he'd been through.

'I didn't see his face,' Jamie said bluntly, staring off at the dwindling light behind the screen, haunted by a memory Lottie couldn't begin to know.

There was something about the Goat Man; he had a way of getting into people's heads, and Lottie was going to make sure it didn't happen to anyone else.

'So you really spoke to him?' Saskia asked, trying her best to stay calm, and Lottie noted a subtle glint in her eye that hinted at danger.

'Yes, well, he mostly spoke to me.' A steady hand reached for his forehead, rubbing his temples uncomfortably. 'He wore a goat mask, with huge horns like a demon, and he had two other masked people with him, a bird and a rabbit. I cut the bird in the stomach with Ingrid's knife but I doubt it was a deep cut.'

'They only wear the masks when they need to hide their identity; I saw him without it only once.' Her voice cracked and she looked away.

'Saskia,' Lottie began, gently placing a hand on her knee. 'You're not in Leviathan any more, remember?'

Her wide brown eyes darted between Lottie and Jamie. 'I'm fine. It's just . . . You don't know what he's . . . the things he can do.' Shaking her head, she looked down at Lottie's hand as if it were a foreign object. 'I was so scared to disappoint him.'

'Disappoint him?' Jamie asked, a connection being made. 'He used the same word when he spoke to me. I understand the effect he could have.'

Lottie clung to his choice of words: 'could have', not 'did have', not 'can have'.

'He didn't mention you.' His words were sharp and quick like a knife.

Saskia recoiled. 'I expected as much,' she said, a sour smile crawling on to her lips.

'He doesn't care about any of the kids he tricks; there was never anything you could have done to disappoint him because he doesn't care, but he's exceptionally good at making you think he does. I nearly –' Jamie cut himself off. 'He said he wanted to be a "father to the world", that everyone should have a choice about how they live. But he acted more like a god.'

Saskia nodded, opening her eyes again, shoulders lifting like she was shrugging off whatever nasty creature from Leviathan had been clinging to her back. 'I know that. I needed to hear it.' She sniffed, attempting a weak smile. 'Thank you.' She gave herself a final shake, her hair springing out of its knot. 'He has dark brown hair, long, and he's tall, pale skin, a little jaundiced.'

It took Lottie a moment to realize Saskia was describing the Master of Leviathan, something they'd been trying to get her to do for over a year. She pressed her lips together in concentration, readying her pencil as she let the image take over her mind.

'Ingrid used to tell me he's very handsome, sharp jawline, heavily lashed eyes, like a stag she said; I think she was trying to shove it in my face that she gets to see him.'

'They're based in Japan,' Jamie added, which reignited Lottie's worries that they'd tampered with her grade, with an even darker thought trailing its fingers through her mind. What if that girl on results day with the red nails really was being controlled by them?

Could the Master of Leviathan really be manipulating everyone that much?

'His accent is hard to place, like a mix of many different ones, and his voice is low.' Jamie chewed the thought in his head for a moment. 'It's almost pleasant, oddly familiar.'

'Familiar?' That seemed completely absurd and Lottie was sure she'd heard him wrong.

'Yes,' Saskia added, thinking hard. '"Familiar" is a good word.'

'I'd guess, from the way he spoke, he's in his forties.'

'Agreed,' said Saskia. 'From the brief moment I got to see him he had frown lines and crow's feet, curved eyes and sharp bones, but he was in shadow. Everything about him looked harsher, darker.'

Lottie let the two of them hash out what they could remember of their mysterious foe, jotting everything down while trying to form an image of him on the paper.

Long dark brown hair
Frown lines
Crow's feet
Tall
Handsome
Pale
Ageing (forties?)
Sharp features

Looking back at her from the paper, a face began to emerge, one that was so completely ridiculous it made Lottie choke involuntarily. She realized the portrait held a remarkable resemblance to Ellie's dad, an idea so nonsensical she nearly laughed.

Beside the drawing she made a note of his attributes.

Strange accent
Familiar?
Petty, and has a God complex

174

With one last look at her notes she added:

Possibly obsessed with the princess of Maradova and her Partizan

'Did either of you get a better look at his eyes? Any scars or markings?' Lottie asked, not looking up from her sketching. Silence met her question, so deep it made her snap her head up to find their stares locked on her.

'Hazel.'

'Green.'

They spoke at the same time, the words blurring together, but it wasn't the mixed messages that caught her off guard. Both of them were looking so intently at her that it made her feel like a puzzle, as if something about her was sparking a connection.

'They're the opposite of yours,' Jamie said.

Lottie didn't know how to respond, while Saskia slowly nodded, still not looking away.

'OK. I think we've made a good start here. We should go and let you have some rest, Jamie.' She smiled, pretending not to notice the strange way he continued to stare at her. She imagined a red rope between them, a line of fate holding them together, tightening with the memory of his fingers clinging to her wrist, begging her to stay.

Saskia, thrilled to leave, gave Jamie a reassuring pat on the shoulder before eagerly heading out of the door, while Lottie lingered. They needed more information, and they needed it soon, but until Sayuri shared what she knew they were on their own.

Lottie started to walk away in the now-dimming sunlight, and she turned to see her shadow stretch, melting into Jamie's in the middle of the amber glow.

She didn't want to leave and, strangest of all, she felt that he didn't want her to either, waiting for something more from her, though she didn't know what.

'Keep rested, Jamie,' she whispered. 'I promise we'll find out who he is.'

23

In the small hours of the morning Takeshin Gakuin hummed blue in the half-moon light. Filled to the brim with the sweet smell of damp earth, drenched in soothing silence. Not a single footstep on the wooden decking, nor a whispered voice, only the lone chirping of insects hidden in the flowers. It was beautiful and calming, and if Lottie wasn't on an important mission she might actually have been able to enjoy it.

In the distance was her mark, skulking through the school, dressed in her black pleats, glossy hair tied back and hidden under a terrifying demon mask that could only have been made by Miko. Lottie had been waiting all night for Sayuri to return, memorizing her schedule, knowing where to hide, and at 3 a.m., smelling of petrol, Sayuri appeared, removing her Pink Demon helmet, which she hid in the bushes, to replace it with a mask, before making her way into the school. But she did not return to her bedroom. Sayuri was clearly on a mission too, and that's precisely what Lottie had been hoping for.

Banshee knew something. They knew what Leviathan wanted from Takeshin, and Lottie was sure they had information about the Goat Man, and she would not rest until she got her hands on it.

Sayuri knew exactly where she was going, shadows stretching around her, making monsters on the walls, and Lottie mirrored them, falling in perfect time behind her, stepping whenever she stepped, moving whenever she moved.

She stalked her, ducking behind bushes, peering over walls, and she imagined herself as one of the many felines in the school, a vampire cat – and her prey was information.

Part of her felt guilty about following Sayuri around without her knowing, but that part was easily drowned out by the vision of Jamie tormented by who he'd met on that rooftop, and Ellie torn up inside with guilt. Lottie felt like she was losing them both, and the only way to save them was to stop Leviathan.

It was just as they were approaching the headmaster's office that Sayuri stopped abruptly, and Lottie had to tiptoe behind the wooden wall, tripping over a dirt step and landing firmly on her butt in a very un-catlike way. Covering her mouth to stop from squeaking, she watched, curious and confused, when Sayuri looked around, slinking to the other side of the museum wall like she'd spotted someone. But she was looking in the wrong direction to have noticed Lottie.

With one cautious peep round the corner of the headmaster's office, Lottie saw that the glass door to the museum was wide open – and someone was already inside.

The statue of Kou Fujiwara outside the museum glowed in the milky light, her sword almost quivering with anticipation. Her bronze eyes were watching anyone who entered her preserved office space. And right now her sights were planted firmly on Haru, who was emerging from the sacred place with a frustrated look on his face, one that didn't match his usual demeanour.

When Lottie had started following Sayuri, she'd never imagined Sayuri was following someone herself.

Terrified to make a single sound, Lottie melted back as far as she could into the wooden wall, begging her heartbeat to slow down, convinced the Partizan would be able to hear it.

How could she have thought this was a good idea? If Leviathan got her now, she couldn't even blame them; she'd basically served herself on a platter.

Only Haru was nowhere to be seen. There was not a trace of him anywhere, except the door to the museum slowly shutting in his wake.

Sayuri moved like a leaf in the wind, fluttering effortlessly through the gap as it shut behind her.

Lottie cast one more tentative look around, still not convinced that Haru had moved far, until she saw him, a smudge in the distance, heading back towards the boys' dorm.

Sure he couldn't see her, Lottie took her chance, crawling along the ground and kneeling at the feet of Kou's statue to watch through the glass door.

The museum was a piece of history frozen in time – only it had a guest. In the milky moonlit reflection Sayuri knelt down over the ancient low table in the centre of the *tatami*, facing away, moving with ghostly speed where she trawled through papers from a small unlocked chest. And beside it, open to the exact same page, was the book Lottie had found in the library. The book that told of Takeshin's secret treasure.

Everything became clear, and just as it crystallized in her head the ghost on the other side of the glass turned and Lottie's eyes locked with the Pink Demon.

Lottie could now see the mask for what it was, a fanged catlike creature, with the drooping round eyes of an evil spirit. If Lottie had seen such a thing by surprise, she would have been sure it was a menacing *yōkai* come to play a trick on her.

There was no point in shying away, no use in trying to back out of this. Lottie reminded herself to be brave, and slowly she pushed open the door.

Silence enveloped her, the door closing behind her without a sound, shutting out the regular world, specks of dust illuminated in the air. It was dreamy with the scent of pine, and alive, golden cats painted on the age-old chest staring out at the room, guarding the artefacts. Starlight hit the glass, the school beyond obscured, like she'd travelled back in time.

The two of them stared at each other, Sayuri still hidden behind her mask, surrounded by shadow.

'Leviathan are looking for the secret treasure, aren't they?' Lottie asked at last.

On the table she could glimpse a collection of carefully organized papers, yellowed with age and covered in characters Lottie couldn't read. She knew Haru must have been looking through the same box, and guessed there were clues in there that he hadn't been able to solve.

Without a word, Sayuri swept up the papers into the box and locked it away in a large chest. Turning back to Lottie, she lifted the mask, letting it rest on her head like a second pair of eyes, but the face beneath was no less scary.

She looked furious, only it wasn't the anger of betrayal or malice directed at Lottie. This was the distinct frustration of helplessness, and Lottie knew it all too well.

'You're trying to find the treasure before Haru does.'

It wasn't a question; it was obvious, and it explained Sayuri's behaviour when she'd found them in the library at the start of the course.

'You shouldn't have followed me.' Her voice was cold, with no semblance of her usual tranquil air. 'I could have you fail your course if I wanted to.'

'What's the treasure?' Lottie asked, letting the threat roll off her.

'We don't know, and you should stay out of it.' Sayuri rose slowly, not taking her raven-black eyes off Lottie.

'Sayuri, don't you see . . . ?' Lottie tried to take hold of her hands but it only made the other girl scowl. 'We're on the same team. I can help –'

'No, don't *you* see?' She took a step forward, face low enough that the mask on her crown flashed its eyes at her. 'That's probably why Leviathan want you here, to solve this mystery for them. Seeing as you're so good at that.'

'We don't even know for certain that they do want me here. It's improbable.'

'Is it? Or is my connection to my family so frayed that I'll never, ever be able to solve this mystery?'

For the first time since Lottie had met Sayuri, a moment of complete honesty bloomed on her face like a rare flower. There was no Pink Demon, no queen of the school, only a lonely girl trapped by burden, forced to push back against the pressure put upon her.

Lottie knew what it was like to feel alone in the world without a connection to your family, and she knew how difficult the burdens people placed upon themselves could be, and she didn't want anyone else feeling like that. Even without knowing the details of Sayuri's family life, her instincts told her to help.

'What if it can't be solved?' Lottie said firmly, taking a bold step forward. 'What if it's impossible unless we work together?'

'What nonsense –'

'I saw something in the Kiri Shinrin. The lost princess Liliana –'

'Why were you in the Kiri Shinrin?' Sayuri's eyes narrowed on her, understandably suspicious.

'I followed a cat, like Miko told me to do.'

Sayuri looked completely lost for words, and before she could respond Lottie finished her story.

'Liliana's the founder of Rosewood, and I saw her house sigil carved on one of the trees – a lily.'

'I thought the founder of Rosewood was a man?'

Lottie faltered. 'Look.' She took another cautious step towards her, and Sayuri allowed it, the two of them close enough that Lottie could smell the fiery tang of petrol fumes. 'Rosewood has many secrets, and I believe Takeshin does too – and that they're linked.'

It was strange to be so close to her, like one of the cats from the school, eyeing each other up, not sure how either would react, but they needed to trust each other.

'The founder of Rosewood was not who they said they were. She had to pretend to be a man in order to be taken seriously; it was the only way she could start the school. She was really the runaway princess Liliana Mayfutt, who was my ancestor. I have a feeling that she knew Kou, that our

182

ancestors are trying to tell us that we need to work together. I have Lili's tiara, and I'm waiting to get her diary. Maybe once it arrives we can –'

'Your ancestor?' Sayuri pulled away from Lottie quickly.

'Yes, we're both descendants of our schools. On my mother's side I –'

'You're not the princess of Maradova.'

There were no words to be found, only crushing silence as Lottie drowned in the deep black of Sayuri's eyes. That she could have made such a stupid, obvious mistake sent waves of nausea through her, the prickly heat of sickness making her sway.

'I, let me . . . What I meant was –'

'You're a Portman.' The heavy finality in Sayuri's voice made it clear there was no backing out of this error; Lottie was trapped forever by her mistake. And Sayuri continued with all the fire of a volcano erupting. 'I didn't know people had Portmans any more. Ellie's so angry – she's the princess, of course!' She let out a humourless laugh. There was a bitter note that made Lottie recoil.

'Sayuri, you can't tell anyone, please.' Lottie tried to grab at the edge of Sayuri's sleeve, but the leather fabric slipped away.

'I wouldn't dream of it!' Sayuri snapped, turning back so sharply she practically sliced the room in two. 'Do you think me completely dishonourable?'

Sayuri's bottom lip quivered. It was the only vulnerability Lottie had ever seen from her.

'Sayuri.' Lottie's voice wavered when she tried to speak, still not understanding why the other girl was so against them being a team. 'This doesn't change anything. I still believe that if we work together, we can –'

'Stop it!' Sayuri roared, turning to leave. 'You and your princess still have your Partizan, and he's a very good one.' There it was, that hint of regret again. 'You have your team and I have mine, and you should all just stay out of this.'

Sayuri had lost Haru, her Partizan, her friend and maybe the last semblance of family she'd felt close to, and watching Lottie, Ellie and Jamie was nothing but a bitter reminder for her. Sayuri didn't hate them; she envied them.

How must she feel to see them bicker and fight, drifting apart, when she would give anything to get her connection back with Haru? The truth unwrapped in Lottie's mind like the moon emerging from behind a cloud, so clear and bright, yet unreachable. Why would they keep Haru around and not report him? It wasn't just to spy on him. Sayuri couldn't bear to see him go.

Lottie thought of Sayuri's parents and wondered how lonely she was.

'Sayuri, stop.' Lottie was amazed she sounded so calm, and to her relief Sayuri paused in the doorway. 'I'm going to prove to you that we should work together. I promise you that. We will be a team.' Lottie clenched her fists. 'And I want you to promise something in return. If I can solve this mystery and help you find the hidden treasure, you have to work with us. You have to give me whatever information you have on the Master of Leviathan.'

'That will never happen.' Sayuri spoke so quietly Lottie almost didn't hear her, before she stepped out of the door. 'I'm going to bed, as should you.' She let the glass begin to close behind her.

But even through the fog of the night it felt so clear to Lottie now. The source of their problems wasn't Leviathan; it was that they hadn't been working together.

24

There were five separate sounds in the compound on any given night. Ingrid liked to listen very hard and pinpoint all of them. The creaking pipes, footsteps in the hallway, the generator humming, owls hooting outside. But the fifth sound tonight was one she didn't usually hear, a sound she hadn't heard in a long time. Her own tragic mewling.

A deep ache kept her up at night, endlessly licking her wounds, nursing the pain in her wrists. She'd had to wait until they were back at the compound to get proper medical assistance, and she'd soon learned that her wrist bones were covered in tiny surface cracks like dried-up mud. Hairline fractures so small and insignificant, yet they made her delicate arms swell up in ugly lumps that she had to hide away under lengths of bandages.

There was something almost pleasant about the pain, that dull, throbbing bruise deep within her flesh, and there were marks too, sturdy purple handprints that completely covered her tiny body. It made her feel like she had a special connection to the Partizan who'd given her these gifts; she only wished she could return the favour. And, of course, she mustn't forget that Jamie Volk had also stolen one of her knives, which meant she needed to take something of his too, something of equal value.

'Ingrid?' She rolled over at the sound of her name, a tall shadow in the doorway that she should have heard coming. 'I have news.'

Phi was a broad, big-muscled Siberian girl who'd made a hobby of challenging any man who doubted her strength. She'd been part of Leviathan long before Julius or Ingrid had joined. Supposedly she'd known the Master at his lowest moment and was regarded as a saint in the compound.

'Sit up,' she growled. 'You look pathetic.'

Ingrid flinched, but did as she was told. 'What's the news?' Her voice came out in a groggy purr, attempting to sound enthusiastic while a small part of her wondered where Julius was, if he was still on mandatory rest, and, if not, why he wasn't also being informed of anything.

'He's pleased with how his meeting went with the Maravish Partizan.'

Ingrid's mouth filled with saliva, and she licked her lips in anticipation of the praise, which would turn the sting in her arms into delicious trophies.

'When do we bring him home?' Her hands were nearly shaking. All she wanted was to bring in Jamie, bring the Master his ultimate prize and bask in his approval. She'd failed him once and had seen how furious he'd been when Saskia had slipped from their side. That girl still owed them an eye.

'We would have the other night if you hadn't made a fool of yourself,' Phi replied.

Swallowing her disappointment, Ingrid focused on Phi's gunmetal-grey eyes. She towered over everything and everyone with a deadly fixation like a walking tank.

'Stop acting so bitter,' Phi grumbled, taking in Ingrid's face.

Ingrid clenched her teeth, itching to tell her that if they'd been on time, and not left her alone with the Master's favourite toy, she wouldn't be so *bitter*.

But they *had* come eventually. She remembered how grateful she needed to be. There was no way she could let them know she was having these impious thoughts.

Get the Partizan; make the Master happy. That was the one thing Julius and Ingrid had been sure of, but recently it felt messy, uncertain.

'The princess.'

Ingrid looked up again, a bloodthirst coursing through her like fire, a burning need for revenge.

'What about her?'

'He's considering their relationship,' Phi said, picking at her eyebrow, an absent-minded twitch. 'We think they're too close; it might hinder our plan.'

The princess, the princess, the princess. What was so special about the princess?

Ingrid had suggested multiple times that they should just abandon the princess of Maradova, that there was no helping her.

The Maravish monarchy represented everything they were against, the root of it all. Yet Ingrid simply couldn't shake how much she hated that senseless spoiled little girl, who'd tripped her over in the Tompkins Manor and ruined everything.

188

Her fingers tensed in a way that sent pain shooting up through the bones. She relished it.

'What does he need me to do?' asked Ingrid.

'Haru believes his master and the princess are only days away from finding the hiding place, but there's been a change of plan. First, we're going to allow the princess to find what's hidden in Takeshin and we'll take it later. He thinks it might change her mind a little. And, second, he's decided we need to send someone to get closer to Jamie. Make the transition easier.' Phi let out a grunt that was almost a laugh before adding, 'And if that fails, there's always the Hamelin Formula . . .'

Ingrid struggled to hide her delight. 'Just give me the orders and I'm there.'

'No! Haru will be taking care of it. He's already got closer than we'd anticipated.'

'What?' Ingrid's hands clenched painfully, all that delicious expectation deflating into nothing.

'He wants you to stay as far away as possible. That's your order.' Phi spoke casually, as if this wasn't the worst news Ingrid could ever have heard. 'From what he saw on the roof, you are far too reckless when it comes to the Partizan, and he wants you to stay away from all targets until further notice.'

Jamie was being ripped away from her. The one thing that would make the Master truly value her.

A million thoughts and questions exploded in her mind. Was the Master mad at her? What was so special about Haru? Why wasn't she getting her way?

Arms crossed against her chest, Ingrid cradled the wretched pain, letting it fuel her anger. This was the princess's fault.

She'd taken her prize away and foiled them too many times, and now she'd turned the Master against her.

'OK.' She acted disappointed so as not to give too much away. 'I understand.'

Phi narrowed her eyes suspiciously, and Ingrid made a great show of whimpering as she touched her wrists.

Phi let out a long sigh before offering an attempt at comfort. 'Just focus on getting better, and if you need any more painkillers, come and find me.'

Ingrid didn't say thank you; it would have been too out of character. Instead she sniffed loudly, as if embarrassed by her outburst. 'I'll get better soon so I can be useful again.' She wiped the tears from her cheeks as Phi left. Then, as soon as she was sure Phi was out of sight, she let the snarl crawl on to her face. Wincing, she picked through her jacket to find her salvaged blade; a slick of Haru's blood still stained it from Jamie having thrown it. The feel of the steel spider made her shiver with anticipation, terrible acts of revenge and torment bubbling in her head.

If they weren't going to let her get close to Jamie again, she would find another way of getting even.

25

Of all the stupid things Ollie had done in his life, of all the half-thought-out, nitwitted ideas, this was by far the most . . . fun.

Standing knee-deep in a stream under the bridge of one of the most prestigious schools in the world, goggles over his eyes, and heart racing like he was preparing to do an Olympic dive, Ollie took in his ragtag accomplices and pondered how he'd found himself here.

Binah had told him there was a diary in Rosewood that they needed to retrieve, part of a puzzle that Lottie was trying to solve. These other two boys, both of whom Ollie had seen on the news, had agreed, as if it were totally normal, to let Binah lead them on an illegal and dangerous mission.

They'd waited until nightfall and Binah had chosen an evening with a full moon to give them the best chance of spotting the glint of the metal hatch, but the only downside was, it was creepy as hell.

'OK, Ollie, time to shine.' The waterproof torch was held out to him by a grinning Raphael, and even in the dark his teeth shone bright white like they might be glowing.

Raphael was strange to him. His expensive cologne made Ollie's nose twitch, and he was beautiful in an unfair kind of way, the kind of attractiveness reserved for Hollywood actors who make it seem completely effortless.

Percy, on the other hand, had little in the way of charisma. His eyes were sunken and bruised like he didn't get much sleep, and he was almost as pale as the moon. Yet there was something about him, an awareness of sorts, that made Ollie feel as though nothing would get past him. It was both unnerving and completely disarming.

Maybe there really was something special about Rosewood students after all. The thought made him wince, remembering how he'd heard nothing from Lottie all summer. Swamped in his own thoughts, he caught Binah's eye, and he was sure from the way she pouted that she knew what he was thinking about.

The only way Ollie could explain how he felt for Binah was a 'friend crush'. He understood she wasn't interested in romance, and he had no interest in that; what he craved was her approval. He wanted to impress her, to be helpful, to make her laugh. If she was the great mind of their generation, he wanted to be her trusty sidekick.

Shaking off the thought, Ollie nodded to his comrades, wading out and sticking his head beneath the surface. He lay down, letting the muddy water pour over him. Binah had wanted him for his 'coin-diving experience' but it was impossible to see anything and he felt the water up his nose. It tasted of grass not salt, and it wasn't the crystalline liquid of the sea that he was used to. It struck him as a complete fluke that anyone could have found anything under this water, though he desperately didn't want to let Binah down.

The only thing he could see was the moon's reflection, but there was something strange about the scene; it looked like there were two moons on the water's face. One of them was significantly larger and raised slightly, glittering.

It was right there, just about hidden under the water's surface. He bobbed back up. 'I've found it!'

It was Raphael's turn next, the muscle who made a great show of pulling up the hatch. Raphael gently lowered each of them down the secret passageway, the water gently lapping at its lip. Binah first, light as a feather with her tiny frame. Then Percy, only a little heavier but still skinny and easy to manoeuvre. Raphael was extra careful with him, constantly signing and reassuring him, and at once Ollie understood what he was seeing.

These people, Lottie's friends, had experienced things that had bound them forever, things that had meshed them to each other, and he was an outsider, only able to look in, like an ornament in a snow globe, watching the world around him but never being able to engage.

'Do you trust me?' Raphael asked teasingly, holding his hand out in an imitation of Aladdin.

'It's not you I don't trust; it's my girth.' He was sat on the edge of the hatch, soaking wet, legs dangling over, preparing to lower himself. 'I'm a lot heavier than those two.'

But, even as Ollie spoke, Raphael wrapped his arms round him and helped him down, not even blinking at the embarrassing intimacy of it all – he was far too confident for that.

'Told you I was strong,' said Raphael as he dropped down and closed the hatch.

'Yeah . . .' Ollie trailed off, once again regarding this ragtag bunch, clothes soaked through, the heat around them making little tendrils of steam. They looked like magic in the dark of the tunnel, a pixie, an elf and an Adonis.

So what was he?

They began to make their way down the tunnel, wet stone splashing beneath them with Percy leading the way, all in an expectant silence, none of them daring to make a sound above their soft footing in case they were discovered.

Occasionally Ollie could hear what sounded like steps above them, or the creak of a floorboard, and his heartbeat would thunder, warning his body to be silent, even though he knew it was probably his imagination.

Binah pointed where there was a crawl space and they each got low. It was intensely claustrophobic, and for the first time in Ollie's life he had a vision of true fear, a breath-stealing image of the ceiling crumbling over them, leaving them trapped forever. When they finally reached their goal, a cut-out in the wall with a tiny door just like Alice might find in Wonderland, he decided to cross caving off his list of things to try. Binah held her ear up and nodded to Percy that it was safe, and so began Percy's part of the journey.

His acquired ability to get around quietly and unseen might have come from a less than ideal situation, but now they were going to use it to their advantage.

The pale boy carefully nudged the door open to reveal wood.

For a brief moment Ollie thought they were walled in. But Percy, with an almost unnatural quiet, pushed the wooden object out of the way to make just enough squeezing space for all of them.

194

And they were in! Ollie was in Rosewood Hall, that mysterious world that had eaten up his best friend and turned her into a fairy-tale princess. The place he'd heard so much about, that always seemed like a made-up land. Now it was real. And it overwhelmed him.

The scent of roses and lavender, honey and peaches gripped him, sucking the air from his lungs and replacing it with flowers. Pungent, heady flowers crawled inside him, wrapping him up in a spell.

It felt as if the school itself were a spirit, and it wanted to know who he was and if he were allowed to stay. He thought he might never breathe again – it was too much and it made his lungs ache.

Then at once, like emerging from the sea, he broke through the surface and became accustomed to the scent, his head no longer heavy with the intensity of it all, and he looked up to see the others staring at him.

Shaking his head, he signalled for them to continue, but he caught the flash of Binah's smile, and the knowing glint had him questioning what he'd just experienced. Without a word, he smiled back at her, relishing the brief moment where he felt like the school had accepted him, that he was part of the team.

They followed Percy through the grand school, moonlight submerging the dark wood and golden wall carvings in a milky glow. There was a groaning, the wind winding through cracks in doors and windows like murmured voices. It felt like walking through a museum, the whole school an ancient relic full of ghosts, and they were on their way to find some of them.

Percy seemed part of the magic and Ollie didn't know that stillness like his could exist. He moved through the grounds like a shadow, his footsteps making no sound, not a peep as he passed through doors and gates, and sometimes the silence was so intense that Ollie was sure he was hardly even breathing.

They reached a tower with a locked door, but Percy was undeterred, pulling out a hairpin, and, like someone out of a kids' spy film, he unlocked the door.

They reached a giant statue of a bird with stone steps round leading up the tower. It watched him, he was sure of it; the statue was watching him, the bird's eyes the eyes of the school itself.

A plaque beneath the bird read 'Elwin'. Binah walked up to it and began grappling with the middle letter. Ollie watched, curious, until at last she gave it a sharp turn, causing cogs to grind, and the 'W' slowly became an 'M'.

A door creaked open and Ollie saw what could only be described as a secret passage. It led down into a dark basement that was decorated with items that he recognized in an instant: fairy lights and hand-made bunting, floral upholstery and pressed flowers. This was Lottie's touch.

The whole room was curved, a circular cavern with cold stone walls, made warmer with the golden fairy lights and glowing stars that hung from the ceiling by invisible string. It was like stepping into the Milky Way. A blackboard in the middle had 'Have a good summer' written in multicoloured bubble writing: Lottie's. In stark contrast to the cosmic and colourful decoration were piles of carefully covered paintings and a mahogany desk that looked about a million years old, with stacks of papers, journals and books that looked even older. All these ancient items were gathered in a recess with a respect that gave it the energy of a shrine.

'Who else knows about this place?' Ollie asked through shaky breath.

'It's our friend Lottie's.' Raphael grinned, clearly immensely pleased with himself and his friends for having a secret base. 'She found it, and only we know about it.'

Ollie resisted the urge to inform him that he probably knew Lottie better than any of them, but he wouldn't have been able to anyway, because Binah rushed over to the dresser and began searching through its contents.

Ollie felt tainted watching her, like he was spying on something very secret.

The other two boys looked like they felt the same, but there was also a hunger to learn more about the unknown parts of their school.

'Binah, should we really –'

'FOUND IT!' Binah shot up, a leather-bound book in her hands that looked about ready to turn to dust. Binah flicked through the pages, then froze. 'My goodness!'

'What?' Ollie asked, the three boys looking between each other. 'What's wrong?'

'Nothing's wrong,' Binah replied, distracted, her eyes scanning the dusty pages. 'Only that it feels a little odd, you know?'

'What does?'

Closing the diary, Binah pushed her glasses up her nose, the light glinting off the frames. 'For the first time in my life I have absolutely no idea what any of this means.' She smiled, carefully placing the diary in a waterproof bag. 'We'll just have to hope Lottie can figure it out on her own . . .'

26

The art department was virtually empty. Scraps of material and streaks of paint covered the giant oak table where Miko sat opposite Lottie, adding the final touches to Aoi Tōyō's hair ornament with aggressive concentration.

Since Lottie's conversation with Sayuri at the museum, they'd started to fall back into a routine again, Miko giving orders, the two of them methodically working on their pieces, and all the while Lottie waited for a message from Binah, knowing there was nothing more she could do until she got that diary. As far as she knew, Haru had made no other attempt to find the treasure; it was almost weird, like he'd given up, but Lottie wouldn't be lulled into a false sense of security. She needed to find whatever was hidden if she had any hope of getting Sayuri to work with them.

In front of her, Lottie's sketchbook lay open, filled with drawings of the vampire cat, alongside a hideous demon Goat Man with an odd resemblance to the king – if the king was scary and had horns.

Pushing her hair back, she tried to clear her thoughts. The question remained, buzzing in her mind in a way that gave her a headache: who was the Goat Man? And what did he want?

She'd thought the idea that everything connected back to the Maravish princess had been absurd, but the more she thought about it, the more she feared it was true.

Takeshin, Saskia, Jamie, Tompkins – you could connect the dots, and every time it took you back to the princess and Rosewood.

And if this was true, what would that do to Ellie?

'It sure would be easier to find the Master of Leviathan if we had more info.' Lottie tapped her chin with her pencil. 'If only we could all join forces and share our information.' Pouting, Lottie stared down Miko, fluttering her eyelashes.

'*Urusai!*' she muttered, crinkling her nose like she'd smelled something bad. 'Put it out of your mind. Sayuri and Emelia told us not to work with you, so I do what they say.'

It had become their own personal routine, working on costumes and bickering over Leviathan.

'If you're not going to help us, at least let me add the tiara design to our Aoi Tōyō costumes.' Lottie tried to put on her most reasonable voice.

'No. No tiara. The energy will confuse the dance.'

'Not if Aoi Tōyō is good enough.'

'No tiara. No treasure. No Leviathan info.'

'Then what about Sayuri's family?' It had occurred to Lottie that it might be helpful to know more about them if it was a secret passed down through the generations.

'You're being nosy.'

'Please, Miko, I just want to help, and Sayuri didn't give you any orders to not talk about her family.'

Miko let out a long sigh, a strand of her blue hair falling over her left eye like a scar.

'She lives with her grandfather, her dad works in Singapore and her mother is absent.'

'Why?' Lottie knew how intrusive she was being, but she couldn't shake off the desire to learn more.

Miko scowled again, rolling whatever she was about to say around in her head.

'They had a death in the family, her mother's sister; they were very close. It was hard on all of them.'

'What happened to her?' she asked before she could stop herself, remembering the sad look on Sayuri's face.

Miko looked away, tapping the table distractedly in a way that was unlike her.

'She was dealt a lot of sadness; she lost a baby. Eventually that sadness ate her up completely.'

The words clung in Lottie's head, the awfulness of it all, how one terrible event could bleed through a whole family, spreading stains of sadness down to each generation.

'Miko-chan? Lottie-chan?' A recognizable voice called through the art rooms, and she could practically hear the smirk on his lips.

'*Hai!*' Miko called in response, clearly relieved to have a distraction.

Rio emerged round the corner, carrying two bags, one of which he handed to Miko, filled with materials she'd requested, and the other he slapped right on top of Lottie's sketchbook.

Lottie looked up at him in irritation.

'This arrived for you today.' He smiled down at her as if he'd just done her the world's biggest favour. 'You're welcome.'

She reached into the bag, fingers meeting with soft padding and paper. Miko and Rio watched her curiously as she opened the package and pulled out the contents, a gift it seemed, wrapped in canary-yellow tissue paper that reminded her of . . .

'Binah!' Lottie said.

Good luck solving the mystery.

The moment the wrapping fell away, a transporting scent took over the room. Roses, pungent and sweet and bursting with a tantalizing call back home, back to Rosewood Hall. Lili's diary.

It was so wonderful that it ached to even hold it. Her clue, her key to hopefully solving Takeshin's mystery and teaming up with Sayuri.

A bookmark poked out of the diary, yellow, the colour of Stratus. With trembling hands Lottie turned to it to find water-damaged pages. She could just make out the words in English.

1642
In a most curious turn of events the boat has landed and
we find ourselves hiding in Japan, where I am unwelcome
and more welcome than ever, for I have met a girl named
Kou. She is my age and comparably improper . . .

It hit Lottie like a lightning bolt. It had to be the same Kou! It had to. That's why the name felt familiar; she'd seen it before in this very diary. Liliana had stowed away to Japan during the *Sakoku* period, when no foreigners were allowed to enter Japan without permission, and that's why she'd never been found.

How did she get there? Did she know that's where she was heading?

She turned the page, expecting more, her fingers twitching with anticipation for the whole story.

Only there was nothing. The next pages spoke nothing of Japan, or of Kou, or any such adventures. Someone had torn out all the pages. It was as if a whole section of Liliana's life had been erased from history.

What followed instead were pages of sketches that seemed to have nothing to do with anything. Suns, moons, sparkling trees, horned catlike creatures and magpies in great flocks, and one image that caught her eye above the others – a sword. Even on the paper it looked sharp enough to cut the world in two, with an intricate handle that showed masterful precision.

Reluctantly she pulled her eyes away from the elaborate drawings and turned to the only other page with writing on from before Lili arrived in England.

Twirling calligraphy spread out to take up as much room on the paper as possible, but there were just seven words. A list.

A cat
A hiding place
A sword

Lottie skimmed through the pages a few more times, slowly losing hope that she would find something else, anything at all that might give her a clue to the puzzle of the hidden treasure. But no – nothing.

She very nearly didn't notice the centre of the book. It was frayed, a page removed just like the others, except it had been taken out right up to the spine with deliberate precision, barely perceptible tear marks that one could almost miss. She pondered the missing paper, running her fingers along the jagged edge, nose so close she could smell the decades of dust.

How odd, she thought, *that someone would take such special care with this page only.*

'What's that?'

Lottie looked up, jolted out of her thoughts by Miko's voice, and slammed the diary shut.

Miko watched her suspiciously, eyes narrowing over the ancient relic.

'It's . . .' Lottie's words caught in her throat, unable to articulate what the diary meant, what it was. 'I have to go and find Ellie.'

She packed up her stuff before they could question her, Miko's voice following her on the way out. 'Don't forget our show is very soon!'

'Yep!' Lottie shouted back, jumping over a box of paintbrushes, and feeling for the first time in a while that she was getting closer to the truth.

It should have been easy to find Ellie; she had a free day, so was going to keep an eye on Jamie. He'd made an almost complete recovery, which was fantastic news, except for the fact he was on the move again, so they had to keep watch in a way he wouldn't notice, finding things they needed to do that gave them an excuse to be near him. Just as long as they kept Haru from being with him alone. It was unclear if Jamie had figured out what they were doing, but if he had, he hadn't said anything.

Lottie had not missed a single shift, using any excuse to be by his side, relieved to see him well again, so it came as a surprise to her that Ellie was nowhere to be found.

'She went to the dojo,' Lola and Micky said in unison, wiping flour from their noses.

'But she doesn't have class today.'

Shrugging, the twins lowered their faces in concentration over the intricate raindrop cake they were decorating.

Lottie couldn't really blame them for not having more urgency about the whole thing, since neither of them had any idea that Haru was not to be trusted. Lottie wanted to keep it that way. The twins deserved to have a break.

After the storm, the weather had settled into an oppressive heat, humid and warm, with lone clouds rolling above the school like a sleepy shoreline.

On her way to the dojo she passed Kou Fujiwara's museum, the glass-doored building a strange anomaly in the traditional setting. She hadn't spoken to Sayuri since their run-in, the two of them barely even looking at each other, and whenever Lottie tried to catch her attention she was met only with cold indifference. Looking up at the statue of Kou, Lottie couldn't help wondering how it felt to see your ancestor every day while feeling so disconnected from your family.

It wasn't hard to find Ellie. She heard her before she saw her, a series of feral grunts echoing from the back of the dojo, from the exact place Lottie had found Jamie during the storm.

There was an animal mania blazing from the girl she saw practising strikes, teeth bared like fangs, attacking the air with lightning precision. It didn't feel like her princess. Ellie had vanished, in her place a twisted, bent-limbed creature.

Instead she saw Aoi Tōyō, the maiden, consumed and reborn into a powerful monster of rage and fire.

'Ellie?' Her voice dragged her princess out of whatever storm was raging in her head.

'Lottie? What are you doing here?' The speed at which she pulled the mask back over her face felt like whiplash.

'What am *I* doing?' Lottie spluttered. 'You're meant to be hanging out with Jamie. Is everything OK?'

Picking her stuff up, Ellie gave the grass a humourless smirk. 'He doesn't want me around, Lottie. He hates me.'

'Ellie, that's not true, he's –'

'The best thing I can do for him is get strong enough to prove he doesn't need to look after me. That none of you need to put yourself in danger for me.'

'Ellie, that's not how this works . . .'

'I don't want to be weak any more, Lottie. Jamie was so . . .' Her eyes misted over, the dark cloud coming low, wrapping her in the horrible memory of seeing Jamie so injured and helpless. It hadn't occurred to Lottie how scary that must have been for Ellie, and she felt so stupid for not thinking of it sooner.

'I've been having these nightmares, Lottie.' Ellie's voice had turned small. 'I'm walking through the long corridor at home, the one with all the paintings of previous rulers. When I get to the framed portrait of Claude the light distorts it, and all of a sudden it's me. I'm in the frame.' Shuddering, Ellie looked down, face obscured.

But before Lottie could reach out to her, Ellie shook herself. 'I found your phone!'

'What?'

'Your phone. I found it smashed up. What happened?'

'Ollie sent me something,' Lottie confessed. 'I was angry and . . . it was an accident.'

Shaking her head, Ellie looked down at her hands like she couldn't recognize them, then, worst of all, she turned that same look of confusion on Lottie.

'I did this to you. The Lottie I know would never do something like that.' Her voice was shaking, and Lottie felt her eyes go right through her. 'I'm a bad influence, just like they said.'

'Ellie, no, I told you already –'

'Didn't you hear what Banshee said? What if it *does* all lead back to me? What if it *is* my fault?'

Banshee.

Simply hearing it took Lottie right back to Kou's museum: Sayuri's anger, Banskee's determination not to join forces with them.

'We'll solve this, Ellie. We'll figure out who the Master of Leviathan is and you can put this silly idea that it's all your fault away. All we need is each other, remember?'

As soon as she said this, she knew that none of it was true. Whatever information Banshee had, they needed it. They needed Banshee's help, and Lottie needed to start preparing for the worst. That it might all lead back to the princess of Maradova.

Ellie threw her bag over her shoulder, and Lottie could see the sweat on her brow. 'It's not good enough. I can't keep relying on everyone like this,' she said.

'Ellie, what are you –'

'Our showcase is only two days away.' The dark cloud inched closer to Lottie when Ellie brushed past her, making her skin prickle. 'If I can beat Jamie, maybe he won't have to worry any more.'

'Jamie doesn't want that, Ellie, I'm sure of it. None of us do.'

But Ellie wasn't listening; she was striding off towards the dorms with a brief wave. 'I'm going to go and find someone to practise with me. I'll see you at dinner.'

It wasn't until Ellie disappeared out of view that Lottie realized she hadn't had a chance to tell her about the diary, and it became very clear that there were much bigger issues to deal with before she could solve Takeshin's secret.

27

Jamie and Ellie had known each other their whole life. From the moment Ellie was born a lifelong bond had been written out for them, a bond of protection, devotion and – most of all – duty. It was the bond of a Partizan, and today Ellie was going to break it.

'You all ready for the showcase?' Anastacia asked.

Ellie found it impossible to answer. Sweat was building up under her *kote* gloves, but it wasn't about the showcase; she'd felt like this for a while now. It was a feeling she'd nearly overcome, but it had surged inside her again since the festival, and she knew the only solution was to get stronger.

'Yeah,' she said at last, chancing a glance at the audience sitting neatly and cross-legged on the other side of the dojo like an array of lotus flowers.

Everything leads back to you.

Bad influence . . .

They'd already warmed up and meditated before the audience had arrived. It was only a small crowd; any Takeshin summer-school student could watch the morning showcase, but it was mostly friends of the kendo pupils. Ellie had never considered herself claustrophobic, and yet even this little group of people set her heart racing. People she barely knew, people who might hurt them.

Squeezing her eyes shut hard, she pushed the thought from her mind, trying to calm herself again.

A flash of colour from a blue pixie cut and a tall red-haired punk with black between them let her know that Miko, Rio and Wei were among the watchers, all barefoot, and beside them, fidgeting, was the one thing that kept her grounded: her best friend and the girl who she could never let know how terrified she really was, Lottie Pumpkin. Like the adorable little princess she strived to be, Lottie fluttered her fingers in a painfully cute greeting over in their direction, her face etched with worry. Worry for her, and worry for Jamie. All they did was make her worry.

On the other side of the room, towering over everyone, tall and powerful in his kendo gear, Jamie was chatting with Haru and Sayuri, oblivious. Ellie watched as he waved back at Lottie without smiling, a dark knight, undefeatable, foreboding and fierce in his *kendōgu*. But she knew now she'd seen him injured and vulnerable that he was human, just like the rest of them. So today she was going to prove to him that he didn't need to protect her. That he never needed to put himself in danger again.

The thought set her fingers trembling, so she squeezed her hands into fists. Since she'd seen Jamie sick and injured in the infirmary, Ellie hadn't been able to get the image out of her head, and the knowledge that it was her fault stuck in her gut.

I have to be stronger. I'm too weak. I put everyone in danger. It all leads back to me.

At last Haru and Sayuri moved to the *kamiza*, the higher area of the dojo intended for the teacher and any special guests, while Jamie put on his *men* and took his place at Ellie's side, entirely oblivious to the storm raging under her mask.

'Thank you, everyone, for coming to our showcase,' Haru began in Japanese, with Sayuri translating next to him. His voice sent goosepimples over Ellie's skin. He was too cheerful, too easy-going and soft for a Partizan, and even now that she knew it was for show it still lulled her every time he smiled. It was further proof that they couldn't trust anyone. Nowhere was safe.

'This is not a tournament or competition,' Haru continued, and Ellie thanked goodness for her helmet so that no one could see her expression. 'Today is a demonstration of all the skills and disciplines the summer-school *kendoka* have learned during their time at Takeshin Gakuin. They will come up in pairs to show you *waza*, or "techniques". Usually it takes many months, or even years to get to this level in *kendo*, but with our advanced course you will see how far Takeshin students can go.' Ellie barely registered his phoney smile, the time inching closer to the moment of truth. 'Would the first pair please come forward?'

Each pair walked to the centre of the ring and engaged in a match, although there was always a clear winner. It was the regular formalities: centring, bowing, respects being paid. All the rigorous energy filled the room with a rubbery smell from the mats on the floor, the sound of *shinai* on *shinai* like a crackling firepit, and the dizzying heat of the suits gave the distinct sensation of being trapped in a burning building.

Second to last were Anastacia and Saskia. The Partizan helped her master to her feet, something that was not allowed in the practice of *seiza*, but Haru let it slide. Trying to pay attention, Ellie found herself fidgeting restlessly. The two girls were having too much fun, and Saskia even let Anastacia get a few hits in, even though it was obvious she was just being nice.

The display sent a sweat trickling down Ellie's spine, and she was overcome with the feverish need to get up and face her own Partizan, to prove to them all that she could do this. That she didn't need protecting.

'Ellie and Jamie,' Haru called finally, making Ellie jump. For a split second Ellie's mind went blank at the sound of her name, as if she'd been plummeted into someone else's body. How could her friends act so calm around Haru? Still feeling displaced, she rose to her feet but was unable to look over at her Partizan. They were the last ones to fight, and having been sat in *seiza* for over thirty minutes Ellie's legs felt stiffer than usual.

In the centre of the ring Ellie still refused to look at Jamie directly as they measured the space between them. She was terrified of bringing back the memory of his sickly face. The rubbery smell seemed to grow more intense and pungent, the heat of her suit like lava, tight and suffocating.

She had to stay calm. With one final deep breath she looked up.

Mask to mask, the sheer size of him was undeniable, a mountain looming over a hill. When they were children, she and Jamie had always been similar in height and build, skinny little things. But while Jamie had been reserved and unassuming

211

in his size, Ellie had been a boisterous and scurrying creature. Now there was no comparison. Jamie had grown and morphed into a brooding beast, whose body pulsed and expanded with his inner torment. He transformed every burden he lay upon himself into getting stronger, bigger, more powerful, while Ellie had remained delicate, boyish and lean. Even Lottie was starting to catch up with her in height. The more Jamie trained to protect her, the more they were growing apart.

An imaginary spark in the air like a trail of gunpowder told them both it was time. They met each other's eyes, black and golden. Gazes locked, they bowed at a fifteen-degree angle, *shinai* held firmly in place, arms unmoving.

The room held its breath, her grip tightening, heartbeat slowing, and so it began . . .

Lottie was as taut as a kendo sword, constantly side-eyeing Sayuri, but, every time she looked at her, Sayuri's gaze was serene, impenetrable.

This was the longest time they'd been in a room together since the museum and it was painfully awkward. Had she told anyone? What would Lottie do if she did?

It made it impossible to entirely concentrate on the match in front of her. She just had to hope they could trust her, and, besides, there was something much more important she needed to fix.

They had to stop whatever Leviathan were planning, and they had to find out who this terrible Goat Man was, but they couldn't do anything until they started working together. Looking at the scene unfolding in front of her, it seemed she had some serious work to do.

Lottie was not going to pretend she knew anything about kendo. From what she'd picked up it was mostly about discipline, but from the moment they stepped in the dojo Lottie sensed the same fiery tension that had been present when she'd found Ellie training. It was not the calm, focused energy she'd been told to expect and it was obvious to everyone who it was coming from.

The atmosphere was a rubber band stretching and stretching, threatening to snap at any moment.

'*Yappari*.' Miko caught Lottie's attention. She was watching Ellie and Jamie intently, all the while chewing the corner of one of her decora nails. 'She's stuck inside her own head.'

A loud whack echoed through the hall from Jamie blocking Ellie's strike, the move so fast it was barely visible. Before Lottie could even register what happened, Jamie's feet glided him into a counter position like some kind of fantastical box step, where he whacked Ellie's mask directly on the side. The second the hit took, he threw his bamboo sword above his head and stepped backwards out of her reach.

'Whoa!' Rio's mouth was agape. 'He's amazing.'

'Your Partizan is very impressive,' Wei affirmed, genuine interest sparking in his eyes.

Lottie still didn't understand, but it was plain that she'd witnessed something remarkable, and it only made the tension increase.

The two fighters got back into position, and Lottie thought her eyes were playing tricks on her, because Ellie's bamboo sword was shaking.

Once more they were centred, once more the bamboo snapped together, and once more Jamie got the winning hit.

This time it was different, a little more spectacular, his footwork intricately spinning him, flipping Ellie's *shinai*, striking her chest and moving effortlessly behind her, swift and easy like a shadow moving with the sun.

Time looped, endlessly repeating bursts of combat, with Jamie coming out victorious again and again. Lottie could see Ellie panting, the suit rising and falling. Centred again, with everyone on the edge of their seats ready for the final round, something changed – the split-second flash of Ellie's weapon was met with a different sound, a more robust pounding as the two bamboo swords struck each other. Ellie darted with such speed that it seemed she might be about to land a hit. The breath caught in Lottie's throat, milliseconds stretching out into an eternity. She was going to do it!

Silence spread through the dojo, and it was just when it seemed a universal truth that it crumbled in front of them. The moment burst, as Jamie did what he did best, and won.

He was a looming darkness, unbeatably quick and deadly. The final hit was on Ellie's left glove, barely even a tap, yet the confidence in the strike was finite, his *shinai* rising above his head again, marching backwards, the shadow receding.

Thundering, awe-struck applause echoed around them, but Lottie couldn't partake. Something was wrong. Miko felt it too. Ellie was practically vibrating, static sparking around her.

'No!' Ellie screamed, pulling off her helmet and throwing it to the floor where it landed with a loud whack.

A collective gasp sucked the air out of the room, the applause drying up to be replaced by a bitter taste at Ellie's actions. Sayuri and Haru rose to their feet, yet even they were hesitant, having never seen such a shocking display in their school.

'I can't!' Ellie's voice was that of a whimpering child, face contorted with sweat and despair, black hair sticking to her face. Her huge dark eyes darted frantically around the room, glazed over, her breath raspy and laboured. She backed away, trembling. Ellie let out a frantic cry and pulled off the rest of her armour, while Jamie stood still.

Frozen by the display, Sayuri's words echoed in Lottie's head. *You and your princess still have your Partizan, and he's a very good one . . .*

Lottie couldn't let their bond be destroyed permanently. She had to do something.

Saskia ran up and tried to offer a word of comfort, but it was entirely the wrong thing to do. 'Ellie, you've got to calm down; it's only –'

Ellie growled. 'Get away from me!'

She made to shove Saskia away, but Saskia blocked the move lightly with her forearm, causing Ellie to tumble into the wall, smacking her shoulder. The shock of the impact seemed to cause a crack in her mind, clarity coming back into her eyes. She suddenly registered what she was doing and how many people were watching.

'Crap, Ellie, I didn't mean to –'

Ellie cut Saskia off with a snarl, but this time the sound was weak. She turned to her spectators.

Rubbing her shoulder, she kicked the helmet on the floor. Lottie tried to reach her, but it was far too late. Ellie had stormed out of the dojo, abandoning her shoes, abandoning all of them.

'Ellie!' It was a pathetic, desperate call that floated in the broken atmosphere of the room.

The door slammed shut behind her princess, and Lottie felt deep inside that she'd failed her somewhere, that the rope connecting them was lying broken on the ground. But she wasn't giving up. She shot a look at Jamie, a fiery determination building inside her, and she knew exactly what had to be done.

28

They both still needed him.

Jamie looked at Lottie in the centre of the circle. Her hair was a tangled mess, hanging down her back from the heated room, and her left hand clasped her chest.

'She ran away,' Lottie whispered.

From the moment he'd seen his princess and her Portman kiss in the chocolate factory he'd felt loneliness lingering within him. Whatever they shared he felt locked out of it, isolated from the strange bright magic Lottie held. They had each other; they didn't need him.

'I need to go after her,' Lottie said, her eyes focused on Sayuri, not Haru.

'Yes, of course.' Sayuri gestured to the door.

It was cooler outside the dojo, and the heat of the day hadn't had time to grow yet, the morning giving the grounds a dusty topaz colouring. Footprints in the dirt path and a knocked-over stack of boxes suggested Ellie had run up the steps towards the forest.

Lottie's eyes were glued on the horizon. 'This is very bad, Jamie.'

'I don't think she's gone far.'

'How can you know?'

'We can find her. It's simple tracking, but it would be best if I came with you. It's likely she went up the path into the forest and –'

Lottie shook her head, her cheeks flushed. 'I'm not going; you need to go after her.'

Jamie faltered. 'I very much doubt I'll be of any help. You're the one who's good at –'

A strange sound pierced the air, shocking him enough to stop him talking, and it took him a minute to realize it had come from Lottie. It was halfway between a growl and an exasperated groan, and it caught him completely off guard.

'This is between you two! How are we ever supposed to take on Leviathan when you two can't even look at each other?' Her hands curled into fists. 'You barely speak any more. Don't you see? She blames herself for everything. You both do, and you're both so . . . so . . . STUPID!' She was hardly able to look him in the eye, and he could have laughed if not for how much she was shaking. 'You've snapped the rope in two and it's your responsibility to put it back together. We can't let the vampire cat get her!' Jamie had absolutely no clue what she was talking about. 'I can't be the only one holding us up!'

Tears brimmed in her eyes, and he felt his hands awkward at his side, no idea what to do.

'You're our Partizan,' she said, finally gaining control. 'We need you.'

Her tears spilled over, and Jamie felt the breath build up in his chest.

Our Partizan, us, we.

The breath within him came out in one great sigh, dizzyingly relieved.

'Fine.'

'Really?' Lottie's whole face lit up, an expression so shining and full of hope that it was like staring at the sun. He had to look away.

'Yes, but I can't promise I'll be of any help.' He wasn't entirely sure why he agreed to it, maybe because it meant being useful, or because it made him feel responsible. Or maybe, possibly, it was because he knew Lottie was right.

It wasn't hard to find Ellie.

The only problem was that Jamie had no idea what he was supposed to do when he caught up with her. Lingering on the edge of the treeline, where the morning light couldn't penetrate, his mind conjured up images of when he'd followed Lottie into the Rose Wood. It had been the middle of winter and freezing, and he'd found her curled up under a giant oak tree. It had been so easy then, scarily so. He knew exactly what she required, and she'd understood so completely that he hadn't needed to say anything at all.

The idea of him ever doing that now seemed unfathomable, so distant from where they were today, and yet hadn't Lottie come to him? Out in the storm?

It's just you. You're the one causing all the problems. You and your princess are going to suck all the good out of the little pumpkin.

Pushing the voice away, Jamie stepped through the shadows of the forest.

The moment his feet touched the mossy ground a floating silence like a deep sleep surrounded him. All the sounds and smells of the school beyond filtered away, leaving him alone in the earthy grove of moss and bamboo. Strange foreign birds whistled in the trees, accompanied by a constant buzz of insects.

A sharp howl broke him from his thoughts. Ellie!

Every Partizan instinct overtook him, and he took off at lightning speed further into the woods. Feet floating above the roots and moss, he effortlessly avoided every obstacle, darting through the trees. 'Ellie! Hold on!'

He could see movement in the dappled light of a clearing. And in the midst of it was Ellie, barefoot and dirty and . . . laughing.

Had his fever returned?

In front of him was a giant bamboo tree, so thick it seemed like the arm of a god reaching up out of the ground. But that was not the strangest thing. Propped up against the trunk was his princess . . . and she was surrounded by . . . cats.

'Jamie!' She looked up, and all the cats turned to him, shocked to see him there. They were all different shapes and sizes: a huge fat ginger cat with a grumpy face, a tiny pure white kitten, a set of mottled grey skinny things and a mishmash of tabbies. All of them were rubbing their heads against Ellie, pawing and scratching at her playfully. Off to the side, away from the others and licking its paw, was the biggest black cat Jamie had ever seen, fur so dark it looked like it was made of the night sky, with eyes the piercing yellow of stars.

'Silver vine,' Jamie said, unable to stop a surprised laugh as he gazed around. 'This whole area is covered in silver vine. Cats love it.'

The huge black cat sauntered over to him, winding between his legs and pushing him towards Ellie and the tree, which he reluctantly allowed. His princess continued to stare up at him, anger and regret burning on her face.

'What are you doing here?' Her voice was so full of rage that one of the tabby cats hissed. 'Shouldn't you be celebrating your perfect performance?'

'I'm your Partizan, Ellie.' He began walking round to the other side of the bamboo tree, the cat trailing his heels. They both slid down to the flower-covered grass. 'It's never going to be a fair fight.'

'Saskia let Ani get some hits in,' Ellie retorted. With the bamboo tree between them, their backs were mirrored but not touching, both of them looking out into opposite sides of the forest.

It had been so long since they'd really spoken to each other.

'Would you have wanted me to do that?'

She didn't reply, but they both knew the answer was no. They sat with only the noise of the leaves and the cats around them, the eerie and evocative calm taking over. The cats settled comfortably into happy purring marshmallows, wriggling for attention.

'You don't even like me, Jamie,' Ellie muttered, the words so quiet they almost got lost in the woods. 'Why do you even want to protect me? I'm not worth it.'

Halfway through stroking the black cat, Jamie froze. He was ashamed. Lottie was right; in his obsession with not becoming obsolete, he'd hurt her in another way.

'Ellie, I do like you. The way I act, it's all –'

'You hate me, Jamie. You hate me so much you barely even speak to me, and yet you're always putting yourself in danger for me. I can't take that responsibility – I hate it!' Her words echoed around them, causing a flock of birds to take flight. 'I'm the stupid spoiled princess who's reckless and good for nothing and bad at everything. It's all my fault, always.'

Jamie couldn't believe what she was saying. How could she not realize that the whole reason he'd become distant was because of how much she was growing – how clear it was that she would eventually not need him or Lottie any more?

'How can you say that? You've come so far since starting at Rosewood.'

'No, you don't understand, I . . . I'm scared *all* the time. I can't get anything right, and just –' she went quiet again, a tired acceptance – 'no matter what I do, Jamie, you're always going to be better than me, and I'm always going to be the problem.' He could hear her take in a long breath before she let out the next words. 'I'm holding you all back.'

Jamie couldn't respond, the shame in his chest blooming through his body. For so long he'd prided himself on putting Ellie first, on not getting distracted by Lottie or anyone else, but when Ellie had actually started to flourish he had made her feel like a failure.

You're the worst Partizan ever. He couldn't silence the angry voice in his head, too overcome with his own inadequate self.

'It's stupid,' Ellie continued, before he had a chance to speak. 'You should be king. You and Lottie should get married and the two of you should rule Maradova together. That would be better for everyone.'

It was an attempt at a joke, he knew that, but her words shocked him. All his training, all his hard work, was to make sure that one day Ellie would take her rightful place on the throne. Not once in his whole life had he ever considered himself worthy to take on that role, and yet imagining it now made his mouth water, halfway between hunger and a convulsing need to be sick. It was nauseating, not because he hated it but because part of him – an awful, disgusting part of him – realized he liked the image.

King of Maradova, with Lottie as the real queen.

Thinking of her brought up her image, not the fake queen image, but the real Lottie who had carried him when he was sick, who had helped Ellie be a better person, who had stared at him with furious resolve, demanding that he and Ellie must reconcile. How could he have gone all this time without realizing Ellie felt the same way he did?

'It's true – you are very annoying.' He leaned back against the tree, and he felt Ellie tense behind him. 'You're brash and outspoken, not to mention constantly getting yourself into trouble.'

Ellie stayed silent, the cats looking up at her curiously.

'And I wish I was as brave as you.' Jamie sagged, and he could feel the earth shift as he said it, softening. 'But I can never let you know that or it'll go straight to your head.'

'Jamie, I'm not –'

Cutting her off with a long groan, he stroked under the big cat's chin, letting it rub its face against his arm.

'Lottie was right,' he said. 'You need to stop blaming yourself. You need to try, for her sake, even if you don't believe it yet.'

223

'And what about you?'

'I'm not sure yet,' he admitted.

He reached out for her hands, so small compared to his. He knew she was crying. 'I have to confess something.' He squeezed the hot flesh of her hand, the sensation transporting him back to when they were children.

'I saw you, Lottie and you, in the factory.' Ellie tensed, and even though she didn't speak a word he knew they were both there, back in that sugar-dusted world, so sweet that it hurt his teeth. They were both thinking of the kiss.

'I think we all need to start being more honest with each other.' As soon as he said this, the cats stood up, possibly hearing a distant call. They vanished into the forest, leaving the princess and her Partizan alone.

He didn't need to say any more. He knew Ellie understood what he was still unable to say, what he'd had to admit to himself after Lottie found him in the storm. Lottie was important to him, and not just because she was Ellie's Portman, not because he was her Partizan. Like the sun itself, she was an unstoppable force casting light on everything she touched. He wanted to be in that light, to feel her warmth and protect it. He just wasn't sure if anyone was worthy of it.

'Lottie's waiting for you,' he whispered.

'No,' Ellie replied. 'She's waiting for us.'

29

Peeping through the heavy velvet curtains, Lottie was filled with a giddy, nervous energy. It felt like she was back at Maradova during the summer ball, ready to be presented as the fake princess. The crowd sent out a deep hum of chatter, the lights low. But it wasn't just the play that had Lottie feeling so excited, through her peephole she could see Ellie and Jamie, and they were sitting *together*.

She'd done it; she'd got them to be a team again, and that meant it was time to turn her attention to more important things. Lottie should have been focusing on the play, making sure it went well so she could get enough marks to get back into Rosewood, only there was something much bigger at stake. She still hadn't even begun to solve the mystery of Takeshin's secret treasure.

She was running out of time.

She had to find something – a clue, anything – that could help her find this hidden treasure. It was the only way to get Sayuri on their side, and get the information Banshee had. She was still convinced there was a clue somewhere in the diary, that Rosewood and Takeshin were connected, that *they* were connected.

'*Kabocha-chan . . .*'

Lottie turned to see a beautiful and terrifying black cat on its hind legs. This was the feline Rio, a performance so perfect it still made Lottie catch her breath. She looked over her and Miko's work, the black silky fur that gave way to a spectacular secret. No detail had been overlooked in the costume and the result was a stunning beast that would make anyone's blood run cold.

'Are you nervous?' Rio asked with a cocky grin.

'I'm not nervous,' she whispered, shaking her head. 'I'm concentrating.'

The lights in the auditorium dimmed, a spotlight spreading over the stage from where Sayuri stepped out from between the curtains. Her porcelain skin glimmered even brighter, and she looked to Lottie now like an unbending spirit.

She introduced the plays in Japanese – lines Lottie had heard over and over during rehearsals so she understood what was being said.

'Welcome, Takeshin Gakuin summer students. Tonight we will be showcasing the best of the theatre courses. From acting, costumes and make-up to lighting, music and set design, we hope to immerse you into some wondrous and terrifying tales. The three short plays tonight are all inspired by Kou Fujiwara's three favourite folk stories: *Tanabata*, *Kaguya-hime* and, last but not least, Fujiwara Sensei's most beloved story, *Nabeshima Bakeneko*. We hope you will think fondly of our school's founder while you enjoy the fantastical display.'

Then the darkness behind the curtains enveloped Sayuri, and with one collective intake of breath the audience was ready.

226

At the back of the theatre Sayuri reappeared beside her Partizan. Haru leaned over and whispered something to her that made Sayuri turn rigid.

Before Lottie could dwell on it, the music started and the audience vanished into darkness.

The first play was *Tanabata*, and told of two star-crossed lovers brought together by the girl's father, a god, but forced to separate by him too. Tears made of dancing ribbon bled from her eyes, a fabric river of woe growing on the stage that moved her father enough to let them meet on the seventh day of the seventh month every year. But it was not enough; she could only meet her lover with the help of a flock of magpies, who would make a bridge for her over the river that separated the two. If the magpies failed, they could not meet and would have to wait another year.

Magpies, made of black and white tissue paper illuminated in rainbow lights, fluttered above the audience in dazzling flocks, moved by hidden fans on the stage.

Lottie's mind's eye burned with the image of the magpies in Liliana's diary, flocks of them covering the pages. It was uncanny that something so similar to the pages of Lili's diary would also appear in one of Kou's favourite plays.

Moments later, the second play began, the velvet curtains revealing papier-mâché bamboo forest behind, shrouded with dry ice, a single sparkling trunk, thick and glittering, in the centre of the stage.

About to look for Sayuri in the audience, Lottie froze, pulled back to the scene in front of her. A scene she knew so well she could practically feel the mossy earth beneath her toes. The stage had become Takeshin's own woods, the Kiri

Shinrin, with its endless fog and the single impossibly large bamboo hidden within it. And it was there again, the pictures in the diary of the sparkling tree. Even though they weren't bamboo trees in the diary, she couldn't help feeling they were connected, that it was a sign.

There was so little time until they left for England, so little time to piece this together, and in the back of her head, frayed like the edge of the torn paper in the diary, were those strange words, and the unlikely possibility that they were important.

> A *cat*
> A *hiding place*
> A *sword*

'Kabocha-chan?'

A voice dragged her from her thoughts. Miko, blue as ever, but more of a navy in the shadows backstage.

'We are next.'

Lottie nodded, but her mind was still half stuck in the mystery of Liliana's diary. It was as if she were split in two; her body was here in the theatre, nervous and excited, but her soul had been spirited away by the performances and stories, floating across the school in a cloud of curiosity.

'Where is your head?' Miko asked, her eyes narrowing suspiciously. 'You are somewhere else.'

Locking eyes with Miko, Lottie let everything sink in, the diary, the trees, the fairy tales, the page with the mysterious list, Sayuri and herself.

'I think there is a secret hidden in these plays,' she whispered in the dark, clutching Miko's arm, just as the curtain came down and thundering applause filled the room.

Miko slowly plucked Lottie's hand off her. 'Then you'd better set up our one quickly so you can figure it out.'

Still in a daze, Lottie tiptoed out with Miko and the other stagehands, propping up the wooden bed that would be Aoi Tōyō's doom. They draped a ghostly sheet of gauze over the left side of the stage, where shadows of the monster cat would grow and reveal their creation, and in front of both they spread hanging vines to create a garden that would melt away when the prince left.

Lottie was so focused on finding some hidden detail in the play that the last thing she expected was for something to go wrong.

A terrible retching sound echoed where there should have been flutes, but the sound was not the worst part. Rushing past, her hand covering her mouth, was their Aoi Tōyō, the fair maiden, the prince's favourite, and she was being sick.

'*Sumimasen!*' the poor girl mumbled in apology, hurrying out of the theatre.

They formed a line in her wake, Rio, Miko, Lottie and the others in the vampire cat production, staring in bewilderment at the now-empty space where their Aoi Tōyō had been.

'Did we just lose our maiden?' Rio asked, the dumbfounded look on his face completely at odds with his elegant make-up.

All Lottie knew was that she'd been looking for a sign, anything to get through to the impenetrable queen of Takeshin, and if she was going to understand what these plays were trying to tell her, she needed to get as close as possible. What she needed wasn't to watch passively from the sidelines, she had to be a part of it completely. She knew it as a fact. She needed to be in the play.

'I'll do it,' she said. 'I'll play Aoi Tōyō.'

Miko and Rio stared at her, mouths wide open in a way she relished, and they gaped even more when she added, 'But I'm wearing my tiara.'

The spotlight slowly came up on Aoi Tōyō, peaceful among the low-hanging paper vines that made up the garden. Fog surrounded Lottie's feet, where her white robe brushed the stage. They had tried their best to comb her hair smooth.

Of all the terrifying, life-threatening things she'd been a part of, this was somehow the scariest thing she'd ever done.

Her head felt tingly where the tiara lay on it, and she was glad to have it as a reminder to be brave, but that was not why she'd demanded it be a part of the show.

She was looking for a sign, proof of Rosewood's connection to Takeshin, a clue to solving this mystery for Sayuri, and if this was one of Kou's favourite plays, she wanted to bring a bit of Liliana into it too.

You're telling a story, she reminded herself. *Just this time you're telling it with your body, not your words.*

All appearance is performance . . .

She let those words Rio had told her sink right down into her core, allowing the make-up and the costume to spark something inside her. It made her feel powerful. She felt the change within her just as the audience did, her body transforming in front of their eyes to that of the beautiful,

230

serene maiden. It was magic, and it had the scent of roses and moss, two worlds combining inside her. Lottie Pumpkin didn't exist any more; it was only Aoi Tōyō.

The dance began. It felt like she'd been through the choreography with their maiden thousands of times, she and Miko determined to get the movements just right. But now, here on stage in front of the whole school, it was more fun than she could possibly have imagined. Twirling and skipping, she felt both graceful and free, the robes fluttering around her like wings.

It felt incredible to be Aoi Tōyō, to be young and full of life and splendour. Forgetting the audience entirely, she wanted to dance forever, but as quickly as it had begun the prince appeared, and it came to an end.

Aoi Tōyō stared at the prince, their movement blending together into a rigid march of a dance, mirroring one another. She was his favourite and marrying him was her duty. It made her stomach sink.

All the freedom of her previous display was gone, replaced by something unyielding. The prince and his favourite maiden stepped in time together; she had no choice but to follow the patterns of his body.

In every reading of the vampire cat Lottie had always felt sad for Aoi Tōyō, that the happy ending didn't include her, but now she felt sad in a different way. Aoi Tōyō was stuck, chained down by the burdens of expectation and responsibility.

The lights went down, but the ache in Lottie's chest remained, Aoi Tōyō's heart sore with despair. She climbed into the bed, the vines and flowers of the garden disappearing above her to give way to the eerie calm of the bedroom set.

Aoi Tōyō lay in the soft flowing silk, the blue spotlight growing around her, unsuspecting of the terrible creature approaching.

It flashed behind her eyelids like a tattoo in her mind: the cats in Liliana's diary, the stone cats at the shrine, and the cats everywhere in the school, all merging together.

A fan wafted the calming scent of pine and lavender through the dark room, lulling the audience into a sleepy sense of security.

Darkness moved over her, the illusion of night-time morphing into a solid shape behind the gauze. Rio convulsed and writhed in a twisted dance until the sheet dropped, revealing the monstrous vampire cat. He pounced on the sleeping maiden, metres of red yarn spilling from Aoi Tōyō's neck and rolling down as the beast feasted on her blood.

This is for the best, whispered a voice deep in her mind.

A hatch in the bed swallowed her up and a collective gasp from the audience let Lottie know that the trick had worked; her body had seemingly been devoured into nothing.

She was under the stage, chinks in the floorboards letting her see everyone watching, the show still unfolding above. Violins screeched and Rio turned to the audience, shedding his silken black cloak, which melted away, folding and unravelling with an intricate ribbon system Miko and Lottie had devised, to reveal a pool of glossy fabric and hair, with a great white and red robe that flowed over the ground, rippling with simmering power. Under his monstrous body stood the deceptively beautiful fake, the vampire cat in the skin of Aoi Tōyō, an angelic demon. Curving his limbs and spinning, Rio

232

performed a mesmerizing dance in the single red spotlight, deceiving and deadly.

Lottie watched, amused by the shocked faces of her Rosewood friends who'd never seen this talent of Rio's. The twins' mouths hung open, eyes sparkling. Even Saskia and Anastacia couldn't hide their fascination; every person in the audience was enraptured by the lethal display of feminine beauty.

And in the centre of her vision were Jamie and Ellie. They were sitting together comfortably, the awkwardness that had curled round them starting to rot away like a dying weed. But there was something more, something between them, a shared emotion while they stared up at the space on the stage where Lottie had once been.

This was a feeling that Lottie had never known before, their own invisible rope that she was not connected to. But now, for the first time, she understood it. That Lottie could never have seen it before felt unreal. The weight of obligations, fears and pressures had made Aoi Tōyō so vulnerable to the vampire cat. How easy it was to give in to it, to let it take you over. Kou and Liliana must have felt it too, and that is why the tale was so important to them.

Black as tar, oozing and thick, it spread like oil, creeping towards its victims. *The creature in the story isn't just a monster; it is what consumes you. The dark dread that blooms in your chest, heavy and sinking, until it eats you up.* Everyone reacts to it in a different way: anger, seclusion, distrust.

Lottie had seen it in Ellie; she'd seen it in Jamie. The creature was obligations, fears and pressures, the loneliest combination, and it wasn't only her princess and her Partizan that had been bitten by it.

30

Applause like a thunderstorm roared through the audience as the curtains came down, snapping Lottie out of the Aoi Tōyō spell.

In the story the vampire cat had been killed and the villagers had won, but the real one was still lurking and she finally knew how to defeat it. Still hidden under the stage, Lottie watched the audience; right at the back of the theatre one person stood as still as a statue, not clapping at all. Sayuri Chiba.

Sayuri's ink-black eyes locked directly on hers through the little crack, her gaze so sharp it made Lottie take a step back, tripping over a box of masks, her tiara slipping sideways.

Lottie tried to right herself. They needed to act now. The only way to solve this mystery was to work together, but to get Sayuri on her side there was one very big thing she needed to do.

It was the first rule of her mantra, the simplest of all. *Be kind.*

It wasn't Sayuri whose mind needed changing. She wasn't some game that Lottie needed to beat. Sayuri was just a girl, as scared and isolated by her responsibilities and worries as

234

any of them were, and the only thing Lottie needed to do was apologize, and she knew exactly how to do it.

Wrapping her robe tight round her, Lottie ran up the steps to backstage to find her bag. Rummaging quickly, she found Lili's diary and tucked it carefully into the fabric of her Aoi Tōyō robe.

Smiling politely, she made her way to the backstage door. Lottie was so determined, so engrossed in her mission, that she almost went right into Sayuri.

She managed to step neatly out of the way as Lottie came crashing out of the back of the theatre into the balmy night to where she was waiting on the dirt steps.

'Sayuri! I'm sorry.' Lottie bowed so low her hair lapped at the ground, the billowing Aoi Tōyō costume draping round her. It was loud outside, a symphony of singing insects and rustling bamboo swaying overhead. 'I'm sorry that Ellie and I took our Partizan for granted,' she began steadily. 'I'm sorry that we may have brought Leviathan to you, and I'm sorry for all the pressure this has put on you. You have a million things to worry about and I don't want to be one of them. So, if you'd like it, I have this for you. It's Liliana's diary.' She paused to grab the diary from her robe, holding out the pages, but feeling more like she was holding out her own beating heart. 'I think it has the clues to solving Takeshin's mystery. If you don't want to team up, I respect that, but I want you to have this.'

She kept her head down, watching the dirt creep up the ends of her tangled curls, tinting the moon-stained gold with a muddy brown. Slowly, like letting a feather float from your palm on the wind, she felt Sayuri remove the diary from her hand.

'Stand up.' Her voice was low, at odds with her dry expression. Lottie did as she was told, acutely aware of the sweat building over her theatre make-up. 'It was quite a rude awakening to discover you were a Portman. It is never fun to be confronted with the fact you might not know as much as you think.'

Lottie swallowed hard. 'I can't apologize for not revealing my role as Portman,' she said firmly. 'But I hope that this diary can make up for any trouble Leviathan have caused you. It was my ancestor's, and I think, maybe with your knowledge, it's the key to solving it.'

It hurt, more than she could believe, to give away the diary – but they had to stop Leviathan, and if this is what it took, if this was the way to get Sayuri to share whatever info Banshee had, she'd do it.

'You'd really give me something so important to you?' Sayuri eyed her suspiciously.

'I would.'

Something passed over Sayuri in that moment, a ghost of a thought. 'I won't take it.' Lottie felt her whole body collapse. 'But if you so insist on there being a clue in here, I'll allow you to show it to me.' Sayuri placed the diary back in Lottie's palms, curling her hands round Lottie's own to hold it snug between her fingers again. 'Only I cannot be blamed if there is no link at all and you humiliate yourself.'

Her skin was warm and smooth like summer flowers, sending a feeling of calm through Lottie, and she realized quite suddenly that this was the first time they'd ever touched. Tears pricked her eyes, only now realizing how much it had hurt her to give the diary up, and how kind of Sayuri it was not to take it.

Biting her tongue, Lottie could tell by the way Sayuri looked away again that they both felt it. That when it came to their schools, there was no such thing as coincidence.

Moving further into the shadows of the building, further away from the laughter and chatter of backstage, Lottie opened the diary, effortlessly locating the passage about Kou.

'There's no proof that that is my Kou,' Sayuri said bluntly.

'I know,' Lottie agreed, 'but look.' She turned the pages to the sketches: the glowing tree, the horned cats, the flocks of magpies, suns and moons.

Sayuri's eyes grew wide. 'Those drawings . . .'

'I didn't notice until I was watching the plays tonight, but they're all references to Kou's favourite stories.'

Fingers trembling, Sayuri grabbed the diary, pulling it towards her. Eyes ablaze, she looked at the images intensely.

'Turn the page,' Lottie prompted, and slowly, with great care, Sayuri turned to the enigmatic list on the single page.

A cat
A hiding place
A sword

'What is this?'

'I'm not sure, but look –'

Before Lottie could finish, Sayuri spotted the ripped-out page and she jumped up, her robe flying around her like a petal storm.

'Come with me,' she whispered, ducking low to check quickly around as if she expected someone to be following them.

Without a word of explanation, she flicked the diary shut and grabbed Lottie's wrist, the two of them gliding through the school like ghosts, white-robed and feet barely touching the ground. Lottie followed without question, letting Sayuri lead her with such speed that she felt that they were flying.

They arrived at the big glass door that led to Kou Fujiwara's museum, their reflections staring back at them from the darkened interior. Without the context of the play, Lottie looked scary in her Aoi Tōyō costume, a spirit in the glass with a jungle of bamboo spewing like a spider's legs behind her. Only Liliana's tiara resting on her head gave any indication of her true self beneath the make-up.

Sayuri looked around, opening the door behind her back and ushering Lottie in quickly.

'If this is the key . . .' she began, gesturing for Lottie to take a seat on the floor and keep low, 'we need to know we are not being watched.'

Lottie nodded, heart thundering away. Sayuri opened one of the cat-decorated chests, carefully pulling out the small one Lottie had seen her searching through the night she'd followed her.

'This is full of Kou's unfinished work.' She sat beside Lottie and set the box down in front of them.

The distinctive scent of the museum began to curl round Lottie, spilling over her, the two of them wrapped up in Kou's world. It was deathly quiet, all the sounds of the school beyond safely locked out, its insect sounds and hot oily air giving way to silence and peace.

Last time, Lottie had felt like an intruder in this space, a ghost drifting through a secret world locked away in time. Now she was at one with the scene, a time traveller. Even her Aoi Tōyō robes felt right.

'This makes little sense to me,' Sayuri confessed, staring at the diary where she'd placed it beside the chest. 'That your ancestor should know mine in a time so unspeakably unlikely. But if my theory is correct, and you are correct, then I've found the key.'

'It's like magic,' Lottie offered, not caring if she sounded childish.

A smile spread over Sayuri's face as she reluctantly allowed herself to get caught up in the story. 'Yes, like magic, I suppose.'

Pop! The chest sprang open, pressure releasing. Sitting still and silent like a good child at school, Lottie watched Sayuri methodically lay out each worn paper and scroll until at last she held up a single piece of parchment. It shone silver, enchanted, and Lottie could see only three horizontal lines of Japanese text spread over the whole page.

'Open the diary to that list.'

Lottie turned back to the page with the frayed edge.

The paper fluttered, resting between Sayuri's middle and index fingers as she held it up to the moonlight, and with all the careful energy of casting a spell she placed the paper in the heart of the diary.

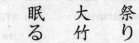

The characters meant nothing to Lottie, and yet when

united with the diary they felt like the most important words in the world.

She felt it just as Sayuri did, a reunion deep inside her, an invisible force slotting together that had always been misaligned. The paper fitted perfectly, its ragged edge an exact fit in the diary.

Tumbling waves of understanding washed over them while the pinewood scent of the museum fused with the dusty smell of the diary. It felt as though they were possessed, that Liliana and Kou were inside them and that they were smiling.

'What does it say?' Lottie asked, her voice barely even a whisper.

'*Matsuri* means "festival",' said Sayuri, pointing to the two characters on the right. Then her finger moved to the middle word, as she read the characters from top to bottom. 'The next word is *ōtake*, this means "the great bamboo". And finally *nemuru*, "sleep". It doesn't make any sense on its own, but if you put the words together –'

'It makes a haiku,' Lottie said, counting the syllables out on her fingers.

The pages aligned to reveal a poem in two languages, and they read it together, their voices becoming a chant that drifted into the air like a spell.

> 'A *cat – matsuri*
> A *hiding place – ōtake*
> A *sword – nemuru.*'

The words were like someone else's memories inside Lottie's head. The firefly glow of the bamboo tree, the cat

240

that led her to it, and Kou's sword, the blade that watched her enter the museum. That same bamboo tree that miraculously held the Mayfutt symbol in its stem.

'Sayuri,' she said, almost breathless, gazing up into the other girl's eyes. 'I know . . . I know where the treasure is . . .'

'LOTTIE!'

The two girls jumped.

'Lottie, we know you're in there. We can see you!'

It was Jamie and Ellie – and she'd completely forgotten about them.

31

'What's going on here?' Jamie asked, eyes blazing.

As her princess and Jamie opened the glass door, Lottie felt the spell snap. Sayuri's secret was the first thing in years she'd experienced that felt private; she wasn't sure she could or should share it with Ellie . . .

'You two.' Sayuri pointed at Ellie and Jamie. 'You're going to help us stop Leviathan.'

Even Lottie could hardly believe the words that came out of Sayuri's mouth. Jamie stared. Sayuri and Lottie stood before them silently . . . until the elegant queen of the school started to shoot out commands. 'You're going to escort us into the woods.' She turned and walked out, expecting them to follow. 'Now.'

It was odd to see her taking on the commanding role of the Pink Demon with Jamie and Ellie, but these demands meant she was treating them like part of her gang.

'Come on! We'll explain on the way!' Lottie called behind her.

It was time to find out what Leviathan had been looking for, and even though it thrilled her, Lottie knew this was only the beginning, a stepping stone towards her true mission. To discover the identity of the Master of Leviathan.

They paused outside the supply shed by the gym, Sayuri picking up torches and two spades and a trowel intended for the horticulture course, while Lottie explained how she'd asked Binah to retrieve and send Lili's diary.

'Your princess and I believe there is something hidden in this school that Leviathan want,' Sayuri said to Jamie and Ellie. 'We think they've been hoping I'll find it for them, like they hoped you would find the Hamelin Formula.' Lottie noticed how she had skirted round the problem that Haru was also searching for it. 'We've put all our knowledge together of our school founders,' Sayuri finished, gazing around her as they reached the Kiri Shinrin, 'and this is the most logical hiding place of the treasure.'

'Oh, really?' Jamie's gaze shifted to Lottie. 'What did Lottie tell you about Rosewood's founder?' The look of warning was so strong that Lottie almost spluttered.

Sayuri didn't miss a beat. 'That she was born a woman but pretended to be a man so she could start a school in a time when women were not often taken seriously. Very inspirational.'

'With this diary and the museum we managed to piece together the puzzle, to reveal a haiku. We think it's talking about the great bamboo tree in the Kiri Shinrin – the one the cats like,' Lottie added, beaming at Jamie innocently, hoping he wouldn't ask any more questions. Fog licked at them from the edge of the trees and Lottie knew they could all feel the haunting pull of the bamboo forest. Only this time there was something more. Instead of hearing only the rustling of leaves and creatures, she could sense a low hum of recognition, as if the forest were waiting for them.

It was a subtle movement, but Lottie noticed that Sayuri balled her hands into determined fists before taking a big step into the trees.

Ellie was next, followed close behind by Jamie. The two turned in unison, both holding their hands out to Lottie.

'Oh.' She wasn't sure what else to say or whose hand to take so instead she took both. 'Thank you,' she replied quickly, deciding to ignore their uncomfortable expressions, skipping onwards to catch up with Sayuri.

Weird, she thought, wondering if Jamie was being nicer for Ellie's sake. She couldn't think of another explanation.

Soft moss cushioned her footsteps, the night-time buzzing with creatures fluttering about. It had been weeks since she'd followed the big black cat into this forest, and she still had faded marks from the worst of her insect bites. This time nothing bit her, nor Sayuri, though it looked as if Ellie and Jamie were not being offered the same courtesy.

'It's your royal blood,' Lottie whispered to Ellie with a giggle when she tried to bat away a mosquito.

'Then what's Jamie's problem?'

With a grunt, Jamie marched forward to the front of their troop, swatting in front of his face irritably.

Lottie hung back for a second, watching them walk on into the bamboo, and for the first time she really let it sink in – that they were doing something together, that they were a pack again.

The deeper they ventured into the woods, the more the calm crept over them. They were very quiet, all the giddiness and prickliness melting off them until it was just the sounds of the Kiri Shinrin and their steady breath floating together.

There was something waiting for them in these woods; Lottie could feel it like a heartbeat below the ground, and it wasn't just the hidden treasure – it was truth. And she knew whatever they found here was going to change things.

'Here.' Jamie's voice was low, barely audible above the forest sounds.

They entered the clearing, one after another, blue light from the moon shining through the trees where the bamboo sparkled in a wash of fireflies.

'This tree.' Sayuri's voice was filled with wonder, her hands stroking the great bamboo.

A glance of acknowledgement passed between Ellie and Jamie.

Lottie guessed this was where they'd found themselves after the kendo demonstration, but she'd never pressed them about it.

'It has to be beneath this tree. Under the Mayfutt mark.' Lottie walked ahead to join Sayuri, the beat of the forest pumping harder with every step closer to its heart. She turned to Ellie and Jamie, both standing at the edge of the clearing, the looks on their faces a mix of shock and awe at seeing a symbol from home blossoming all the way on the other side of the world.

'How did I miss this?' Jamie asked, running his fingers curiously along the indented bark.

'I think we were a little preoccupied,' Ellie replied, and the two of them shared another look, making Lottie wonder once again what exactly they'd discussed.

'Well?' Sayuri said, cutting their moment short. 'Aren't you going to help dig?'

A smirk crept over Ellie's mouth as she rolled up the sleeves of her uniform, while Jamie nodded, stepping forward to strike the ground with his spade.

A soft hand reached out for Lottie's as they started to dig, a warm pulse against her skin. It was Sayuri's, but she wasn't nervous or scared of what they'd find. Her hand wasn't shaking – this was solidarity. The mingling heartbeats fell in time with the beat of the Kiri Shinrin.

Kou and Liliana had hidden something here, something for their ancestors to find, and after hundreds of years today it would be revealed.

A hard thud sang from the end of the spade, sending a thrill through Lottie. They'd found it. It was real.

What emerged was a dirt-covered chest, though it was much larger than Lottie had imagined. The skin of the wood was etched with circles and crescents in varying sizes, like the cycle of the moon.

Torchlight shone over the mystery box, a click sounded out and it was open. They eased back the lid, revealing the centuries-old secret. The object shone so bright it nearly blinded them.

'Oh my.' Even Ellie was frozen with shock.

In all Lottie's imaginings she'd never in a million years thought they'd find something so . . . lethal.

Sayuri delicately lifted their sacred gift from its hiding place where it glowed blue in the starlight. It was no longer lost to history, but real and alive.

It was Kou's sword, just as the myth had said. The blade was so sharp it sang, the air quivering around it. It was dangerous and deadly, with a handle of heroic detail, suns and moons engraved in dramatic lines on either side. Instinctively Lottie reached for her tiara.

Perfect, strong, unstoppable and glowing from within with that same strange magic as her tiara. This was the sword from the statue of Kou, the sword from all the drawings, alive once again.

But why would Leviathan be looking for it? It didn't feel right. It didn't feel like the truth she'd been looking for.

'Careful,' Jamie warned. 'Even a small amount of pressure could cut you.'

Instead of heeding his words, Ellie reached over and gently stroked the edge. 'Ow!'

'Ellie,' Lottie chided, grabbing her hand to see the damage.

A thin red line grew on Ellie's pale skin, not too deep, and yet the blood spilled in an elegant trickle. There was something strangely pretty about it, a lethal beauty.

They were enraptured by it, none of them moving, until suddenly Jamie started to take his shirt off.

'Jamie!' Lottie spluttered. 'What are you doing?'

Ignoring their confused expressions, he carefully took the blade from Sayuri's hands and bundled it up in the shirt. 'That thing is incredibly sharp. I'm wrapping it so it's safe to carry back,' he replied, ever practical.

Ellie rolled her eyes, the magic of the blade vanishing into Jamie's shirt, yet Lottie and Sayuri couldn't drag their gaze away.

It was such an odd sight. Jamie, towering and bare-skinned with glowing golden eyes in the moonlit forest. There was something fairy-tale about it, like he might be a great muscular centaur. Or possibly a demon.

'There's something else in here,' Ellie called, snapping both girls out of their hypnosis. 'Actually, there's a bunch of stuff.'

Lottie and Sayuri leaned in, the beams from their torches dancing over the carefully placed piles of history.

'What's this?' Lottie asked, reaching to pull a coiled snake of matt gold out of its resting place, while Sayuri grabbed a bunch of papers and a book, scrutinizing them in the milky light.

Lottie stared down at the coil in her hand, before carefully holding it up to her own matted curls, realization dawning.

This was Liliana's hair. It hung like a long pendulum, drifting back and forth in the misty air, planting a story in her mind. She saw, as clear and warm as the lock of hair in her hand, how important Kou and Liliana's friendship had been, that it had allowed them to shed their skin and be true to themselves. While it swung in front of her, she could see Ellie and Sayuri behind the golden curl, and felt in that moment, that for the very first time, she understood her ancestor completely. She quickly placed the lock back in the chest, catching Jamie's eye just in time to see that he'd noticed. That he also knew what it was.

'It's a time capsule . . .' Sayuri trailed off, looking at the paper. 'It's centuries' worth of my family's history and secrets. Everyone in my family who's ever found it has left something behind.'

Even in the dark Lottie could see the ice melting from Sayuri's eyes. It was a feeling Lottie knew well, to feel so disconnected from your family – and then to have it all open up in front of you like a book.

Lottie went to look at the letters, placing a comforting hand over her shoulder. 'What's this?' she asked, pointing at the cursive script.

'I'm not sure.' Sayuri peered at the papers. 'It looks like letters to my auntie. Love letters from before she passed away.'

Ellie rushed over to take a look. 'Who's it from?'

'It doesn't say, but this letter . . . it's awful.' Sayuri's voice was shaky in a way Lottie had never heard before, and Lottie couldn't help leaning over to read.

To my beloved Kana,
It pains me to send you this news in a letter, although I fear it would be dangerous for both of us if I did so in person.

Whatever you decide to do with the child after what I am about to tell you, please refrain from contacting me. There is nothing either of us can do to change this.

You know better than anyone how important my family is to me and all that I must do for them, and I beg you to remember this when I tell you my solemn news.

My mother has arranged a bride for me from another royal family and I am to be wed in five years' time. I must vow myself solely to her and to use this time to establish a strong and beneficial relationship.

This will not be easy for me, and I will think of you – and the life we made – often, but I have a duty to my country that I cannot turn my back on.

I do not expect forgiveness, and I will carry this with me until I die.

I am sorry, and I love you.

Lottie felt tears stinging in her eyes, her heart aching for this woman she'd never met and her terrible lover, remembering what Miko had told her about how Sayuri's mother's sister had passed away, that sadness had consumed her.

'I don't understand,' Jamie grunted. 'Why would Leviathan want any of this?'

Then Lottie saw it. The mark at the bottom of the letter where there should have been a signature – a mark she was sure she'd seen before.

It made her feel sick, the very idea that what she was seeing could be true, that what she was thinking might become real.

'We need to go back to Rosewood,' she said faintly, taking the letter from Sayuri. 'I think I've seen that symbol before, and there's something in the school that could prove it.' She felt her fingers shaking, but she continued, knowing she had to face this head-on. 'I'm probably wrong, but I want to make sure.'

'What is it?' Ellie asked, eyebrows furrowed with worry.

'Can we just . . . ?' Lottie looked at Ellie, her heart hurting. 'Let's not talk about it until I'm sure, please.'

They all stared at her, none of them sure what to say; she hardly even knew what to say herself, dreading what this discovery could mean for all of them.

A question played over and over in her head. Why would Leviathan want this?

'If it's OK, Sayuri, may I borrow this?'

Sayuri slowly nodded. 'Take care of it.'

'We need to head back.' Jamie kept his face neutral, but Lottie could see the concern creeping in, absorbing Lottie's unease like it was his own. 'We don't want anyone finding this place, and it looks like whatever Leviathan might have thought was hidden here is gone.'

They silently began burying the chest again, putting all the pieces of history back in the ground – everything except the sword and the letter. Lottie allowed herself one more glance at the coil of hair, that glowing part of Liliana, the tendril of gold that she'd cut away and buried with her friend's secrets, and she wondered how much more to their story was there.

Dirt covered the history once more, and yet that same pounding wouldn't leave Lottie's head. It weaved and spluttered inside her, snaking into her consciousness with a terrible burden. It was time to go back to Rosewood and figure out who the Master of Leviathan was. She felt it deep inside her that the truth was just over the horizon. So why was she suddenly so scared to find out?

PART THREE
しょうがない
Shōganai

Japanese phrase:
'It can't be helped'

32

The cars were waiting in a formal line along the driveway of Takeshin, a colourful brigade ready to take the international summer-school students to the airport.

It should have been a moment of relief. Lottie knew she'd got enough marks to make up her grade – Sayuri had confirmed it for her – but she couldn't relax, knowing the truth was waiting for her at Rosewood, whether they wanted it or not.

'I'm actually gonna miss this place,' Ellie said with a laugh, wrapping an arm round Lottie's shoulder to take in the school one last time, completely oblivious to the fear growing inside her friend.

Down at the end of the driveway, Takeshin Gakuin looked almost like a castle, an ancient fortress of secrets. The Kiri Shinrin lived in the same space as the Rose Wood, and as much as Lottie had grown to love Takeshin it was time to go back. And to face the final secret.

Watching her fellow Rosewood students bask in their last moments in Takeshin's grounds, Lottie couldn't help envying them. Things were never going to be the same soon; a pounding drumbeat of truth had followed her out of the bamboo forest, and it promised to alter their lives forever.

'I'm going to miss it too.' Lola looked like she was about ready to burst into tears, clutching Micky's arm like he was a teddy bear. 'We should come here every year.'

It was obvious to everyone that Lola and Micky had thrived at Takeshin more than any of them, completely unaware of all the Leviathan trouble, basking in the sweets and the attention they got from all the students who found them so cute.

'Don't worry, guys.' Lottie patted Lola on the shoulder with a smile. 'We'll take a little bit of it with us, I'm sure.'

Like magic, Miko appeared in front of them, hands firmly on her hips, with Rio and Wei towering behind her. The little blue heart she'd drawn at the side of her eye winking at Lottie behind a loose strand of hair.

'*Kabocha-chan.*' Miko nodded at her.

Lottie returned the gesture, mirroring her stance.

'The boss wants to see you.' Rio couldn't resist ruffling Lottie's hair as they wandered past her to say goodbye to the twins and Ellie.

'Good luck,' Wei added, not even a twitch on his face.

Just before she continued on her way to the twins, Miko paused and grabbed the hem of Lottie's skirt, the action catching Lottie by surprise. 'Lottie-san, thank you.' Her voice was low, eyes glued to the ground, a furious blush spreading over her cheeks. 'Thank you for whatever you have done for Sayuri. She looks happy. Thank you, Lottie.'

'Oh. That's the first time you've called me Lottie.'

'Yes,' Miko replied bluntly, letting go of her skirt and marching off to join Rio.

Sayuri was waiting at the end of the cars, holding two small envelopes and dressed in a long white summer gown and cloak that floated around her like butterfly wings. She looked so delicate, so shimmering and ethereal, but Lottie could see the edge in her midnight-black eyes.

'Princess.' Her lips curved knowingly and Lottie couldn't help rolling her eyes as she smiled back at her.

'Pink Demon,' she said in return.

Sayuri handed an envelope to Lottie. 'Here, as promised.'

Excitement twitched through her, knowing what was in the package. It held the power to change everything, and with unexpected reluctance she peeped inside.

'I don't understand?' She stared at the contents of the envelope. She'd anticipated information on Leviathan, but all she could see was metallic fragments.

'I stole this from Haru's bin in his room. It was one of the first things he was asked to do when he joined Leviathan – to take this to the design centre and destroy it.'

'But what is it?'

'We don't know, and we've never figured it out, but we know it was important to their leader, and he wanted it gone.'

Evidence. Shaking the package, Lottie watched the little crumbs of metal swirl about, muted silver, something that might once have been pretty but was now dulled. A sudden light caught her eyes; a single shining rock among the fragments, possibly a gem of some kind, was glowing up at her. It was so unexpected that it made her quickly close the envelope, hiding away from the gemstone that felt like a watching eye.

'Do you have the letter?' Sayuri asked, her tone turning deathly serious.

Lottie nodded. 'Yes. You can count on me.'

'I know. That's why I'm also giving you this.' Before Lottie could react, Sayuri opened the other envelope, revealing a glossy black snake tied with red string. A perfect strand of her silky hair. 'I saw that strand of hair in the chest, and I want you to bury this in Rosewood.'

Lottie coughed. 'You cut your hair?'

'Only a little at the back. Look.' She pushed her head forward to reveal a blunt clump, just below her ear. 'I did it with the blade; it was like cutting butter.'

Lottie stared at her in disbelief and admiration, her hand clasping her own overgrown locks.

'I believe in this, Lottie.' A semblance of a smile crept over her face as she closed Lottie's fingers round it. 'I'm trusting what you think you've figured out. Once you confirm it, I want you to embrace whatever it is, no matter how hard that is to do.' She smiled at her, a genuine smile filled with trust and warmth. 'We're a team now, Lottie.'

With a deep breath, Lottie silently agreed, reaching out to wrap her arms round her new friend, unable to articulate the dread growing inside her, knowing that Sayuri understood.

You can do this, she told herself.

But the truth was, they both knew, she didn't even have a choice.

Ellie watched as Saskia, Jamie and Haru appeared at the same time, lugging everyone's suitcases to the cars. It still baffled her that Saskia was so effortlessly good at pretending to be fine with Haru.

That Partizan training, she admitted reluctantly.

She half-smiled at Jamie as he made his way to one of the vehicles and felt a wash of relief when he returned the gesture. It was so normal being around him again.

After he'd found her in the woods, they both knew things were going to be different. Somehow she'd always known that one day something would come between them – she'd just never expected it to be something they had in common.

'What are you looking at?' Anastacia asked, sliding over next to Ellie. Her hair was up, something she didn't usually do unless they were training, and it looked good, showing off how much stronger her delicate frame had become. They were all changing so much, constantly growing.

'I'm not sure,' Ellie replied uncertainly, her gaze falling on Lottie. She'd changed too; they were nearly the same height. Lottie's hair had grown loads since they'd met, a tangled weave of her old life – a Lottie that Ellie had never known. But the thing that struck her the most was how much she looked like Liliana. That unstoppable princess Ellie had admired as a child was right in front of her eyes.

Whatever Leviathan had been looking for in Takeshin, it wasn't there – or at least that's what they were telling themselves. Lottie had hardly been able to look at her since they'd left the Kiri Shinrin, and her smiles had turned pensive. The strangest thing was, Ellie was scared to ask. It was like she knew, they all knew, that something was waiting for them at Rosewood.

Her line of sight was abruptly cut off by Haru marching forward to assist Jamie, equipped with a happy little smile as usual. It was creepy. Over the last few weeks he'd been as quiet as a mouse, an invisible presence around them, sneaking along in the background like a menacing spirit. Supposedly he'd been looking for the hidden treasure, so why was there no urgency? Simply being in the same room as him put a bad taste in her mouth.

What are you planning? she thought. *What do you want with me and my Partizan?* She'd be glad to see the last of him.

Jamie knew Ellie was staring; she could not have been more obvious. But he decided to ignore it. Soon they would be back at Rosewood, and he could put all the madness of the summer behind him. At least he hoped so. The only problem was that he felt like something had followed them out of the woods, like the future was staring right at him. He could see it etched in the nervous way Lottie smiled at them.

'Let me help you with that.' Haru's calming voice floated over from where the Partizan leaned over to take one of Ellie's suitcases.

'No, I'm fine, I –'

But Haru paid no attention, taking the case effortlessly.

Curious: that was still the only word Jamie could truly come up with to explain Haru. No matter how much he pondered the strangely soft Partizan, he could never quite figure him out. Even after a whole summer together, he was an enigma, so warm, yet so distant, like sunshine.

Jamie reached down for Lottie's case, an oversized pink case that she'd bought with her Portman funds, in stark contrast to Ellie's battered sticker-covered black case.

His elbow nudged Haru's side. The other Partizan flinched, grabbing his stomach like he was in pain.

A hazy, rain-soaked memory flashed like lightning in Jamie's mind, the smell of a growing storm catching in his nostrils and a boy in a mask struck by one of Ingrid's blades that Jamie had thrown.

They stared at each other, the sun beating down over them.

Jamie felt his skin prickle, his instincts taking over, fearful and ferocious. But it was Haru. It made no sense. Haru couldn't be that masked bird boy on the roof; it was impossible, ridiculous. He quickly put the thought out of his head, not allowing it space to grow.

'Will you miss me?'

Jamie was caught off guard. 'I . . . What?' The alarm began to fade, the pounding in his head softening, replaced only by confusion and Haru's gentle smile. 'I don't know. I suppose I'll have to be away from you for a little while to find out,' he replied, barely concentrating on what he was saying.

Something glinted in Haru's brown eyes. 'Maybe we'll meet again? Maybe sooner than you think.'

Before Jamie had time to dwell on this, something bumped him in the knee, hard.

A cat. A big black cat with yellow eyes that he recognized instantly from the woods.

With a fierce resolve, the oversized creature continued to bump his legs, rubbing against him just as it had done by the great bamboo tree.

'Vampy!' Lottie's high-pitched squeal caught the large feline's attention. She rushed over, shoving a white box in Jamie's arms and leaning down to scoop up the big brute of a cat. It made a strange noise halfway between a purr and a grumble, its legs sticking out in begrudging acceptance of its cuddly fate.

Oh God, he thought, suddenly realizing why he felt an affinity for this creature. *He's like me.* 'You know this cat?' he asked.

'Know him? Vampy saved your life!' Lottie nuzzled a cheek against the creature. 'He came to find me in the storm and showed me where you were.'

The cat's glowing yellow eyes locked on Jamie and he could practically hear its sarcastic drone telling him, 'You're welcome.'

As she placed the cat back on the ground, it began to mewl, calling the attention of everyone around them.

'He wants to go with you,' Miko told them. She gave Jamie a hard look, as if he had something to answer for.

'Well, that's tough luck for him,' Jamie replied, turning back to the car, placing Lottie's case in the boot. But he was only met by hissing and more leg bumping.

'You can't ignore the cats.' Miko was adamant, her eyebrows knitting together.

Sayuri swept forward, picking up the purring cat and shoving it in Jamie's arms. 'It's decided,' she said. 'The spirit of Kou has spoken and you must take the cat back to Rosewood.'

Jamie stared at everyone, sure they must be joking, but not an inch of humour sparked on their faces, save for everyone from Rosewood, who broke out into laughter. The cat gave a tiny mew of satisfaction but Jamie was sure he could hear what the creature was really saying.

'I win.'

33

They arrived back at Rosewood Hall two days before school was due to start. Evening light sank over the grounds as they pulled up through the golden gates.

There were no reporters to be seen in the empty hours of the day, an eerie stillness surrounding them when they climbed out of the car. Lottie hoped that the journalists had become bored of the story, but part of her knew now that there had been more to the media coverage than they'd wanted to admit.

Few students arrived before induction day, with only a handful of lone students and groundskeepers around. Anastacia, Saskia and the twins had headed home and would be joining them tomorrow, leaving Lottie, Ellie and Jamie nearly completely alone at Rosewood.

It was time for the moment of truth.

Walking up the path to the reception hall felt like they were walking to trial.

The hall echoed when they entered, almost empty, the settled dust stirring, catching in their noses. It felt like walking into a tomb.

A solitary secretary sat at her desk, waiting to sign in early arrivers.

Riddled with jet lag and nerves, they each gave their names and were admitted entry, until finally it was Lottie's turn.

'Name, please.' The summertime secretary was a tired-looking woman with greying red hair and long fingers, yawning while she tapped away at the keyboard on the giant oak desk.

Her friends knew Lottie had got enough extra marks at summer school to make up her overall grade, but they needed to hear it. They needed the school to welcome her back.

'Lottie Pumpkin.' Her voice barely wavered, accepting whatever was about to come their way.

Fast fingers clacked at a keyboard, taking them closer to the answer they'd been waiting for. Looking up at them, the secretary's face was unreadable, and Lottie squeezed her eyes shut.

'Thank you, Charlotte. Here is your return package. You can come back tomorrow at noon to collect your timetable.' Ellie and Jamie barely moved, all of them hardly believing it was true, that everything they'd done had been worth it. 'Oh, and, welcome back.'

'Thank you,' Lottie said. She desperately wanted to feel the relief she deserved, but it didn't come, because this was so small compared to what she had to do next.

They all stepped out into the grounds together, into the evening air. The lavender sky was dotted with twinkling stars, the moon peeping through a cloud of deep indigo. It gave the flowers a drowsy coat, the deep rose and lavender scents a happy dream.

'Well done,' Jamie grunted, awkwardly patting her on the shoulder.

'Yeah, good job, Lottie. We can rest now,' Ellie said, but her words only made Lottie's heart sink more.

They walked quietly up the path, to the Ivy dorm, and something shifted. The trees began to rustle, while Vampy nestled in Lottie's arms, sleeping soundly, his heartbeat thumping against her chest.

She felt surrounded by a melody made of three distinctive sounds: the endless beat of the Kiri Shinrin still following her, the burning rustle of the love letter in her bag, and the gentle twinkle of the metallic fragments Sayuri had given her.

When they reached Ivy Wood, night-time had reached its stillest point, milky blue shadows falling over Ryley as he greeted them by the pond.

Jamie made to head up to the boys' dorm but Ellie stopped him.

'Erm . . .' She coughed, raising her eyebrows indignantly. 'I think you're forgetting something, Jamie.'

Following her signal, Lottie handed Vampy to him, smiling apologetically at his furious expression.

'I still think it's unacceptable to be sneaking a pet into the grounds; if the cat gets caught, I'm handing you both in.' His face was dead serious while the cat nestled itself against him.

Ellie smirked. 'Oh, please, I'm sure that's not the worst thing someone's smuggled into this school.'

A dry smile crept over Jamie's face, a look Lottie remembered from a long time ago, an expression she'd thought was gone forever.

'What do you mean?' he asked, effortlessly grabbing his bag and hauling it up over his shoulder. 'I smuggle weapons into school all the time.'

He turned to Lottie and she stared at him blankly, not quite finding a smile.

Both Ellie and Jamie watched her suspiciously, circling in front of her like a pack of wolves. 'Are you OK?' they asked in unison.

'Yes,' she repeated, already zoning out. 'I'm just very jet-lagged, and there's lots to do.' The pounding in her head was still going, getting stronger and more distracting.

'Lottie's right. We need to set up our room, and I'm pretty tired.' Ellie yawned and stretched. 'Goodnight, Jamie,' she called, heading up the path.

'Goodnight, Ellie.' But as he spoke his eyes didn't leave Lottie's, sending shivers through her.

She knew there was no point in putting on a smile for him, no point in pretending it was all OK. He knew, as she did, that the truth was coming for them.

Tomorrow Lottie was going to do the hardest thing she'd ever done, and prove once and for all whether Ellie and her family really were at the centre of Leviathan's plans, and if she was right, she could never look at the Maravish royal family the same way again.

34

For the first time in a long time Jamie didn't wake up before his alarm. The chirpy trill of Judy Garland singing him good morning was strangely jarring and it was only made worse when a large fluffy face appeared in front of his own.

'*Mreow,*' the cat grumbled.

'What do you want?'

The cat stared at him, purrs vibrating against his chest. Stifling a yawn, he picked up the big attention-seeking brute and put him to the side of the bed so he could turn off his alarm.

7 a.m.

It felt particularly odd to have his phone in his room; it felt like more of a crime than having the cat, and part of him was looking forward to handing it in later.

Back to normality.

Only there was no normality now, because he couldn't get Haru out of his mind. He'd infected his dreams, that summer-breeze smile twisting and melting into a grinning bird mask.

Haru isn't part of Leviathan, he told himself. Because if he was, then nothing made sense any more.

Rubbing his face, Jamie tried to push the thoughts out of his head, trying to persuade himself he just felt weird not having Percy in the room with him. But he knew it wasn't that. He felt out of place. When he'd decided to share his feelings with Ellie, it was the first time he could remember ever choosing to relinquish control and it made him squirm to think of it. Everything felt so messy now and all he wanted to do was get out of this cage of a room and burn off some steam.

Catching his reflection in the mirror while he pulled a black shirt over his bare skin, Jamie felt as though he was looking at a stranger. A lock of hair fell over his face as Vampy came to stand beside him.

Shadows under his eyes gave away a lack of sleep and he remembered Ingrid looking up at him while he squeezed down on her wrists and shuddered.

Who are you? he asked the mirror, but what he really meant was, *What are you?*

His vision warped, the image in front of him morphing into a terrible black-cloaked figure, horns extending from his head, coiling out like a ram's, and Haru was there, smiling beside him.

He blinked and the image was gone. Shaking his head and pushing his hair back, Jamie reached for a pair of jogging shorts.

He wasn't doing this any more. He wasn't going to be paranoid. And he wasn't going to let the sickly darkness that the Goat Man had left behind seep into him.

They were so close to revealing his identity; he could see it in the way Lottie kept drifting off, her mind wrapped up in a puzzle she was on the verge of solving. It made her visibly anxious, but strangest of all it was making him nervous too.

'Are you coming?' he asked Vampy, but the cat didn't budge, instead choosing to circle the one bag Jamie had yet to unpack.

Without looking, Jamie knew what was inside. Watching curiously, the big black cat rubbed against the bag.

'Vampy!' Jamie chastised, but the cat only stared at him.

Reluctantly he picked up the bag, cursing himself while he unzipped the front pocket. It still smelled like his room in Maradova, cinnamon and spice, proof that he hadn't touched it the entire time they'd been away.

He pulled out a royal-blue-velvet box, so unassuming and simple, yet what it held had been whispering in his ears for months.

He watched his hands take the lid, and all the while soft fur rubbed against his bare legs, Vampy moving in little figures of eight between his shins, purring at him in satisfaction.

'OK, you pest,' he grumbled, and with furious distaste he opened the box.

A silver wolf stared back at him, glittering gems awoken from a long slumber.

It had been a long time since he'd properly looked at his wolf pendant, and seeing it now felt like rediscovering a lost part of himself.

The wolf – the one thing they all had in common. If you had one of these, you belonged to the Maravish royal family; you were part of the pack.

He remembered how tense he'd been when they'd given one to Lottie, knowing the responsibility it carried, only to discover it was he who didn't feel worthy of it.

Shaking his head, he put the box down and made his way to the door.

The cat moaned again, vibrating at his feet.

'Sorry, Vampy.' He slipped on his running shoes. 'I'm still not ready.'

Lottie awoke to the endless thumping of a heartbeat pounding away like a drum against her chest. In her sleepy, confused state she thought it was Mr Truffles, come to life in her arms, and she quickly pushed him away.

Only once her stuffed pig was lying on the floor, drooping to the side in outrage at his mistreatment, did Lottie realize the sound was coming from inside her.

'Sorry, Mr Truffles,' she said, placing him back on the bed and planting a kiss on his forehead.

Her recently fixed phone screen read 7:15 a.m., fifteen minutes before her alarm was due to go off. A few other international students might start arriving at the school over the course of the day so she needed to do this now, while she was sure she could be alone.

'Hey.'

Lottie nearly jumped out of her skin, frozen in the act of putting her pink jogging sweater on.

'You're awake? It's quarter past seven. Who are you, and what have you done with my princess?' Ellie stretched out in her black bedding among pillows and fluffy cushions.

270

Even though they had both been very tired, Lottie had demanded they take some time to remake the room, refusing to let Ellie sleep on a bed with no sheets, which she was clearly thankful for now, and, besides, Ellie needed a good night's sleep with what was coming their way.

The wooden floor was warm beneath her feet, sun streaming in through the chiffon curtains in amber streaks that made the floor look like gold. Their room felt like home again, with handmade decorations and a motley collection of books and posters. It was strange the way the once clear-cut divide between Ellie's and her own stuff had begun to blur, melting into each other like a Rorschach test made of pink fluff and teenage rebellion.

'You going for a run?' Her eyes were already closing again.

'Yes, I've a lot on my mind. A run might help.' Lottie watched her princess's breathing begin to steady.

'I'm so glad we're home,' Ellie murmured, a smile spreading before she completely zonked out.

'I'll see you in half an hour,' Lottie replied. A small part of her felt guilty for leaving Ellie behind, but she knew that it was better she wasn't there. This was something she needed to do alone.

'Sorry, Ellie,' she whispered, putting on her wolf pendant and squeezing it until the polished silver dug into her palms, leaving little red marks. Tucking it under her vest, she grabbed the envelopes Sayuri had given her: one with her hair, and one with the mysterious metal fragments.

Closing her eyes, she meditated on what she was about to do, visualizing the exact spot in Lili's study where the proof

271

was hiding, taking it and going into the Rose Wood to be completely alone before she revealed the truth. Only then would she bury Sayuri's hair under the great oak tree. It didn't seem too difficult.

As she bent down to pick up her backpack, the wolf pendant freed itself, dropping over her chest, the little gem eyes reflecting the rose-gold velvet box that held her tiara.

'I'm afraid you're sitting this one out,' she told it, turning to leave.

On her way out, she thought she heard the debris inside the envelope rattling ominously. She knew she was only imagining it, but it didn't stop her from feeling uneasy.

35

Tiptoeing down to Lili's study, each step took Lottie closer to the heart of the school. At her side in a bag was Sayuri's hair, her only friend in the darkness, and she imagined her like a spirit beside her, willing her forward, reminding her that she had to do this, no matter what it meant.

Liliana's study was creepy without anybody to cushion the haunted feeling, the shadows looming larger, the air cold like ghost breath on your skin. The torchlight made big yellow circles on the floor.

It would be so easy to turn back. So easy to ignore the truth. But instead Lottie clenched her fists, marched to the desk and slid open the left drawer. There, right where she'd left it, looking back at her in the topaz light, was the letter she'd received at the start of summer from the king. And at the bottom was his symbol.

The very same symbol that was at the bottom of the love letter to Sayuri's aunt.

Stupid.

Ingrid could hardly believe how stupid the Rosewood Hall set-up was. It was completely closed off and yet entirely exposed. Anyone could just walk right through the woods; what was even the point of the gates?

Her Partizan training kicked in, an instinctual drive to map out the surrounding area and locate every weak spot. If she had someone to protect, she would place watchers in the woodland, people to keep guard, so she had to assume that's what they'd done too. A school full of rich, important children was bound to be riddled with security.

It had occurred to her that she might simply walk through the front gate and pretend to be a student but she couldn't risk it. She could just imagine the smug look on Haru's face if she got caught on her rogue mission.

His name sent violent volts of anger through her and she furiously clenched her fists until pain shot up her arm. Sweet horrible pain. Why did they all like him so much? Why was it never her? She deserved her revenge. She deserved to take something from that disgusting marshmallow of a princess, and she was going to prove her worth.

Someone needed to get that letter they'd let the princess find, and Ingrid was going to make sure it was her – but most importantly she was going to make sure they would never see it again. No letter, no plan, and then they could move forward with the Hamelin Formula.

A grin spread across her face as she imagined Jamie's expression, warped and pained, when he saw the little gift she would leave him on his princess's face. But the image began to deform, morphing into that twisted demonic look, the empty gold eyes, an endless void of nothing reaching into her as the terrible monster bore down on her, breaking her deep inside her bones.

She blinked the image away, her breath catching, and she realized she was cradling herself, her bandaged arms wrapped round her own body. It was a horrible picture and she shook her arms free, fresh pain tingling from within.

Stupid.

The symbol on the king's letter burned inside Lottie's head. That triangle, with three surrounding circles, in red ink – it was undeniable. It had shone in the torchlight, teasing her, and there was no hiding from it now; it was the same symbol that had been on all the love letters at Takeshin.

Lottie needed to go somewhere that would give her strength, a place where she could process what it all meant. The letters felt heavy in her bag where she stood at the edge of the Rose Wood, her mind twisted like the roots beneath her feet.

In her mind the Rose Wood was a tangled maze of brambles and roots, with no way of knowing where you'd come from or where you were going. That was not the wood that greeted her today.

There were no paths in the Rose Wood, which was almost entirely untouched by people, but the way to the great oak tree was as clear and easy as if someone were guiding her.

Lottie pondered with each step.

The king's strange reaction to them going to Takeshin.

His own mark on that terrible letter.

It was the kind of written proof that could cause a huge controversy, putting the Maravish royal family's very integrity on trial.

So why on earth would Leviathan want such a thing?

Lottie couldn't figure it out, but it told her with absolute clarity what she'd spent so long telling Ellie in her head. That everything Leviathan did led back to her and her family.

Strangely nervous, Lottie pushed herself towards the clearing, which was glowing amber. It was a beacon calling her forward, and she would not leave it until she understood what was going on.

The plan was simple. Ingrid would trek through the Rose Wood, and emerge on the east side of the school by the Ivy dormitory, which she would stake out until she caught the princess alone. The ease of it was laughable; it was practically an invitation. But what she hadn't been anticipating was the strangeness of the woodland. It rippled as she approached it, a distinct cut-off point between the dense forest and the rest of the world where the trees became dense and dark, and the ground beneath them cold. Ingrid stood at the rim of the shadows, age-old oaks towering over her, sunlight and shadows in criss-cross patterns across her legs. She spat on the ground like a cat coughing up a hairball. She wasn't sure why she did it, but she smiled down before continuing on into the woods.

The second she was under the cover of the trees, a great chill wrapped round her. Only seconds ago she'd been too hot in her black catsuit and backpack, and now she was cold – and not just cold, freezing. It was as if the Rose Wood existed in an entirely different climate. Deeper in, pockets of sunlight provided moments of warmth but it didn't stop the goosepimples building on her flesh. She hissed in irritation, continuing on and catching her foot in a bramble, thorns biting her legs.

The hands of the Rose Wood were gripping her tight, holding her back. With a furious shriek, she reached for her knife and in one great strike that sent a million volts of pain up her arm she cut into the brambles, slicing them clean off her.

'Overgrown pit,' she snarled, swinging her blade again, grinning as she tore another scar in the woodland. With each swipe of the blade, a fresh ache of pain blossomed from her wrist, a glorious bruise that she cherished – proof that she deserved what she was going to take.

After fifteen minutes, her breathing turned heavy, thrilled by the damage she was causing. It wasn't until she reached a large clearing that she stopped to look at herself. Thorns had torn her catsuit, and welts and red lines of blood flared up along her skin. The woodland had bitten and scratched her with every step she took. Ingrid imagined how she must look right now, bandages unravelling, her matted hair tangled with twigs, insects and dirt.

Monster. The word screamed in her head, and with it the distinct sound of a girl's voice, a voice she was sure she knew.

Ducking low, Ingrid began to prowl, finding a sturdy tree to climb up, deathly silent, until she saw a clearing in the distance filled with golden light and the biggest tree she'd ever seen. The tree's branches spilled out over the woodland, crowning the forest in dappled light. But it wasn't the tree that had Ingrid so thrilled. She'd thought the wood hated her, but now it gave her a gift.

Nestled under the oak tree was the princess herself.

Ingrid's mouth twitched at the lack of scratches on the princess. She was entirely untouched by the Rose Wood, with not even a speck of dirt on her. Her hair was longer than she remembered, curling locks of wheat cascading down her back. Ingrid felt her fingers curl in anticipation round the knife in her hand, heartbeat racing.

Ingrid harnessed all her self-control. She needed this to be perfect.

The sun-warmed patch deep in the heart of the Rose Wood was radiant, the air ignited by the buttery light that poured through the leaves. The only sounds were the gentle wind through the leaves, distant streams and sweet birdsong.

The oak was somehow bigger than Lottie recalled, a wrinkled mass of ageing wood that towered over the clearing. It hummed and creaked, the roots beneath her feet pumping life through the woodland.

'Hello, old friend!' she called out.

Everything around the oak was still and untouched, a welcoming cocoon of silence: a secret place that called to you when you needed to be alone with your thoughts.

Lottie had found herself here on the anniversary of her mother's death, and now she was here again, to try to understand the mystery of Leviathan.

She began to dig, finding the perfect spot to lay Sayuri's hair just under the huge oak tree. It was oddly therapeutic, and let her clear her head.

Why would Leviathan want those letters?

Dig.

Who is the Master of Leviathan?

Dig.

What do they want with the princess and her Partizan?

As she dug, Lottie could discern a ringing in her head, a distant bell getting louder and clearer the more earth she dug up. After a while she'd almost entirely forgotten why she was even digging, her mind distracted, so it was alarming when her trowel struck something hard.

Blinking down, Lottie found a wooden chest much the same as the one in Takeshin.

She moved the earth aside, revealing its full extent. It was almost the same as the one they found in Takeshin, but instead of moons the chest was engraved with wavy-edged orbs. It was a sun box.

And, although she did not dare dream it, Lottie was sure she knew what it would contain.

The lid eased open with a creak, and what was inside took her breath away.

It was a sword of legend to match Kou's, a curved blade in the radiant grip, like the sliver of the moon coming to meet the sun, so sharp it whistled.

As she reached for it, something else caught her eye, a small roll of fabric.

Beneath the swathes of cotton lay a glossy black snake made entirely of silk. It slipped between her fingers, smooth and malleable, a glossy rope of ebony. Holding it up to the light, Lottie pulled out Sayuri's hair and placed it beside to find that they were almost identical.

It was Kou's hair.

Lottie snapped out of the spell and dropped both locks of hair into the chest. She could hardly believe what she'd stumbled upon, and how it had been right in front of her eyes this whole time.

It was so painfully obvious now – how the bamboo tree mirrored Rosewood's oak, and all the glowing trunks in Lili's diary. How on earth could she have been so blind? The clues had been there, telling her there was a gift for her as well: a gift from her ancestor, Liliana. And not just any gift: a sword.

Stroking the handle, Lottie felt the careful engravings. It had been waiting for her for hundreds of years, sleeping in the ground, ready to be awoken.

A thought formed in her head like a chant. *Right in front of you.*

The words repeated in her mind, a dawning sense like the sun rising over her. Everything slipped out of vision. The woodland, the sword, even her own body, melted away, her thoughts vanishing into a maze with one clear answer at the centre.

Why would Leviathan want a letter Ellie's father had written?

But the question she hadn't asked herself was far more important. *How did they know the letter was there at all?*

These past few weeks they'd been trying to find who the Master of Leviathan was with abstract facts – his height, his accent, the drawing she'd put together – all the while trying to convince herself that Ellie wasn't at the centre of it all, but the puzzle pieces were right in front of her, real objects and clues that she couldn't deny.

The Master of Leviathan.

The idea made her dizzy, hot panic and crystal clarity colliding inside her while she fumbled frantically with her backpack to retrieve the envelope, pouring the fragments out into her palm.

The Goat Man.

Hand trembling beneath the muted grey shards of silver, the single gem rolled into the centre of her palm, staring up at her again, just as it had the first time she'd looked at it.

Pale skin.

With her other hand she shakily reached for her pendant.

Long dark brown hair.

The pendant was distinct, instantly recognizable on another member of the pack. It was a firm reminder that you were part of something bigger, that you belonged to the Maravish royal family.

Green eyes.

They glittered with truth, the eyes of the wolf confronting her with a terrible, inescapable reality.

Familiar.

Lottie's heartbeat slowed down so much she thought it might stop completely, everything becoming languid, the air thick. Because the fragments in her hand were piecing themselves together, the single precious stone staring down its sister at her neck, its face ripped apart, along with its owner's connection to the family.

This was a wolf pendant, exactly the same but shattered into shards.

Claude Wolfson.

The name struck her so hard she felt the wind knocked out of her.

She had wondered why her drawing of the Master of Leviathan looked so much like King Alexander, and she'd

281

prayed so hard that it didn't lead back to Ellie and her family. But it was all there, staring back at her in the eyes of the wolf, forcing her to rethink everything.

Ellie's Uncle Claude was the Master of Leviathan.

It was a truth she'd been so afraid to uncover, but now she knew it, nothing would ever be the same.

This is why Leviathan wanted the love letter King Alexander had sent, because it could destroy the Maravish royal family's reputation if anyone knew he'd got another woman pregnant. It was dreadful to think that the sadness in Sayuri's family could lead back to Ellie's father. That everything led back to the Wolfsons.

Putting the broken wolf away again, Lottie stared at the bark of the tree, knowing she had to tell everyone, but knowing that would be the hardest part.

Only she didn't get a chance to move. There was not a moment to let the truth rest inside her, because something wicked was creeping up on her: a monster in the woods stalking its prey.

She saw the shadow first, growing bigger around her in the silence. But by the time she realized it was too late – there wasn't even time to scream. The scratched hand appeared like a cat's claw, covering her mouth, while the other came down hard on the back of her head, tangling in her hair and pulling her up painfully.

Lottie knew who it was before she saw her snarling face.

'Hello, Princess,' Ingrid purred, dangling her like a mouse. 'I've been looking for you everywhere.'

36

There is a specific kind of fear that feels like acceptance. A prickly calm in which your mind cocoons you from reality. It says, 'This isn't happening,' or, 'It will be OK in a minute.' It lulls you into tranquillity, cradling you in a false idea that everything will be fine so long as you are very quiet and very still.

This was not the kind of fear Lottie was feeling.

'Would you quit struggling?' Ingrid hissed, pulling sharply on Lottie's hair again. Even with her mouth gagged, and all odds against her, Lottie wouldn't stop fighting, wriggling and kicking. She would not be helpless. Not again.

Grabbing her shoulders, Ingrid turned Lottie to face her. She was a dreadful sight, covered in scratches and welts, her once-sleek hair a knotted ratty mess, caked with mud and leaves. And worst of all: her eyes.

When Lottie had been little, her friend Kate adopted a cat called Coco from a shelter. It would bully anything small; its eyes would go wide, deep black pools of mania, unblinking and unpredictable. If you saw them, you knew it was too late – Coco was going to get you. But Ingrid was human, and seeing that same mania in her was like staring into madness itself.

'If you don't stop struggling, I'll drive this knife right into your hand.'

Lottie believed her.

Satisfied, Ingrid dragged her along the ground, muddying her clothes, and propped her up against the oak tree with a hard thud that nearly knocked the wind out of her lungs. Ingrid clearly had a plan that she'd been nurturing for a while and Lottie dreaded to find out what it was.

She looked tall, a great monster that eclipsed the sun, staring down at her with malicious intent. There was something odd about thinking of Ingrid as tall, since she was significantly shorter than the other members of Leviathan Lottie had encountered, and yet something had grown within her, a poisonous spite, deforming her and stretching her.

'Now listen very carefully to me, Princess.' Her breathing was uneven when she spoke. 'I'm going to remove your gag and we're going to play a game. But if you shout or scream, I'll tear your fingernails out, like this. Do you understand?' To emphasize her point, Ingrid took the tip of her knife and pushed it slowly under the fingernail on Lottie's pinkie, just far enough to give her a taste of the pain. She gasped, the pink nailbed turning purple with the pressure, and she quickly nodded to make Ingrid stop.

Ingrid leaned forward, fumbling with the ties at the back of Lottie's head, her scratched skin coming up to her face, and she could smell her. Iron and sweat tingled in Lottie's nose.

There were two other things Lottie noticed as her mouth was freed.

The first was that Ingrid hadn't spotted the sword. And the second was that Ingrid was shaking.

You need to run; you're good at running.

It wasn't her voice she was hearing; it was Jamie's.

You have to run as fast as you can.

The only problem was she had to get free first.

Ingrid was a Partizan. She knew the Partizan tricks. If Lottie was going to do this, she had to do it her own way. Behind her thoughts she could almost hear the ringing of the sword and she thought of Sayuri in Japan counting on her to solve this and tell her the truth.

She had to get away and warn them about Claude. There was no option to fail.

'What game are we playing?' Lottie asked as calmly as she could, and it appeared to work, a spark of surprise flashing across Ingrid's face. Although her chances were slim, Lottie knew that there was something different about her. The frenzy in her eyes, her uneven breathing. She was not thinking with the usual Partizan precision.

'The game, Princess –' a wry smile had spread over her lips, dried blood crusting over her chin – 'is truth or dare.'

It was Lottie's turn to be surprised.

'If you fail to answer or do your dare, I'll cut a line in your skin. Got it?' Ingrid stared at her, genuinely seeming to want her to answer.

'And what happens if *you* forfeit?' Lottie asked in response, an idea forming.

The look on Ingrid's face turned venomous, her eyes narrowing at Lottie. Clearly Lottie was the only one expected to play.

'Truth or dare?' Ingrid asked, plonking herself down cross-legged on the ground. It made for the strangest scene. It was like looking at a monster meditating.

'Truth,' Lottie said, gulping down her terror.

The predatory split of a smile spread back over Ingrid's face. 'Why is Jamie your Partizan?'

The question was a blanket of ice, freezing Lottie in place.

She knew the facts. That Jamie's mother had sought refuge in the palace, that she'd died in childbirth and the royal family had kept him and trained him to be Ellie's Partizan. But the question was so very loaded, and nothing she knew about the Maravish royal family felt solid any more.

Why are you Ellie's Partizan, Jamie? Lottie thought, unable to find any words. She looked up at Ingrid's swirling eyes, wondering what answer she would be hoping for.

'Guilt.' Lottie felt the word leave her throat before she could process it, and it shocked them both. 'He feels like he owes my family and is scared he's not worthy.'

She could hardly believe she had said something so awful out loud.

It took Ingrid a second to process her answer, but her confusion did not last long, and was quickly replaced by menace. 'Wrong.'

It happened so fast that Lottie barely had any time to register it. One moment her hand was her own, and then it was pulled forward as Ingrid grabbed her, raised her arm and sliced so cleanly and quickly that the pain had to catch up with her.

Lottie didn't make a sound. She simply cradled her arm and watched as a dark red line began to pool out from the back of her hand.

'You know what's funny?' Lottie said, using every ounce of bravery to not let her voice shake. She couldn't look at Ingrid, too scared to see that grin, but she knew her calm confused her. 'When I first met you I thought your knives were dipped in poison.'

Words were powerful, and Lottie chose hers very carefully.

A splutter escaped from Ingrid's mouth and Lottie knew she'd been successful. She chanced a look to see disgust on her captor's face.

Ingrid lifted her knife to the sun, inspecting the drops of blood that dripped down like syrup. 'I would never,' she said. 'It would be boring if the fight ended so quickly.' The look in her eye was almost fond. She gazed up at her blade, rubbing her thumb against the cold metal spider that wrapped round the grip.

Her eyes pounced back to Lottie with a look so deadly she felt as though she were being devoured.

'Truth or dare?' she asked slowly, placing her knife back on the ground. But Lottie had seen that Ingrid was distractible. That words could affect her.

'Dare,' Lottie replied, feeling braver than she should have. It was most certainly the wrong thing to say.

Ingrid grinned. 'I dare you to destroy that letter you stole.'

'What?' Lottie spluttered. 'That's not . . . I don't know what you're talking about!' The question made her brain fuzzy, because the way Ingrid said this suggested Leviathan knew everything.

Something changed on Ingrid's face, her smile coiling in on itself. 'You're confused.' Her face came close to Lottie's. 'But that's OK. Let me explain. I want that letter gone, so we can move on to the better plan.' Her breath tickled Lottie's cheek. 'You know, the plan where we dispose of those lying parents of yours.'

'What are you talking about? What have you done?'

A cackle bubbled out of Ingrid, and Lottie thought of Claude, the black wolf of the family, and the awful Hamelin Formula he'd got his hands on, a formula with the power to make anyone do anything he wanted.

Could this possibly be his plan? It seemed too gruesome, too awful to possibly be true.

A milky distant look took over Ingrid's gaze, like she was staring at a vision of the future.

'Once they're gone,' she began, with the dreamy voice of a psychic telling Lottie her future, 'he'll be welcomed with the respect he deserves. Just like Alexis.'

Alexis.

The name caught in Lottie's head like snagging fabric, tugging at a memory she couldn't place.

'Now come on,' Ingrid demanded, cutting Lottie's thoughts short. 'Tell me where that letter is. We know you have it somewhere.'

Her face was twisted with laughter, but this wasn't a woman working towards a team goal. This was a mad girl determined to cause as much damage as possible.

But why did she feel such hatred towards the Maravish royal family? What could have made her this way?

'I . . . I don't understand. What did we do? I don't know what we've done,' Lottie spluttered.

Ingrid looked furious. 'You don't know what you've *done*?' she growled, all the humour vanishing from her voice. 'You took *Jamie*.'

It was all nonsense, venomous rambling that Lottie couldn't understand, couldn't reckon with, and she watched in horror as Ingrid grabbed her knife again. 'And it's disgusting. You and your family are a horrible, lying, repulsive pack of rats. You don't deserve the mercy the Master planned for you. I won't let you get off so easy.'

Lottie tried to lean out of the way, diving to the side, but Ingrid grabbed her hair and pulled her backwards with a hard yank.

'That's a forfeit,' she hissed in her ear, taking the knife and pulling it along her cheek. Hot blood trickled down her face, yet all Lottie could focus on was what lay in front of her asleep in the ground, unnoticed.

'You're weak and pathetic.' Ingrid pulled Lottie's hair again, moving them even closer. Liliana's sword lay mere centimetres away, and Ingrid was too frenzied to notice.

Each time Ingrid pushed and pulled her, the sword glinted, calling to her, getting closer with every haphazard shove.

'Foul, worthless . . .' The words rolled off Lottie. They were scorching embers spitting with fire and fury from Ingrid's bloodied mouth, but when they reached Lottie's ears they burned to nothing. Because Lottie knew they weren't true.

She was starting to understand Leviathan, the story they were trying to spread. It was an unbridled fury directed at the Maravish royal family, as broken and chaotic as the remains of the wolf pendant.

This wasn't about her; this was about Ellie's family – and Lottie had to get out of here. She had to escape and figure out why Claude would do this. She had to find out the truth about the Wolfsons. And to do that she needed to cut herself free.

Lottie leaned forward, Ingrid's hands still wrapped in her hair, pulling and twisting and screeching. She reached to awaken her sword. With one swift movement she swept upward, just missing the tips of Ingrid's fingers, and sliced through her own hair.

Free.

Ingrid fell backwards, losing her grip, wheat-coloured hair slipping through her fingers. There was so much of it, Lottie's golden coils, knots of memories and experiences, everything she thought she understood fluttering down to the ground. And then she ran.

She ran and the woodland flew past her. She ran and the world zipped out of view. She ran and did not look back, not for a second, not for anything. It was the fastest she'd ever moved in her life, and every step of the way she could hear the growling, screeching monster behind her. Exposed roots and slippery moss threatened to trip her, but her feet missed them, the branches and brambles swaying out of her way, a path unwinding in front of her.

Her chest began to ache, her wrist and cheek throbbing, but she kept thundering through the trees.

She was faster than Ingrid! The moment she saw light ahead, the thought that she really had escaped burst in her head, a wash of relief so powerful that it sent tears down her face. But she wasn't clear yet; Ingrid was still on her tail, an erratic thrashing and cursing at her ankles.

Just a little further.

The light through the trees was so close now, but there was something coming towards her: a person she knew so well. An angel come to save her.

Just a little further.

Twigs snapped and the ground crunched as she gave one last furious push.

The familiar scent of cinnamon flooded her nose, and she barrelled into the dark-clad figure, gentle arms wrapping round her.

Panting, she looked up into two golden eyes, stars on the top of a great mountain. Jamie's eyes. Wonderful, miraculous Jamie.

'Get behind me,' he growled.

37

What had led him to take his run in the Rose Wood? Jamie couldn't say for sure.

It was an itching feeling that the school couldn't contain him, that he needed to be somewhere wild, somewhere as chaotic as he felt.

He'd heard it before he saw it, a feral screeching, a terrible beast chasing its prey, and he knew that sound; he'd heard it before.

Lottie!

There was nothing else in his mind, every Partizan instinct taking over, making him take off like a charging bull. Only she didn't need saving; she was coming directly to him. She'd already saved herself.

Lottie bolted through the woodland faster than he'd ever seen her run, her full force colliding with him, and a sword to rival Kou's glowing in her hand, but that wasn't the strangest thing of all.

Her hair was gone. Her golden tangle of locks had vanished. It was now a short crop that fell just above her jawline, a messy halo coiling at the ends like ribbon, practical but chaotic and clearly done with a blade. Jamie's blood began to boil, and as Lottie moved behind him he felt his muscles twitching, that same deadly fury he'd felt on the rooftop in Tokyo crawling through him.

'Get behind me,' he growled, his voice barely recognizable.

Tearing towards them through the Rose Wood, quivering and panting, was a terrible monster.

Ingrid looked far worse than Lottie. Her skin was etched with purple welts and bruises, crusted blood smeared her face and loose bandages dangled from her wrists. And her eyes were cold and manic and capable of awful things.

He knew this fight would be easy. Ingrid was exhausted and unstable, and he should have simply subdued her, but one look back at Lottie, and Jamie found he wasn't feeling so merciful.

But what he didn't expect was for Lottie to make the first move, marching forward to hold the sword out beside him. She was holding it completely wrong, but he didn't stop her.

'Together,' she whispered, her racked breathing taut with determination. 'Ingrid,' she said. 'This is not a fight you can win. Go back.'

Lottie took another step forward, holding Ingrid in place with her fiery eyes.

'Disgusting!' The noise that came out of Ingrid's throat was more like gravel than a human voice. 'If you knew anything at all, you'd both come with me.'

'Is it just you?' Jamie asked, attempting to step in front of Lottie again.

'I should damn well hope so,' Ingrid cackled.

She reached into her jacket for a knife, her movement slow and languid, chest rising and shrinking with the effort. Jamie

293

decided it was time to put an end to this whole thing, the anger burning through him like lava.

'She's not our enemy, Jamie,' Lottie beseeched him, tears stinging her eyes. 'It's not her we need to take down.'

Her hand clutched the wolf pendant, and even with her muddied clothes, the wounds Ingrid had given her and the loss of her hair, Lottie stood tall, unwavering and concerned. Not for herself but for him and probably Ingrid too, despite everything she'd done to her. And she was right. This was why he'd never be satisfied taking down Ingrid. This was why nothing made him feel better. Because she was just a pawn, and he needed to go after the leader.

Turning back to Ingrid, he felt like he truly saw her for the first time, how Lottie saw her – a scared, pathetic kid.

'You, keep your mouth shut!' Screaming, Ingrid held her knife up, preparing to make towards Lottie.

This wasn't a fight; it was barely even practice. It was just that same mewling girl from the rooftop in Tokyo, and he didn't need to prove anything.

'Ingrid,' he began, taking one last step in front of her. 'Lottie's right. Stop.'

There was no way to halt the trajectory of her knife, the blade slicing into his arm. Jamie took the impact without flinching, barely even a scowl on his face.

'Ingrid,' he repeated slowly. 'Stop. Go back.'

The calm that followed felt otherworldly. She looked up at him, trembling hands crumpling away from the blade that fell to the ground. Black hair electrified around her like the fur of a scared cat; she was shaking, staring at her hands like they'd betrayed her. A noise escaped her lips, a hissing, screeching sound, and all he could think of was Vampy, and how much this feral girl had in common with him.

Jamie could see Lottie to the side, eyes wide at the scene before her.

'Ingrid, you won't win,' he said calmly, grabbing her shoulders. 'You need to leave now, before people arrive. Ingrid.' Her eyes fluttered between him and Lottie. 'You're going to leave now, and you're going to tell your master that we're waiting for him, that when he wants to stop hiding behind masks and children we'll be here – waiting for the truth.'

She continued to stare up at him. It felt like he was holding a small animal in his hand, the wound in his arm a fearful bite, and he had to prove to this creature that it could flee, that it didn't need to hurt anyone or itself.

'Oh yes,' he added, letting go of her. 'Take this with you. I believe it's yours.' He reached into his vest where her other blade was holstered, ignoring the blood that was starting to drip down his arm, and pulled out the knife, the black spider winking at him in the light.

A million possibilities flashed before them, every single outcome laid out in front of him. Ingrid could take the blade and stab him again. She could make a lunge for Lottie. She could make to leave and change her mind, or maybe she'd do what he asked, and go back to the Goat Man with his message.

Noise began to sound from within the school grounds, the students arriving. All it would take was someone to stray too close to the Rose Wood and send for help.

'You,' Ingrid said at last, sagging. She turned to stare at Lottie once more. 'Don't tell anyone I tried to destroy that letter.'

'I won't.' Lottie nodded, her voice quiet but firm, and for the first time since he'd met her Ingrid looked calm. Really calm, not the fake catlike calm of a predator, but a girl seeing herself clearly for once. She turned the look back on Jamie. 'I'm only doing this because it's you, but we will have our revenge.' Her eyes fell one last time over Lottie with enough intensity to shatter glass.

The voices were getting closer, students laughing. Rosewood Hall was coming back to life, and Ingrid did not belong here.

She stared down at her hands in disgust, before grabbing her knives and running off into the woods again with the jerky speed of a frightened animal.

And just like that she was gone, with no need to fight at all.

This is what they could do – what he and Lottie could achieve so easily when they worked together.

Ingrid's words slowly seeped into his head. *Because it's you.* What did that mean?

He felt a fresh wave of anger, but he knew it wasn't Ingrid's fault. He knew now it was the Master of Leviathan and whatever dreadful reason he had for coming after them.

'Jamie, we have to find Ellie.' Lottie's voice dragged him out of his thoughts. 'It's all true, everything we feared . . .'

Then her legs buckled, her body exhausted, and he ran to catch her. Lottie knew something, something that could help him find who he really needed to fight.

'Help me back to the school; we need to call everyone for a meeting.'

'Lottie, no, I'm taking you to the nurse. Tell me on the way.'

'No, you listen to me,' she demanded, pushing herself up again, before the last of her strength blinked out.

But, just before she disappeared completely, she got her last words out, and they made his mouth water.

'I know who the Master of Leviathan is.'

38

Lottie woke up in the nurse's office later that day, springing up from the pristine white bed.

Everything in the infirmary was white: lines of white-frame single beds with pretty lace bedding, painted windowsills.

The one thing that was different to what she remembered was the many faces leaning over her when she opened her eyes.

'Am I dreaming?' she asked.

Everyone was there. Saskia, Anastacia, the twins, Percy, Raphael, Binah, and standing either side of her like two guard dogs, her Partizan and princess, Jamie and Ellie.

Seeing them was an instant reminder of what she needed to do, what she had to tell everyone, and she could see on their faces that they'd been waiting.

Lola was the first to make a move, hugging her. 'Are you OK? Do you need anything?'

Lottie winced where Lola's face brushed her cheek. The pain in her hand and cheek was more noticeable now, a wasp sting of an injury, annoying but not unbearable.

'Lola,' Anastacia chastised, pulling her back. 'Give her some room for goodness' sake!'

Lottie had to wonder what on earth they'd told the school nurse. And where was the sword?

'We gathered everyone while you were sleeping,' Jamie said. 'Ellie and I told them what happened. We told the nurse you'd had a nasty fall in the Rose Wood while running. They'll be adding extra security measures to stop people going in the Rose Wood, and hopefully it'll stop people coming the other way too.' Jamie read her mind in a way she didn't even find creepy any more. What she hadn't expected was the way he spoke; there was an urgency to it, like a predator circling its prey.

'And we've hidden the sword, which I hope you'll tell me all about once you've recovered please, Lottie,' Binah added, pushing her glasses up her nose with a flashy grin as if nothing life-threatening had taken place.

'What time is it?' Lottie asked, peeling back the sheets and throwing her legs over the side of the bed to find they'd turned entirely into jelly from running so hard.

'Twelve,' Micky and Lola said in unison.

'You'll need to be careful walking for a few days,' Jamie added, holding a hand out to help her up.

When she took it, light pooled around him, the midday sun holding him in its palm, but there was something strange about it; he was more like a fallen angel, perched and waiting.

Lottie's reflection was revealed in the window behind him. Gauze covered the wound on her left cheek. It would leave a scar, and it would match the one Ingrid had given Ellie last year. It was strange and oddly pleasant to know they'd shared something so terrible.

Her hair curled at her chin with a few mismatched strands sticking out at the bottom, and her first thought was how much she looked like William Tufty. It felt right, as if for years she'd been looking at a spot-the-difference version of herself, and now she was seeing the real image.

'Lottie, apparently you have something you need to tell us all,' Saskia said bluntly. 'Something about the identity of a certain Master of Leviathan?'

It took Lottie a second to realize it really was Saskia, that she was really back in the school.

The memories flooded back to her so fast she wobbled, Jamie and Ellie both leaning in to hold her up.

The pendant, the love letter, the black-framed painting, Claude Wolfson, all the crazy things Ingrid had said about the Maravish royal family, about Ellie's family.

Looking around, Lottie realized there was one big problem. She had to choose her words carefully, knowing they still had to keep Banshee under wraps and that she owed it to Sayuri to keep the secret about Haru.

'I need you all to promise me that what I'm about to say isn't going to change anything, that we're all still in this together and that it's no one's fault.' She placed extra emphasis on the last words.

Her friends, with Micky signing for Percy, all nodded their understanding.

'I'm still confused by it myself, but we're a team, and I know that we can work together to solve this.' Lottie held Ellie's and Jamie's gazes, knowing she was about to turn their whole world upside down. But even Ellie's feelings couldn't be spared; she understood that now. 'I realized that a letter Leviathan were looking for . . . it was from my father. They most likely wanted it to discredit his right to the throne.'

A harsh intake of breath told her that Ellie had felt the words deep inside her. What an awful discovery it must be to find that your father could have done something so terrible.

Lottie pushed on. 'That was my first clue. My next was when I found something that had been given to one of the members of Leviathan by the Master to take away and destroy. I thought it was just a handful of metal shards and a random gem – but there was something familiar about the gem, and I realized it was this.'

Lottie pulled out her wolf pendant, its eyes glittering with truth.

'Lottie, stop. What are you saying?' Ellie's voice was shaking, the sparks of realization setting a storm off within her.

'Only members of the Maravish royal family are given these,' she explained, watching as Binah's face lit up, the second person to understand. 'I thought it was odd that all Leviathan's efforts would lead back to me; I refused to believe it.' Lottie coughed, suddenly terrified of what would come next. 'But I couldn't deny it after I saw the destroyed wolf.'

'Lottie, just say it,' Ellie whispered.

Closing her eyes and taking a deep breath, Lottie felt the power of the new information flow through her. 'I believe with one hundred per cent assurance that the Master of Leviathan is my uncle, Claude Wolfson, who abandoned the Maravish throne and was exiled by the family.'

The silence that followed was deafening. Only Jamie and Ellie stood unflinching at her side, the anchor of dread this news had created pulling them down, lost in an underworld of tangled emotions Lottie couldn't begin to unravel.

'Holy chocolate biscuit!' Lola practically squealed, cutting through the silence. 'This changes everything.'

Even through the seriousness of the situation, it was impossible not to smile at Lola's choice of words, although Lottie's cheek twinged in protest.

'Wait,' Raphael chimed in, rubbing the back of his head, 'how did you get the remains of the pendant?'

Everyone turned back to Lottie, and she could feel Jamie tense at her side, knowing that if she told them about Banshee and Haru he might never forgive her.

'I gave it to her.' Saskia lied so easily. 'I asked her not to tell anyone because I'd been selfishly hanging on to a clue I should have shared. I'm sorry – I should have given it to you all sooner.'

The twins, Percy and Raphael seemed satisfied with this answer, but Jamie remained tense, while Binah watched her like a hawk, both of them making her feel like she might crumble under the guilt.

'Why would your uncle want to cause so much trouble?' Micky asked.

'I'm afraid I don't know.'

It was impossible not to glance at Ellie as she spoke, her gaze darting towards her involuntarily. The sight made her feel like she'd been stabbed in the chest. Ellie's face was haunted.

'I think we should give Lottie a chance to rest now so she can join us for the fireworks later,' Jamie said, although it was clearly more of a command. 'And I think we all need some time to let this sink in.'

Murmurs of reluctant agreement echoed through the room, everyone mumbling 'See you later' and 'Get well soon', but there was an airiness around them all now, none of them sure what this new development meant.

'Oh, and, Lottie –' Lola paused on her way out, peeping back past the door frame – 'your hair looks great!'

Lottie nodded weakly at her as the door closed, before she turned back to her princess and Partizan. 'Listen, guys . . .'

She wanted to explain to them about the terrible things Ingrid had said about disposing of the king and queen, what she thought they might be planning to use the Hamelin Formula for, and her manic rambling about Alexis, but before Lottie could get another word out a set of arms wrapped round her. It wasn't the usual warm and safe feeling she got from Ellie, but a desperate choking squeeze filled with fear and pain. Ellie was crying.

'Ellie,' she whispered, 'this changes nothing. It's all OK.'

'No, Lottie, it's not OK.' A sob escaped her, and Lottie could see Jamie in the corner staring out of the window. 'All this –' her voice was a mess of tears and all she could do was hug her back, gently stroking her hair – 'everything that's ever happened to you and Jamie, and everyone else, it's all because of my stupid family. It's all my fault and now we have proof.'

Lottie's hand froze, her eyes locking on to Jamie's, because they both knew this would happen, but neither of them knew what to do next.

'I'm going to let you two talk this out,' said Jamie. 'I'll make the call to Ellie's parents; I imagine they'll want us to come back as soon as possible.' He headed to the door, glancing briefly over his shoulder, and the look on his face was so confusing, not at all what Lottie was expecting, that it made her catch her breath.

He looked furious. It felt as if it was on her behalf, that he was angry for her, and she couldn't understand it. Before she had time to process it, he was gone, leaving the two of them alone, Ellie's weeping the only sound.

Ellie had never cried like this, not ever, and Lottie couldn't tell if this was a good thing, a step in the right direction, or a very bad sign. All she knew for certain was that it was a change, and that there would be a lot more changes from here on.

And right now she had to tell her what she felt; she had to tell Ellie her own truth.

'Ellie,' she began, the name like a lullaby on her lips, 'I'm going to tell you how I feel, and I'm going to trust that you're really listening, and that you'll believe me.' She waited a moment, Ellie still clinging to her, face hidden. 'This is no one's fault. No one blames you, and even knowing all this every single one of us would still be your friend; we'd always choose you. I promise.'

She felt Ellie shuffle, the breath on her neck becoming deeper, less frenzied, and she continued. 'We're a pack, Ellie,' Lottie said soothingly, stroking her princess's hair. 'You're not Claude, and you're not your family; you're Ellie, and we're our own pack.'

With a loud sniff Ellie's face finally reappeared with massive panda eyes and streaks of black down her face in the shape of teardrops.

Their bodies were so close Lottie could feel her heartbeat, but she didn't think about the kiss, or Leviathan, or Claude, only Ellie, the person in the world she felt most herself with. The person she wanted to hold on to forever.

'Lottie,' Ellie said at last, her voice strained, breathing ragged. 'I don't want to lie to you. I can't tell you I'm OK with this.'

Lottie absorbed the words, feeling them settle inside her like a bruise that might never heal, and in the deep ebony wells of Ellie's eyes Lottie could see her drifting further and further away, and she'd drown unless she did something now.

'Cut my hair,' Lottie announced, surprising herself. 'It needs fixing, and then I can cut yours. It'll be like when we first became friends, remember? When I did your hair?'

Ellie mumbled something, looking away.

'I'm serious. There's no point in thinking about this now; we deserve to enjoy our time back at Rosewood.' She could tell from the way Ellie recoiled that she didn't believe she deserved anything right then, but she persisted. 'Please, Ellie.'

Perhaps there was just the right amount of desperation in her voice, because, although reluctant, Ellie agreed, but the shadow remained over her princess, a dark cloud that Lottie had put there, and part of her began to wonder if, despite her belief in the truth, she'd made a terrible mistake.

39

Ellie stepped back, contemplating her work with a tilt of her head, black hair flopping to the side in wet inky clumps.

Their bedroom was fully aglow, come back to life after its hibernation over the summer, filled to the brim with books and clothes, socks on the dark-wood floor, which was making its familiar creaks, while the sound of students drifted into their motley hideaway on a breeze that smelled of flowers. Yet it felt like they were seeing it through an old TV. A fake happy, a 'play pretend' that they were all following along with for each other's sake.

'Done.' With one last snip Ellie chewed her lip, looking down at Lottie, absently fiddling with a strand by her chin, her mind already drifting off again.

The voice in Lottie's head hissed again, wondering if the truth had been too much, if she'd done this all wrong.

They had dealt with the worst of Ellie's panda eyes, though a faint black shadow still lingered, stuck to her like a tattoo under the skin. She was pretending it hadn't happened, but the evidence was there, the effect this news had had on her, on all of them. But she was trying to pretend she was OK, and somehow that made Lottie feel even worse.

'You ready to see?' Ellie asked.

Lottie nodded determinedly, ready to embrace the new her and everything that came with it.

Liliana's sword was safely hidden under her bed, and thinking about it made her feel a spark of relief, reminding her of the allies she had across the sea. The first thing she'd done when they got back to the room was message Sayuri; it was late in Japan so she didn't expect an answer any time soon, although she was desperate for it, knowing that Sayuri more than anyone else would be able to help her make some sense of all this.

She still hadn't told anyone what Ingrid had said in the Rose Wood, about Leviathan's final plan; she knew she would have to eventually, but she hadn't completely made peace with it herself, and it was clear from everyone's reaction that no one was ready to hear it yet.

'I'm ready,' Lottie said, turning towards the mirror.

It was perfect; all the strands the sword had missed had now been cut sharply and precisely, framing her face in a way that made her look older, leaner.

Fresh, clean, open. That's what it felt like, and it's exactly what she needed to be, who she needed to be.

'I love it so much.' Lottie spun back to her princess, trying to ignore the shadows at the edge of the room. 'Thank you, Ellie.' She beamed at her again, hoping the smile would cover up her inner thoughts, but it was clear by the way Ellie returned the gesture that they were both doing the same thing.

'OK. Your turn,' Lottie said, taking the scissors from Ellie.

The two girls switched places, Ellie taking a seat and wrapping the towel over her shoulders like a royal cape.

Scissors in hand, Lottie felt the power of them, the importance of this moment.

The truth had changed them, and she needed to make sure it was for the better. If they were going to confront Claude, they needed to rid themselves of everything they thought they knew, everything about the Maravish family. Ellie's family.

As Lottie snipped carefully, meticulously checking the length, Ellie could feel the spell of calm taking over – and it was not long before Ellie drifted off, her head flopping sideways like a doll. Each sleepy breath was like a lullaby to Lottie, calm and comforting, and she hoped Ellie could find peace in her dreams. Satisfied, she held a chopped lock of inky hair in the palm of her hand and blew it away.

Putting the scissors down, she placed her hands on Ellie's shoulders, leaning over until they were face to face, their breath mingling together while she slept.

The wolf pendant glittered, dangling over Ellie's neck, anchoring her to the Rose Wood, to everything that had happened.

Why is Jamie your Partizan?

Ingrid's question grew in her mind like a distant rumble of thunder, a grey cloud looming over her that she couldn't ignore.

Why would Claude want revenge?

Would he really want to commit murder?

What could lead a person to do such a thing?

And again the one question she knew meant something, snarling lips whispering in her ear with insidious knowing, toying with her. *Why is Jamie your Partizan?*

The words repeated in her head, but this time they weren't Ingrid's; it was Lottie's own voice. It felt like a clue, the first part of a bigger riddle, a magic spell that would open a hidden door, and she leaned in so close that their eyelashes almost touched. 'Why is Jamie your Partizan?' she whispered.

A gentle knocking at the door made Lottie jump, and sent her scurrying to answer.

'Hey,' she said softly, opening the door slowly so as not to wake Ellie.

She wasn't sure who she expected, and she probably should have been more surprised to see Jamie breaking the rules by being in the girls' dorm, but all she felt was relief.

'Hey,' he said back, his voice barely above a breath. She nearly laughed when she noticed the big black cat in his arms, nuzzling him. She carefully slipped out and stroked Vampy. 'Ellie's sleeping, so we need to be quiet. Do you wanna head out to the pond?'

Jamie nodded, peeping over Lottie's shoulder, a strange expression on his face when he saw Ellie in the chair.

'I figure she needs a rest after the news,' Lottie said, the two of them heading out.

The school was officially back to life, new and returning students filling up the hallways, sun-kissed skin and designer clothes, golf buggies carrying giant suitcases fit to burst. None of them could possibly imagine everything they'd been through that summer.

'You know what?' Jamie said as they sat on the bench in front of the fountain. 'Sometimes I'm glad I don't have any family.'

Lottie spluttered, hardly believing Jamie could have said such a thing, before she added with a dark realization, 'Me too actually.'

Ryley the deer watched them curiously, the bronze flesh of the Ivy mascot rippling with the water's reflection, rose petals from the surrounding bushes swimming at his feet.

She wasn't confused any more, at least she could say that much. They weren't in the dark about Leviathan and what they wanted; it was all becoming clearer, and they were stepping into the truth together. And yet, even as she thought it, she felt that fear again for Ellie.

Vampy let out a grumpy meow, squirming until Jamie put him down.

'Will he be all right in the school?' Lottie asked, watching as he sprinted off to find some food.

'I think he can look after himself mostly,' Jamie replied, scowling at Vampy, but she could tell he liked him just as much as she did. 'We'll be heading back to Maradova this weekend coming,' Jamie said. 'Nikolay took the news, so I'm afraid I don't know what the royal reaction was. We'll have to wait and see for ourselves.'

'And you?' she asked. 'How do you feel about all this?'

Jamie didn't answer at first, staring out into the water.

'You said Ingrid wasn't my enemy, and you were right,' he replied cryptically.

'It's a relief to know that it's Claude, even if it's hard to digest.'

Jamie nodded, but once again she saw anger crack over him like thunder, and it made her nervous.

'I'll make sure they pay, whoever's responsible for this.'

Before Lottie could register what was happening, Jamie was holding a strand of her freshly cut hair and staring at the cut on her cheek with such intensity it made her dizzy.

All the sounds of the school melted away, and the scent of roses and cinnamon was so powerful she thought she might choke.

'Jamie, I –'

Lottie wasn't entirely sure what she was going to say; all she knew in that moment was that she was truly afraid. It was a fear for Ellie and Jamie, a fear that she'd made a terrible mistake in discovering the truth, and a fear that even though she'd uncovered the mystery she still felt like she knew nothing at all. But, before she could get the words out, someone called to her.

'Ah, Lottie, I'm glad I caught you before the opening speech,' Professor Devine announced, her piercing soprano voice like birdsong. Jamie quickly released her lock of hair, the two of them turning away, the brief moment vanishing as fast as it had happened. 'I heard you had a little tumble in the Rose Wood. I'll overlook this time that you were beyond school boundaries. I think your injuries are punishment enough, hmm?' The professor looked at her pointedly, sharp eyes darting between her and Jamie. 'How are you feeling?'

The question felt loaded, dripping with a million possible answers. The truth was a good thing, and with a deep intake of breath she told herself for the first time in a long time: *I will be kind, I will be brave, I will be unstoppable.*

'I actually feel great, Professor. I hope you had a lovely summer.'

311

'Yes, yes, I did, thank you, Lottie, and that's wonderful.' The professor waved her hand through the air absent-mindedly. 'Now, I was wondering if you two could help me with something. We have a new arrival who I think you might know. It would be lovely if you two could show him around the school. He's in my office right now – do please come along and meet him.'

A prickly spider began to crawl along Lottie's skin, a nervous feeling she couldn't shake, and with it the chirping of cicadas, a scorching hot sun and the sleepy, disarming smell of lilies.

'Yes, of course,' Lottie said, she and Jamie getting up to follow Professor Devine.

As if from far away, Lottie could hear the professor talking. She could smell the spicy cinnamon of Jamie's aftershave, only it was drowned out by memories of Takeshin.

The professor opened the door to her office, and what Lottie saw made everything turn black. On the other side of the room was a worry she thought they'd escaped. A warm summer smile that turned her blood to ice.

'This is Haruki Hinamori. I believe you met over the summer,' the professor said. 'He'll be working as my teaching assistant over the year. I'm sure you'll all be happy to see a familiar face.'

Haru beamed at Jamie. 'I look forward to spending more time with you,' he said. 'I'm sure we will have a very interesting year together.'

Japanese Glossary

arigatō gozaimasu – 'thank you'

chigau yō – 'you're wrong'

dashi – a savoury stock used in Japanese cookery

geta – traditional Japanese wooden sandals

hai – 'yes'

hayaku kudasai – 'please hurry'

kabocha – pumpkin

kami – Japanese spirits or gods

kendōgu – protective outfit worn in kendo

kote – gloves used in kendo

matsuri – a traditional Japanese festival

men – facemask worn in kendo

noren – traditional Japanese curtains hung over doorways

oni – a demon

onigiri – a rice ball wrapped in dried seaweed

onnagata – a male actor who plays female roles in Japanese theatre

onsen – a bathing pool heated by natural hot springs

oyasuminasai – 'goodnight'

seiza – sitting in a kneeling position

shakujō – a wooden staff with interlocking metal rings at one
   end which make a noise when shaken
shi – four
shinai – kendo swords
sumimasen – 'excuse me' or 'sorry'
taiyaki – a Japanese fish-shaped cake with a sweet filling
tatami – straw matting, a traditional Japanese floor covering
tengu – a mythical creature found in Japanese folklore
urusai – literally means 'noisy' but can also mean 'be quiet' or
   'shut up'
yamete kudasai – 'please stop'
yappari – 'I thought so'
yōkai – supernatural creatures from Japanese folklore
yukata – a light cotton kimono

A note on Japanese names and honorifics

Japanese names usually consist of a family name (surname) followed by a given name, but in this novel the Japanese characters follow the Western convention when they introduce themselves. When addressing each other, the students used the honorific 'san' after the given name as a sign of courtesy, and 'sensei' is added after a teacher's name.

The suffix '-kun' is usually added after a name when an older or more senior person is addressing a younger or more junior person. The honorific is also often used by people addressing a male with whom they are familiar. (Which is why it's very cheeky of Haru to address Jamie as Jamie-kun!)

'San' is the most common honorific and is a suffix used for acquaintances in public settings such as schools and offices. It is similar to the term Ms or Mr.

The suffix '-chan' is an honorific that suggests endearment. Generally used for babies, young children, grandparents, or among close friends and family. It is most commonly used for women and girls, although it can be used for boys in certain circumstances, for example a boyfriend or close relative. It adds an element of cuteness to a name and will sometimes be used to create nicknames, e.g. *Kabocha-chan*.

⟪ Acknowledgements ⟫

First, I would like to say a very big thank you to my editors, Sharan and Karen, with a special thanks to Wendy who sneakily dotted the names of her siblings around the world of Rosewood. These books are infinitely improved by her magic touch. Thank you to everyone who let me sleep on their sofa, and made me some food or a cup of tea while working on this book. Thank you to my agent, Richard, and manager, Mark, who make all this possible with their constant support. Thank you to everyone in the RWCH fandom for all the fanart, fan-fiction and, most importantly, the memes.

What will happen next for Lottie and her friends?

Read on for a sneak peek . . .

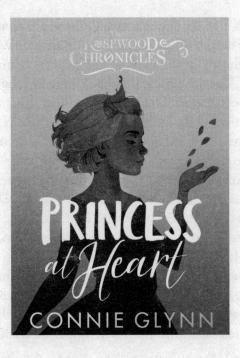

Prologue

When you live by the sea, you can smell summer storms brewing. The tide sucks in the water, whispering out a salty sigh that churns up the scent of approaching rain.

When Ollie was young, he'd been scared of the storms. It was his best friend, Lottie, who'd taught him they were nothing to be afraid of. She'd recount the tale of the Little Mermaid and how her journey had begun with a wild and courageous storm, so ferocious it had sunk a ship.

What Lottie failed to mention was that the mermaid's destiny was to turn into a pile of sea foam. Once Ollie discovered that, the fear stuck with him like a scar. Even now that he was sixteen, the distant rumble of thunder sent a tremor of fright skittering across his skin. Lottie loved the storm because she said it was the start of something new – because no matter how violent the raging winds and rain, no matter how loud the thunder, a storm meant the tension would be released, that the earth would be fresh and cool once more.

But for Ollie a storm meant only trouble.

Summer had come and gone in the blink of an eye. It was time for Ollie to head back to school, and a storm was rolling over the horizon. The humid weather was building to breaking point. His shirts clung to his skin with sweat, and he could never get the sticky feeling off his fingers no matter how much he showered. His mother, Manuela Moreno, however, seemed unaffected, cooped up in her oven of a studio or cooking her spicy dishes in the stuffy kitchen. The idea of being back at school, away from this unbearable heat, actually felt good. More than anything, he needed a distraction.

'Ollie?' His mother's voice pierced his bedroom. 'Hurry up, or you won't have time for breakfast. I'm not letting you start back at school on an empty stomach.'

'Coming, Mamãe!'

Another white-hot flash lit up the blue walls of his bedroom, startling him as he reached for his backpack.

A lot had happened over the summer, most of which he'd had to be updated on by Binah. Ever since Lottie had started at her new school, the mysterious and prestigious Rosewood Hall, his comfortable little world had been turned completely upside down. Despite his disapproval, Lottie had taken a job as a Portman for the royal family of Maradova, pretending to be Princess Eleanor Wolfson. This allowed the real princess to live a 'normal' life. Having met the real princess, Ollie could see why she preferred to remain undercover. Ellie Wolf, the name she preferred to go by, was a thunderstorm in human form. Nothing about her screamed 'princess'. She was all dark eyes and moody stares. The confident way she moved, the lazy way she laughed. She was just like the storms he'd been afraid of as a child, the very same storms that Lottie adored.

And that was just the princess. Even worse was her Partizan, Jamie: a bodyguard who looked as though he'd never smiled in his entire life. Ollie still remembered him leaning against the door frame in the kitchen, as still and patient as death, and equally as foreboding.

Lottie had been thrust into their world of royal conspiracies and secret evil societies, and now Ollie had been dragged in too, everyone banding together to try to find the identity of the Master of Leviathan, a strange and menacing group whose only goal was to destroy the Maravish royal family.

Sitting at the kitchen table, Ollie drifted into a daze, shovelling pancakes into his mouth like an unthinking machine. He didn't even taste the maple syrup. He swallowed down a mouthful and it stuck in his throat, choking him. He rubbed his chest frantically.

'Chew your food, Ollie,' his mother scolded, placing a reusable water bottle in his backpack.

He nodded absent-mindedly, thoughts turning back to the summer and the terrible secrets that had been revealed.

He and a group of Rosewood students had sneaked into Rosewood Hall. They'd ventured beyond the walls into the sleeping school to steal an ancient diary that had belonged to the founder. Reading it, Ollie had discovered that the school's founder was Lottie's ancestor – a long-lost Ottoman princess, Liliana Mayfutt.

Of course, being related to lost royalty would never be enough for Lottie. There was more. The second layer of secrets they had discovered was a set of twin swords, one buried at Rosewood and one at its sister school in Japan, Takeshin. The swords had their own secret – that an age-old and powerful bond between the two school founders stretched back to when Liliana had hidden away in Japan after escaping from the palace in the seventeenth century. After that she'd ventured to England and founded the school there.

But the icing on the secret cake was the most terrifying news Ollie had ever received. With the help of some students at Takeshin, he and his friends had discovered that Leviathan, the mysterious group who'd targeted his best friend ever since she'd started her new life, was led by Claude Wolfson, Ellie's uncle. Wolfson had abandoned the throne, then he'd been exiled from Maradova and his younger brother Alexander forced to take on the role of king. None of them knew Claude's ultimate plan, but Ollie knew one thing with absolute certainty – Lottie was at the very heart of the intrigue, and there was nothing he could do to save her. Not yet.

He shook himself from his thoughts. 'I'll head off before it starts raining.' He kissed his mother on the cheek, grabbing his backpack and one last pancake before heading out of the front door.

A familiar red van pulled up. 'Good morning, Ollie. Glad I caught you,' said a voice.

Ollie smiled at the postman. 'Good morning, Mr Harris.'

'I've picked up a postcard for the Pumpkin household,' the postman said, his sunburnt cheeks turning round and friendly. 'No one's been there for a while, so I thought I'd bring it over to you. You were always good friends with that Lottie girl.'

A menacing rumble of thunder disrupted the air. It rolled over Ollie like a premonition of trouble arriving. Something Ollie had come to realize over the past year was that trouble always sought Lottie out – just like the thunderstorm. A myriad of awful possibilities exploded in his head: news reporters who'd figured out her Portman secret, a threat from Leviathan, news that her stepmother was coming home. The letter could be about any one of these.

Mr Harris pulled out a postcard with a picture of a white-sand beach. Lemon-yellow lettering read: *Havana*. Ollie could practically smell the rum and cheap aftershave wafting off it. There was only one person who'd send a postcard like this. It conjured an image that was far, far worse than any of the possibilities he'd already thought of.

He took the card, trying to be as calm as possible. 'Thank you. I'll be sure to pass it on to her.'

'Say hello to your mother for me, Ollie,' replied Mr Harris as he headed back to his van.

The world swirled. Ollie knew he shouldn't turn over the postcard, that he shouldn't read it. Whatever was on the other side could only be bad news. But Lottie had to know what was coming, surely? With a gulp, Ollie flipped it over. The writing was smudged, probably done in a hurry, but the words were clear, as was all the trouble they would bring.

To my little princess, Charlotte,

It's been far too long, and Beady tells me you're working your way into high society.

She has also brought it to my attention that you have not been living in the old house, so I hope you will understand that it's become necessary to sell it.

Much love,
Your father

Ollie looked up to see Mr Harris's van disappear out of sight, and with it any chance of returning the cursed postcard. He could only hope Lottie would be able to handle the bad news.

1

Night had consumed Wolfson Palace. Ornaments and portraits that dazzled in the sunshine now lay dormant, waiting for life to be kissed back into them like a cursed princess.

Wiggling her toes, Lottie did her best to stave off some of the cold that was seeping through the palace floor. She was jet-lagged after returning from Japan and still feeling disorientated from everything that had happened over the past few days, not least her discovery about Leviathan. Lottie tried to hold herself upright, focusing on the wall of shiny diamond jewellery while the king's advisor went to work around her in the crimson room, side-stepping the purple-velvet ottoman in the centre.

'This won't do.' Simien narrowed his eyes at the reflection in the ornate mirror, his liver-spotted hands firmly placed over Lottie's shoulders, turning her from side to side to get a better view of the puffy-sleeved dress he'd had her put on, which made her look remarkably like a strawberry blancmange. 'Perhaps a high neckline and padded shoulders will balance out that *very* long neck that you've exposed.'

Dizzy with the dressing room's thick perfume clouds, and feeling more like a marionette than a human being, Lottie let her imaginary strings go slack when Simien finally turned back to the dresses, searching through them to find something that would work with Lottie's new messy bob.

'Whatever you think is best,' Lottie called out, hoping to move the process along without giving away her impatience. She had somewhere she needed to be, and she couldn't have Simien knowing that; she couldn't add to his stress.

It wasn't simply Lottie's hair that had everyone on edge; the whole palace felt like it was on a tightrope, ready to topple over at any moment if someone so much as breathed too deeply. Five days had passed since the nightmare in the Rose Wood, and, while Lottie was desperate to figure out Leviathan's plan, first she had to contend with Ellie's family, and that meant she had to be as presentable as possible to soften the blow of the terrible discovery she'd made.

'I think it's best if we avoid a media scandal over your hair. It's the last thing we need,' Simien hissed, tutting to himself.

Lottie couldn't help sighing. She felt like the only person in the world who didn't look at her hair as if it was a disaster or even something to be concerned about. There was only one person who understood, and she was hundreds of miles away in Japan.

Thinking about Sayuri filled Lottie's head with motorbike fumes and sharp, intelligent glances from midnight-black eyes. It made her chest ache like part of her soul had been snipped away. The summer they'd just spent at Takeshin had changed everything. The friends she'd made in Banshee, the motorbike gang, Miko, Rio and Wei, and their notorious Pink Demon leader, the silken-haired Sayuri who'd become more like a sister, were on the other side of the world but felt close to

Lottie's heart. They were linked not only by their schools but by the secrets their ancestors had trusted them with, the twin swords – one of which had saved Lottie by cutting her free.

Lottie felt calm as she stared at herself in the glass, fingers moving up to twiddle the ends of her freshly chopped bob. But as soon as her skin met the curling ends of her hair, memory jolted through her like a static shock. She was gripping the sword, flicking it up with determined abandon through her hair, freeing herself from Ingrid's and Leviathan's grasp, then running until her lungs burned.

Letting go, she tilted her chin up, marvelling at how much older the trim made her look. Ellie had done an immaculate job, the cut framing her apple-cheeked face, leaving her body lighter and revealing a version of herself that felt more Lottie than ever. The only problem was . . .

'You look too much like your real ancestors,' Simien moaned behind her, mumbling a series of curses. 'We need a Wolfson, not a Mayfutt.'

It was undeniable. Lottie looked the spitting image of her ancestor Liliana Mayfutt's male alter ego, William Tufty, right down to the splatter of freckles on the bridge of her nose. Every time she spotted them she felt like the ghosts of her family were watching her and expecting something.

'Don't slouch.' Simien reappeared behind her, holding a butter-yellow dress up to her, its shoulders protruding like stiff whipped cream. 'We need to make sure your princess image is still intact to lessen some of the queen mother's distress over this unfortunate discovery.' He didn't need to say the name out loud. The whole palace could feel the severity of the situation like a hard grip on their necks.

Glancing briefly up at the clock, Lottie felt her patience wearing thin and, just as she thought she'd have to make an excuse and plant a well-timed yawn, Simien, at last, relented.

'This will have to do, I suppose,' the king's advisor said, sighing and tapping at the temple by his glass eye before putting the dress back on the hanger. 'Now make sure you go straight to bed and get a good night's sleep for the meeting tomorrow,' he said, attempting breeziness, but Lottie could hear the grave tone that he was doing his best to hide.

Lottie had one more stop before she retired for the evening. After changing into something more comfortable, she waited until she was sure the rest of the palace had gone to sleep and sneaked out of her bedroom door, listening carefully for any movement.

A floorboard on the stairs squeaked beneath her feet and she froze. Heart pounding, she strained her ears for any response.

Silence.

She crept into the long marble corridor, where the ghostly faces of the previous rulers of Maradova looked down at her from their gilded frames. Ignoring their eyes, she paused at the largest painting.

Alexis Wolfson, the man who'd seized the throne of Maradova hundreds of years ago, stared down at Lottie with piercing eyes, the same wild green as a forest at dusk. His long black hair fell thickly around his broad shoulders. Draped in protective pelts, he looked more warrior than king, but his smile was warm. Gazing up at him, Lottie wondered why she'd never paid this portrait more attention. It had taken

Ingrid's cryptic words for her to notice him, and now she could see why he'd been so adored.

Just like Alexis, Ingrid had said. It was one of two statements she'd shared that day in the woods. The other, and more confusing, was simply: *Why is Jamie your Partizan?* It was a question meant for the real princess, and Lottie was determined to find out what Ingrid had meant. Why was he Ellie's Partizan?

Pulling herself away, Lottie walked to the end of the corridor until she reached the black sheep of the family, and the very person to whom Ingrid devoted herself – Claude Wolfson, Ellie's uncle.

His painting hung in a black frame, a dark reminder of the fate that would befall any royal who turned away from their responsibilities. In his exile he'd waited, plotting, building an army. Now they knew that the mysterious goat-masked man who'd tormented Lottie and her friends for the past two years had been him. But why?

'Hello, Goat Man.' She found a strange satisfaction in using his nickname when he looked so proud. Perhaps this was how Ellie felt whenever she defied authority.

'You can say his name, you know.' Ellie's voice drifted down the corridor, dark and bitter like coffee. 'Everyone's acting like it's some terrible curse word.'

Turning slowly to face her princess, Lottie braced herself, remembering that it wasn't just her image that had changed. Even so, it made her mouth go dry.

In the glow of the moonlight Ellie was dressed in a long black robe fit for a funeral, her face floating in the dark. She looked utterly exhausted. A sheen on her pale skin made her complexion look like alabaster, and the darkness beneath her eyes looked stained with ink. Lottie wondered if she'd slept at all since they'd learned about her uncle being the Master of Leviathan.

Taking a sweeping step forward, there was something dangerous in her eyes.

'Claude Wolfson, Claude Wolfson, Claude Wolfson,' Ellie repeated as if she were calling on the bogeyman, looking around with her hands outstretched. 'See? Nothing happened.'

Lottie flinched at her tone. Ellie was obviously angry.

'You're late,' she said, ignoring Ellie's teasing. 'What's wrong?'

Ellie's face dropped, and Lottie felt guilty as she took in her smudged eyes and chewed lips. She had to believe she'd done the right thing in telling Ellie about her uncle, but seeing her like this it was hard to feel like she was helping anyone.

'I had to steal this from the post room; it could have got us in serious trouble.'

From an inside pocket, Ellie pulled out a postcard, passing it to Lottie so she could see the elegant painting of a bamboo forest on the front. She could smell it, like a scorching-hot summer and the fizzy tang in the air after fireworks.

Flipping it over, Lottie stared at the six lines of simple text.

Dear Princess,
Please keep an eye on Haru for us.
His sabbatical is still regrettably a mystery.
Stay safe, and remember our fates are linked by the sword.
                    Sayuri, Miko, Rio and Wei

'She sent it here, to the palace, for you.' There was an edge to Ellie's voice that sounded like fear, the kind of low-frequency sound you expect from a cornered dog. 'It's dangerous, Lottie. What if someone had seen it?' Ellie groaned, putting her head in her hands. 'No one knows Haru is part of Leviathan except for us and Ani and Saskia.'

Trying to keep calm, Lottie pocketed the postcard. It felt warm nestled next to her heart, despite the terrible reminder that Haru was waiting for them when they returned.

'Is this why you wanted to meet me?' she asked, wishing she could do something to put Ellie's mind at ease.

'No.' Ellie shook her head. 'I need to ask you a favour.' Her gaze wandered once more to the painting of Claude.

'Anything.'

'I need you to promise you won't tell my parents about Haru being part of Leviathan tomorrow. Not unless I say so.'

'Wait, what?'

Ellie's eyes snapped back to Lottie's, her sleepy demeanour melting away. 'I'm serious, Lottie. After what you found out about my . . . about Claude, I feel like my parents are hiding things. Tomorrow I'm going to tell them I'm sick of it.' Ellie's hands curled into fists. 'I can't believe they're not letting Jamie attend. We can't let them keep things from us. We should be vigilant; we have to –'

'Jamie's not attending?' Lottie's mind felt muddled, sure she'd misheard, but Ellie shook her head again, letting her know it was very real.

'It's weird, isn't it?' Ellie looked vindicated for a moment, glad to see Lottie equally as perplexed. 'They won't say why, but they're keeping it intimate, just me, you, Grandmother and my parents.'

The news was like a boulder, knocking Lottie right back into the Rose Wood, Ingrid's voice snaking into her thoughts once more. *Why is Jamie your Partizan?*

Shaking it off, Lottie grabbed one of Ellie's clenched fists and squeezed. From the way her friend's hand trembled, Lottie could sense a long-growing resentment in her princess towards her secretive family. 'Let's see what your parents and grandmother have to say tomorrow. Then you can decide what you think is right for everyone.'

'But –'

'I'm on your side, Ellie, no matter what.' This was the truth – a fact she could always fall back on. Everything she did was for the good of her princess, the girl who made her feel whole. 'And if you decide that's what you want to do after we've spoken to them, then OK.' Lottie spoke steadily but her chest felt hollow at the idea of keeping Haru a secret any longer. 'Can we do that?'

Seconds felt like decades while she waited for a reply, and all the while Claude stared down at them, watching, waiting.

'OK, yeah,' Ellie said at last, her fists uncurling. 'I'll try to keep my cool tomorrow, for you.' A semblance of Ellie's old charm crept back into her smile, but it faded quickly. 'We should probably go to sleep. I'm not thinking straight. I'm tired and it feels weird being back here, and . . . yeah.'

'Don't worry, I understand.' Lottie linked her fingers with Ellie's.

Ellie lay her chin on Lottie's head, wrapping her arms round her neck until they were slotted together. Lottie could feel the flicker of Ellie's pulse where her cheek rested against her neck. She was so warm; it made her want to melt into her, visions of their kiss from so long ago fluttering through her mind as soft as butterfly wings, but then Ellie pulled away.

'I'm sorry,' she said softly, and Lottie couldn't tell what Ellie was apologizing for. 'Let's head upstairs.'

Silently they made their way back to their quarters. They said goodnight at Lottie's door, hands drifting apart. And, as Lottie climbed into bed, her head filled with images of Alexis and Claude, Haru and Jamie, and Ellie, Ellie, Ellie.

But when she thought of Ellie's tired eyes, the way she'd crumbled when they'd discovered that Leviathan's tricks all led back to her family, and the secrets and lies . . . she wondered was any of this really what was best for Ellie?

Was Lottie helping anyone at all?